Blood, Sweat & Queers

VAMPIRIC LOVE STORIES

EDITED BY MARGARET HALL & JAMIE RYU

CONTRARIAN PUBLISHING

Brooklyn, NY * Est. 2024

First published in the United States by Contrarian Publishing

contrarianpublishing.com

This book is a work of fiction. Names, characters, and incidents are the product of the author's imagination and/or are used fictitiously. Any resemblance to actual persons, living or dead, is coincidental.

Summary: Eight LGBTQ+ authors present decadent tales of queer love, all intertwined with the eternal allure of the vampire—stories of desire unbound, of passion unending, and hunger that threatens to consume everything in its path.

Library of Congress Control Number: 2025942370
ISBN: 978-1-965422-07-6
ISBN (ebook): 978-1-965422-08-3

First Edition

Cover illustration by Mazhuir Hussain

Book and cover design by Jamie Ryu

Table of Contents

Content Considerations

This book is meant to be a celebration of queer love and members of the LGBTQ+ community, but it does contain content that may be disturbing to some readers. Content includes gun violence, gore, ableism, sexual harassment, domestic violence, political messaging, suicidal ideation, and death.

Reader discretion is advised.

This book is dedicated to every single member of the queer community—past, present, and future.

We are here. We have always been here. And we will continue to be here.

No matter what.

Foreword

by Margaret Hall

There's just something about a vampire, isn't there?

When I was approached by Contrarian founder Jamie Ryu to co-edit this anthology, I was immediately on board. While much of my professional career has been spent in the theatre, it is no surprise to anyone who has spent more than fifteen minutes in my presence that I *love* a good vampire story. As a teen, I wholly fell under their spell, honing my craft as a writer and refining my tastes as a reader as I worked my way through every piece of vampire fiction I could get my hands on. Now an adult working deeply within multiple branches of the arts, I remain eternally loyal to the monster lurking just out of view.

This collection of short stories honors one of the defining features of vampiric literature: queerness.

The vampire is an inherently queer figure. They live in the shadows, slipping between the lines of terror and temptation. Vampires don't just scare us; they *seduce* us, terrifying us while pulling us closer, daring us to look deeper. They are the monsters we want to touch, even when we know we shouldn't. They exist on the margins of human society, resisting traditional norms of relational behavior. Their queerness is not only defined by their sexuality or gender expression. It is their intensity as the personification of want, of yearning, of taboo desire, that renders them inherently and automatically outside of the societal norm.

A brief history lesson: the vampires we know today are far from the creatures they once were. The original vampires of folklore weren't exactly enticing. They didn't think or feel or fall in love. In the oldest stories, vampires were little more than rotting corpses with an appetite. They clawed out of their graves bloated, stiff, and stained with gore; hardly the kind of figure that could carry a romance novel! These vampires came from deep-rooted folk beliefs, especially in Eastern Europe, where they were feared not for their seductive power, but for their mindless greed. They were far closer to what we now think of as zombies, animated by hunger, and hunger alone. In most folkloric vampires, you won't find internal conflict, or motivation beyond their never-ending, gnawing need for *more.*

The turning point came in the late eighteenth century, as Europe was gripped by the slow-motion horror of tuberculosis, then known as consumption. The disease didn't leave its victims disfigured or foul-smelling; it instead gave them a delicate, otherworldly appearance. It hollowed them out with such slow precision that death seemed more like a final sigh than a sudden shock. Those who suffered from consumption could live for years as their countenance slowly transformed, their skin going pale and luminous, their eyes growing dark and fever-bright, and their bodies wasting away, leaving a fragile shell of the individual behind. At the end of their convalescence, their lips would stain red with the blood that spilled forth from their ravaged lungs, dripping out life as death descended.

In a society obsessed with appearances and symbolism, this new image of death proved captivating. Unlike the terrifying chaos of the plague or the brutality of smallpox, tuberculosis made death look almost graceful. Artists of the Romantic period—drawn to passion, loss, and longing—began to paint the sick not as tragic but as transcendent. Writers described consumptives as delicate angels, too sensitive for the world. Death became beautiful. Pain became profound. The figure of the dying person, wasting, ghostly, and oddly radiant, became something to admire. And it is from this cultural moment that the modern vampire began to rise.

The image of the consumptive body—thin, pale, and burning from within—laid the groundwork for what we now recognize as the vampire's stereotypical look and feel. The monster no longer had to be foul and bloated; it could be lean, elegant, wounded. Its hunger didn't have to be mindless; it could be *romantic*, even erotic. The vampire became a creature suspended between life and death, with a body marked by suffering and a gaze that could slice through emotional defenses. It wasn't just about blood anymore. It was about yearning.

This transformation wasn't accidental. It grew directly out of a society struggling to understand beauty, sickness, and desire all at once. As tuberculosis swept across Europe, consuming the healthy, the young, and the beautiful, people started to believe that an individual's proximity to death could reveal some deeper, hidden truth about their spirit. Susan Sontag, in her powerful essay *Illness as Metaphor*, pointed out that tuberculosis was once seen as "a disease of passion"[1]—something that exposed the true soul of the afflicted. To be sick wasn't just to die, it was to suffer proximity to the transcendental release of eternity. And in the vampire, that idea found its perfect metaphor: a creature that suffered eternally, loved desperately, and walked forever in the shadows.

The vampire morphed into a captivating mirror, a mirror for everything society feared but could not look away from: sickness, sensuality, desire that didn't obey rules. In the hands of Romantic writers, and later Victorian ones, the vampire became

1. Susan Sontag, *Illness as Metaphor* (Farrar, Straus and Giroux, 1978), 21.

the embodiment of all things forbidden and fascinating. A monster who could *feel*. A body that could *want*. A presence that could make you shiver, not with fear, but with the thrill of being seen, hunted, *chosen*.

This is the vampire we know now. Not the brainless corpse, but the beautiful shadow. Not the bloated dead, but the elegant mourner. They are suffering made seductive, danger made delicate. And they carry with them all the ache of forbidden longings, be it physical or emotional, that society so often tries to bury. From the moment tuberculosis painted death in poetry, the vampire stepped forward, red-lipped and waiting.

The three foundational texts of English-language vampiric literature—John Polidori's "The Vampyre" (1819), Sheridan Le Fanu's *Carmilla* (1872), and Bram Stoker's *Dracula* (1897)—are not just landmark works of gothic horror; they are saturated with homoerotic tension and coded longing. Each text drips with desire that dares not speak its name, produced by authors many scholars believe hovered somewhere along the queer spectrum.

In "The Vampyre," John Polidori introduces the vampire not as a grotesque revenant, but as a refined, aristocratic predator, a striking departure from the folkloric tradition.[2] His titular vampyre bears a striking resemblance to Polidori's employer Lord Byron, with whom Polidori was fascinated. The character of Lord Ruthven is less a monster than a man, whose power lies in his unsettling charisma and his ability to command obsessive devotion, especially from other men. His young companion Aubrey is seduced not just intellectually but emotionally, drawn to Ruthven's mystery and magnetism even as he recoils from the dark implications of his nature. Ruthven's danger is rooted in the intimacy of his influence. The queer subtext is difficult to ignore;

2. John Polidori, "The Vampyre," *The New Monthly Magazine and Universal Register* 1, no. 63 (1819): 195–206, https://www.gutenberg.org/ebooks/6087.

the relationship between the two men is marked by secrecy, betrayal, and a strange form of emotional possession. Ruthven drains not only the life from his victims but the psychological clarity from his closest companion, destabilizing boundaries between friendship, attraction, and domination. In a society rigidly policed by the norms of masculinity and heterosexual propriety, "The Vampyre" opened a door, quietly but definitively, to the possibility of queer desire being both thrilling and ruinous, seductive and inescapably dangerous.

Sheridan Le Fanu's *Carmilla* is perhaps the most overtly homoerotic of the three foundational vampire texts, yet its queerness is shrouded in gothic ambiguity. At its heart is a story of fascination and hyperfixation: young Laura is obsessed with the mysterious Carmilla, who enters her life under strange circumstances and gradually becomes both confidante and predator. Carmilla does not hide her desire; she gazes, touches, and whispers, always lingering a moment too long, always too intimate. The connection between the two girls transcends friendship but cannot fully settle into a known category. "Sometimes after an hour of apathy, my strange and beautiful companion would take my hand and hold it with a fond pressure... it was like the ardor of a lover... her hot lips travelled along my cheek in kisses," Laura confesses early in the novel, both enthralled and confused.[3] The lesbian desire here is not metaphorical; it's physical, sensual, and unsettling in its intensity. Yet, Le Fanu's depiction is not entirely moralistic. Carmilla is a monster, yes, but she is also deeply lonely, wounded, and searching for connection in a world that will not allow her love to exist. In its portrayal of desire that defies explanation and control, *Carmilla* anticipates modern queer narratives—tragic, tender, and haunted by possibilities outside of heteronormative oversight.

3. Sheridan Le Fanu, *Carmilla* (London, 1819), 26, https://www.gutenberg.org/ebooks/10007.

Then, of course, there is *Dracula*. Bram Stoker's epistolary novel, widely recognized as the most famous piece of vampiric literature in the English language, is a fever dream of Victorian sexual anxiety, and beneath its surface of moralistic horror lies a roiling undercurrent of queer panic and fascination. Nowhere is this clearer than in Jonathan Harker's first encounter with the Count, a scene soaked in erotic tension and gender role inversion.[4] Harker, the respectable English solicitor, finds himself disoriented and helpless under Count Dracula's gaze, his body penetrated not by fangs alone but by the violation of his self-control. As scholar Christopher Craft notes in his work "*'Kiss Me with Those Red Lips': Gender and Inversion in Bram Stoker's Dracula*," the first half of the novel involves significant acts of voluntary and involuntary submission by Harker, whose horror is laced with a kind of dread-laced thrill.[5] Count Dracula's attacks on men carry a different charge than his seductions of women. They are covert, bodily, and intimate, disrupting the binaries of Victorian gender and sexuality. The novel's broader narrative, too, trembles with queerness, not just in Count Dracula's connection to Harker, but in the deep homosocial bonds among the men fighting him, in Lucy's unruly sexuality, and in the moral panic over bodies that resist control. Count Dracula becomes a site onto which every sexual fear of the conservative class is projected: promiscuity, gender role inversion, foreignness, disease. And yet, the reader is drawn to him—he is compelling, tragic, masterful. In trying to destroy Count Dracula, the novel also memorializes him, placing his queer hunger at the center of its mythology, a seductive threat that lingers long after the last stake is driven.

4. Bram Stoker, *Dracula* (Archibald Constable and Company, 1897).

5. Christopher Craft, "'Kiss Me with Those Red Lips': Gender and Inversion in Bram Stoker's *Dracula*," *Representations* 156, no. 8 *(1984): 107–133.* https://doi.org/10.2307/2928560

It is under the shadow of these three texts that the vampire evolved into an archetype of forbidden appetite: a creature defined not simply by bloodlust, but by the very transgressiveness of that hunger. As scholar Nina Auerbach explores thoroughly throughout her book *Our Vampires, Ourselves*, every age embraces the vampire it needs,[6] and what our culture has needed time and again is a figure who embodies desire without apology. Whether it's the monstrous yearning of Count Orlok in *Nosferatu* or the decadent sorrow of Anne Rice's Lestat de Lioncourt, the vampire's craving is always more than just physical. It is a hunger for connection, identity, touch. And unlike more sanitized romantic archetypes, the vampire doesn't mask their need in politeness. They *feed*. They consume entirely. They transgress, and in doing so, they refuse to perform the chastened rituals of "acceptable" love. In this way, the vampire becomes not just a monster, but a mirror for the queer self: perpetually outside, perpetually longing, perpetually alive.

Today's vampire doesn't just hunger for blood; they hunger for connection, for understanding, for something forbidden. And that desire, outsized, dangerous, impossible to sanitize, has always carried a distinctly queer charge. The moment the vampire became "human", it also became "other" in a way that feels deeply familiar to anyone who's ever loved differently, secretly, or too much.

Throughout modern history, vampire fiction has surged in popularity during moments of cultural repression and liberation alike, functioning as both escape and protest. When you trace the vampire's popularity in the United States alongside various LGBTQ+ rights movements, the correlation is clear. In the early 1930's, during the backlash to the Homophile Movement of the

6. Nina Auerbach, Our Vampires, Ourselves (University of Chicago Press, 1995), n8.

1920s, Bela Lugosi's depiction of *Dracula* allowed the disenfranchised to escape, ever so briefly, into a compelling combination of extreme wealth and resolute desire. By 1976, as the gay liberation movement made countless strides toward equality and equity, Anne Rice had ushered in the era of protagonist vampires with her bestselling novel *Interview with the Vampire*.

While Dracula remains the most famous vampire by name, Rice's rich catalog of characters are, in my view, just as influential. Rice's vampires were the center of her stories, shifted out of the shadows and into the spotlight as the characters audiences were supposed to identify with, root for, and bond to. They were, in one loaded word, *human*. Born from Rice's all-encompassing grief following the death of her young daughter, the first novel in her Vampire Chronicles explores the complicated interpersonal dynamic between two vampires, Louis and Lestat, and their proclaimed daughter, Claudia. Rice never hid the fact that she considered Louis and Lestat to be analogous to herself and her husband Stan, with Claudia aligning with their five-year-old daughter Michele. Rice's depictions of vampirism, queer domesticity, trauma, and forgiveness have become foundational for all vampiric media that has followed. She explicitly encouraged readers to embrace the unknown with empathy rather than cower in fear, setting the stage for all that was to follow.

On *Buffy the Vampire Slayer*, America's cheerful heroine fell in love with not one but two vampires who proved to be complicated men with deep-seated sexual struggles. Both relationships walked the line between eros and annihilation, casting queerness not as a literal sexual orientation but as a metaphor for "the othered" sexual self—strange, magnetic, and overtly dangerous. When *True Blood*, *Twilight*, and *The Vampire Diaries* exploded in the early 2000s, they brought this psychological queerness out into the open. These stories emerged alongside American debates on gay marriage, with characters whose longing and conflict mimicked the slow mainstreaming of queer love; once hidden, now visible; once monstrous, now desirable. The vampire was no longer just a monster. It was a lover. It was us.

What we call a vampire today would be unrecognizable to the villagers who once whispered of bloodthirsty revenants clawing out of graves. In modern lore, the vampire is no longer just a monstrous "other." It is us, refracted. Vulnerable, seductive, tormented, and painfully self-aware, the contemporary vampire hungers not just for blood, but for intimacy, identity, and meaning. That evolution has rendered the vampire unmistakably queer. Not merely in terms of sexual desire, but in the way it embodies the outsider's longing, the refusal to conform, the hunger to live and love differently. This is not accidental. It is baked into the bones of the vampire's literary history.

Now, as the queer community faces down vitriolic hate once more, the vampire is rising once again as a favored archetype to cope with violence, both emotional and physical. The eight stories in this collection utilize a bevy of different tropes, archetypes, and cultural touchstones as they push the boundaries of the vampire romance genre in different ways.

First in the collection is Ezra Wren's "Sweet Crimson Dripping: Overture," a lush, operatic exploration of queer longing across centuries, and the families we find along the way. The richly imagined piece entwines themes of trans embodiment and immortal grief with a gloss of historical romance for a final product that complicates animalistic bloodlust by rooting it in trauma, tenderness, and the politics of being perceived.

Mae Murray's "Blood and Oil" is a haunting piece of eco-horror, mining the everyday banality of evil in the twenty-first century as the setting for transformative rebirth. In the last twenty-five years, the concept of vampirism outside of strictly blood drinking has been heavily explored in fiction, questioning what it means to consume life in alternative ways. Murray's piece is a worthwhile addition to that evolving canon, straddling the worlds of vampire fiction and modern dystopia.

U.M. Agowike's "Teeth Sharper than Moonlight" takes the stereotypical "damsel running from a monster in a diaphanous nightgown" image and transposes it into the world of consensual kink and the role of fantasy in long term relationships. Calling upon both the classic humanoid vampire and the Ancient Greek *vrykolakas*, this monster-meets-monster story is a beautiful bridge between both the old and new depictions of vampirism.

Like many before them, Austen Lee joins the long line of writers that use vampirism to explore the danger that has historically accompanied taboo pleasures. "Suckr" grabs hookup culture, gay bar cruising, and dating app anonymity by the throat, hunting flesh with a predator's patience. While many of the most famous serial killers in the United States have specifically targeted queer individuals, "Suckr" flips the script in a series of unexpected ways that are sure to satisfy.

In Andi Astra's sprawling fantasy "The Girl in The Grove," a vampire queen long resigned to her monstrous nature comes across an injured fae. As the familiar game of power and indulgence shifts, the fae flips the script on everything the queen considers natural. Sensual, sorrowful, and steeped in old forest magic, this tragedy lingers on the slow unraveling of inherited legacy and the courage it takes to want something of your own, if only for a moment.

When a reclusive, bar-owning vampire falls for her human employee in Anna McG's "When the Day Met the Night," desire becomes something far more dangerous than bloodlust. This quiet love story unfolds in the space between safety and secrecy, where trauma and trust brush shoulders behind the bar. Blending the loner-vigilante archetype with the yearning tenderness of mortals who still believe in good, the story subverts the "forbidden love" trope by making safety, not seduction, the primary hunger.

In L.A. Barron's "Still, We Rot," vampirism is state-regulated, monetized, and riddled with bureaucratic cruelty. Set in a crumbling healthcare dystopia, the story reimagines a reluctant vampire as a working-class queer woman surviving on the margins. Drawing from the medical horror genre and neo-vampire tropes, this is a story of rage, refusal, and queer tenderness in a system designed to devour you.

Lastly, Lyndall Clipstone's "Sweetest Midnight" is a sapphic vampire romance set in the cut-throat world of dance, where broken rules lead to bodies broken open. Against the eerie hush of a lakeside summer, it is a tale of yearning in all directions, plunging into the sensual unease of fairy-tale horror. Erotic, eerie, and devastating, "Sweetest Midnight" reclaims the trope of the monstrous feminine and asks: what if the greatest threat to a woman's body is the systems that claim to refine it?

More than ever, uplifting queer stories is of the utmost importance. We hope that this collection of new, queer vampire love stories will soothe your soul, embolden your spirit, and strengthen your resolve to live your lives as freely and as openly as possible. Like the vampire, queer love endures; it shapeshifts, it survives, and it will never be driven back into the dark.

Sweet Crimson Dripping: Overture

by Ezra Wren

The first time Ambrose DeVoreur was stabbed, he was still human. Six hundred and fifty-four years later, he could still recall the feeling of iron ripping into flesh, his gasping breath as the blade pressed into something essential, something soft and warm and full of love and joy. Anger too. Despair. All of it seeped out of him, blooming crimson over yellowed bandages, trickling down the plane of his stomach, pooling at his knees.

"Shall we, darling?"

Ambrose glanced at the man standing in the doorway, lips curved on an ashy, light-brown face, frozen beauty preserved for eight hundred years. Marcel had been older when time had halted his ticking heart. He had been thirty-two. But only Ambrose knew about that. At their lavish parties, he told people he was twenty-seven.

"Let's." Ambrose looked down at his shirt, eyeing the ruffles at the collar, the bronze brocade corset Leonora had tied for him minutes before. He adored this style of clothing, missed wearing it anywhere and everywhere. A smile graced his mouth. Perhaps it was not so much the clothing that he missed but the company he'd kept while wearing it.

Memories of fumbling fingers tearing at his laces flashed through his mind, grazed his neck with recollections of soft cool touch, the sharp points of fingernails at his throat, the press of teeth against alabaster skin.

Ambrose picked his coat off the divan and shrugged it on, following Marcel out to the dim hallway that ran between their suites. Marcel was a handsome man, bearing eight centuries of joy and pain in bright onyx eyes, his rich brown waves swept back from his brow and flowing over the tips of his ears. Ambrose remembered Marcel's long hair from centuries before, brushing his shoulders, thick as velvet.

"What *are* you looking at?" Marcel cast him a sidelong glance.

"Well, since I can't admire my own reflection, I'll have to settle for yours, won't I?" Ambrose flashed Marcel a boyish smirk.

"I know you were unschooled for a very long time, my sweet, but if you're looking at another, then it is not a reflection. Do I need to sit you down with the books about how *light* works again?" Perhaps Ambrose was out of his depths trying to play mischief with its very master. Marcel's eyebrows rose, drawing a crease on his forehead.

"I know how light works." Ambrose tilted his head back, raising his chin. "Perhaps if you stopped hoarding antiques and got me an aluminum mirror, I would be less inclined to stare." Or maybe Ambrose would never get anything done, go anywhere. Not that he could be faulted. Who could have told him, during his human years, that he would one day look upon his own reflection in the mirror and be glad?

Their winding staircase was a *bitch* to walk down in his thickly heeled leather boots, but Ambrose achieved it with the utmost grace, tickling the cool marble banister with the tips of his fingers.

In his mind, Jacques waited for him at the bottom, a black curtain of hair sweeping a cinched in waist, a gorgeous smile on soft lips that would kiss him. Ambrose imagined a hand out-stretched, heavy rings on every digit, long fingernails filed to a point. He imagined taking it, Jacques twirling him in the center of their magnificent entrance hall, brown eyes glimmering as they caught the light of their crystal chandelier. Ambrose imagined laughing. Imagined joy.

The last time Jacques had touched him, they hadn't lived here. They'd lived in Marcel's ancestral manor. The manor where they'd danced, where they'd sat beneath the apple trees in the orchard late at night, whispering to each other, where they'd picnicked with Marcel in their small private clan of three. The manor where Jacques had touched every part of his body and called it beautiful. The manor had long since burned down. And Jacques had burned down with it.

Ambrose turned away from his memories toward the front doors of the château he and Marcel now called home. The car was already waiting below the lavish wide steps, the vast expanse of their green lawns stretched out behind it.

"After you," Marcel said, opening the door for Ambrose. Always the gentleman, since the day they had first met in that dark alley behind the tavern. The same hands that were now curled around the handle had curled around Ambrose's waist, flattening against his bleeding wound. He had called him *darling*. *Poor darling*, to be exact.

Ambrose stepped into the car and sat on the warmed leather, the overly sweet scent of caramel wafting into him, filling his throat with a taste of something from a long gone past, burning his chest with the ache of recollection.

"This car smells sickly," he said as Marcel took his place behind the wheel and drove away, circling the large stone fountain glinting bluish in the moonlight on this pleasant night. The car rumbled down the gravelly drive towards their open gates, beyond which lay the open road that would take them to their destination for the night. "Did you hear what I said?"

"I did. But how about 'Thank you, Marcel, for starting the car?' 'Thank you, Marcel, for warming my seat.' 'Thank you, dear Marcel, for opening the gates.'"

"I would never call you *dear*," Ambrose said, rolling his eyes. A laugh warmed his throat as he turned to look out the window.

"Nor would you ever say thank you, you ungrateful brat." Marcel laughed too, hands wrapped around the wheel of his flashy sports car, one of many. Ambrose had said many times that Marcel would live for 1600 years, because this obsession with collecting vehicles over the last half century must be his mid-life crisis.

In his cold, silent chest, Ambrose wished Marcel would live all the millennia left to come. He was a good man, perhaps the best Ambrose had ever known. Ambrose tore his eyes from the vampire who had not only given him his life but offered to share it, and fixed his gaze instead on the road ahead, on the glimmering lights in the distance, where their pleasure awaited.

Ambrose handed his coat to the man behind the counter and glanced toward the open doors, within which lay the ballroom, all decked out for the party. Marcel sourced two champagne flutes, handing one to Ambrose. Ambrose took a sip, closing his eyes as the flavors settled on his tongue, burning a path down his throat to a stomach that would not keep them.

Something to worry about later. For now, pleasure.

The party was already in full swing—chandeliers dimmed, laughter and conversation drowning out the music booming through the speakers, the air thick with the heady scent of perfume mixed with sweat, hors d'œuvres, and alcohol. Marcel set his empty glass down on a passing tray, shooting a glance at the bar. Ambrose knew to follow his mesmerizing eyes as he leaned in to whisper, "whiskey," to the man standing behind the long, elegant table in uniform.

Ambrose nursed his champagne. He had come to appreciate the sensation of fizzy bubbles on his tongue, scratching away at him, laboring to make their presence known. He had labored once to make his presence known. He never would again.

As his eyes slid over the crowd, they landed on wide, bright green eyes framed with thick lashes on a doll-like face. Her pink lips curved, cheeks warming as Ambrose straightened. He set the flute down on the table, tapping Marcel's heirloom ring to let him know he was about to depart.

Ambrose knew how to step, how to move as though all eyes were watching, how to carry the wind in his shoulders and float as though he were walking on the clouds. Marcel's gift had made him more apt, but even as a human, Ambrose had been quite capable. That was why they had wanted him. That was why they had killed him.

"You're a good dancer," the woman said, looking down at his feet. Her eyes slid up, gliding over his legs, his hips, his waist, pausing at his pale bare throat, until they finally fixed on his face. Her dress took him back ages, the swishing satin skirt glinting like emeralds in the light, the sequins on her bodice shimmering as she moved.

"I have practiced." Ambrose refrained from letting her know that he had been around when this dance was invented, that he had witnessed the fashions shift across centuries, that her dress was not fine enough to be the real thing but still beautiful. Ambrose called a smile to his lips and swallowed back the bitterness coiling into the sweet recollection of Jacques spinning about the great hall of their old countryside manor in a dress not dissimilar. Jacques had worn green better than most people would.

"Your hair is lovely," Ambrose said, eyeing the fire red floret she'd gathered at the crown of her head.

"Wow, look who's talking." Her gaze followed the silken length of his near-white hair swishing at his waist.

Ambrose opened his mouth to thank her when a wind cut through their dance, long fingers slipping into the gaps between his, a hand settling on his waist.

"Apologies, dear, but I have not seen this one in *ages!*" Algernon purred, flashing the woman one of his irresistible smiles. She glanced at Ambrose, then back at Algernon, cheeks flushing, and then she was off, searching for another partner.

"Did you *ask* whether I wanted to dance?" Ambrose arched his eyebrows.

He and Algernon had crossed paths many times over the centuries. They had been new vampires at the same time, heeding to different Sires with very different styles, very different ways of life. Sires who hated each other. On many occasions, the two of them had shared a treat that could have landed Ambrose in a mess. Claude and his underlings were known for their carelessness, the brutal way in which they handled their meals, leaving a trail of bodies in their wake.

"Do not pout, handsome," Algernon said. "It could give you wrinkles."

"But you know it won't." Ambrose eyed Algernon's outfit, an original he'd owned for a century at least. He remembered it from a time before, a time between Jacques and now. Their paths had crossed at a different party in a different city. They had shared more than a meal that night. Algernon was brutal at everything he did. Beautifully brutal.

"I have missed your face." Algernon smiled down at him. What a handsome mouth. He had lips that seemed designed, painted. They were soft, Ambrose remembered. He eyed the straight line of Algernon's nose, the arch of his brows, his dark deep-set eyes, the cutting line of his cheekbones. A man of many conquests. "Tell me, do you like my hair?"

"I think it would be tragic if I say no now," Ambrose replied. Vampires did not *regrow* things. Not fingernails nor teeth nor hair. And Algernon had cut his blond locks short, a mass of curls atop his head, leaving only fuzz along the sides and back. Algernon looked at him expectantly, quirking an eyebrow. "It's gorgeous."

"Good. I like to impress you." Algernon's voice was like rough satin, like a nail scratching over a record, like gasps and moans on hot summer nights while Ambrose called out his name. "Don't take my example, of course." He released Ambrose's hand, taking a strand of his long, pale hair. "This could be spun gold."

"I'd say silver, if you're looking for accuracy," Ambrose replied. "Can you stop touching it with your greasy fingers?"

"My fingers are not greasy," Algernon replied, dropping his hand regardless. His eyes narrowed, brown glinting almost amber—hunger spelled out in a gaze. "They have missed you too."

Ambrose shook his head, instinctively leaning into Algernon's palm, taking his hand again. The music had somehow grown louder, the laughter and conversation drowned out, muted by the man standing before him. His boots clapped against the marble floor of the ballroom, the lights overhead weaving gold into Algernon's soft curls.

"Is that a no, Ambrose?" Algernon leaned into his ear, bending to match the difference in their height. His neck smelled like musk, like an invitation, like *bite me.* "I would so love to remind you of before."

"Does Claude know you're propositioning Marcel's *puppet?*" Ambrose could have bitten Algernon and it would have been less cutting than this. The other vampire pulled away, his young handsome face conspiring to collect itself in the center, pinching. "Isn't that what he said the last time you and I crossed paths?"

"That was... that must have been a decade ago. Time really flies when you have an endless supply, doesn't it?" Algernon pressed his hand, spinning still. "Ambrose, that was not about you. Or even about me. Claude and Marcel's history shouldn't come between us."

"*Us?* Next thing I know you'll be asking me to wed." Ambrose rolled his eyes.

"Now, don't run before you walk, love. I know you and Jacques liked to pretend, but I am not them and I'm not quite yet ready to play house with you." Algernon's laugh cut into Ambrose, burning him right through. If he looked down, Ambrose suspected he would find his corset ruined, red blooming where he had once been stabbed. He shifted, easing out of Algernon's grip, ripping his fingers free, and turned on his heel.

If vampires could cry, Ambrose would.

He had desperately longed for the ability the night their manor had burned down, the night they'd taken Jacques from him.

His eyes were as dry now as they had remained then, on a night worse than his own death. Ambrose strode away, passing through the crowd of dancing couples, meandering until he found an open door that led out to the back garden of the hotel.

The air was biting cold and fresh, pleasant. He didn't need his coat, not really. In fact, Ambrose could be stark naked and he wouldn't be bothered in the least. Still, he enjoyed the warmth, the comfort it brought, and a part of him wished he'd gone to the front desk and asked for it.

Ambrose wandered beneath the starlit sky, passing the neat flowerbeds and dainty fountains until he came upon a maze of tall hedges, the perfect place to hide. The music played on, streaming out through the windows and doors of the ballroom, easing its step until stomp turned into tiptoe, tickling his eardrums as he wandered among the hedges.

His stomach was turning, but not from the champagne that sat inside it, an alien trying to stick to barren soil.

Pretend, Algernon had said. *Play house.*

Perhaps one could be vicious even without teeth. With the sharpest of fingernails, Jacques had been gentle with Ambrose, tender. With the largest of vampire teeth, able to sire and rend apart, able to rip, Marcel had cared for him as a father might.

But with one phrase, Algernon had torn him down, ripped from him the semblance of healing he had plastered together over two hundred years of loneliness.

Lost in his thoughts, Ambrose wasn't listening for heartbeats as he wandered the hedgerows. He saw the secluded human just as their gasp slipped forth. Ambrose felt like a deer caught in headlights, keenly aware now of the fangs that had slipped out in his frustration, glistening bright in the shaft of moonlight that lit the maze garden in pure silver.

The human stiffened, hands tightening around the edge of a stone bench, color draining from their face as swiftly as water in an unplugged bath.

"I..." The poor thing looked as lost as Ambrose felt. The fear in those lovely blue eyes was palpable, the scent of terror thickening the air between them. *Ah well. No avoiding this now. Might as well make the most of it.*

"May I have a taste?"

How about hello first, DeVoreur?

Seeing Algernon again had thrown him off-balance, his sharp tongue cutting through every polite ritual Ambrose had built over the years. But in the end, Ambrose always asked. He never took. Never forced. Nothing in the world could ever distract him enough to forget about consent.

The human tilted their head to the side, short brown curls flopping nearly to their shoulder. As they shifted, the moonlight cut across their face, exposing the tears streaking their cheeks. "Oh, dear, are you upset?" Ambrose asked.

"Am I dreaming?" The human's voice sounded thinned out, breathing air through the thickness that had previously clogged their throat.

"No, you are not, but if you let me taste you, I can make you forget after. Truthfully, I will have to. This entire exchange, in fact." Ambrose crossed his arms, shaking his head. Silver-white hair flicked past his eyes and over his shoulder. "I will not pry, but it *is* quite dangerous to be roaming about in the dark like this, especially if you thundered away in a huff. Nobody will be looking for you."

"How do you know I thundered away in a huff?" the human asked.

"Because *I* thundered away in a huff, and this was the most plausible place I could think of to come and make a fuss." Ambrose pressed his lips together, glancing at the human. They couldn't be any older than he'd been when Marcel had given him the gift. Twenty-three at best. "It's dangerous. There are..." Ambrose's eyes skidded to the hedges, as though he had the ability to see through them. "Others like me," he finally admitted. "Not everyone is considerate."

"To be fair, I didn't know you existed five minutes ago, and I still think someone spiked my drink for me to be seeing those teeth. Wait." They craned their neck, eyes bulging. "Where did they go? Am I... did I imagine it?"

It would have been easy to say yes, to dismiss it as delusion, but when had that helped anyone? In the end, he would have to look the person in the eye and compel them to forget. Ambrose shook his head.

The human narrowed their eyes, mouth twisting from side to side in deliberation, then sighed and scooted over, patting the empty space on their bench. It warmed something that had refused to die in Ambrose, some lingering human sentiment that would always love these creatures despite the way they'd hated him. He moved closer, covering the distance at a snail's pace, in case the human suddenly changed their mind. If they ran, he'd have to chase them, and that would be unpleasant for both of them.

In the end, Ambrose sat. The stone was not uncomfortable, although he would prefer a cushioned seat, a warm divan in front of a roaring fire, familiar arms around his shoulders, soft lips grazing his skin, gentle hands brushing his hair. He and Jacques had braided their hair together in the middle once, a marbled rope of black and white that joined them in yet another way. Marcel had called them ridiculous when he'd seen them, but the glint in his eye had betrayed his fondness.

"Well, why did *you* storm off?"

"Someone I trusted hurt me in a way I did not expect," Ambrose said. *Trusted.* Did he trust Algernon? He combed a thick strand of hair over his shoulder and began running his fingers through it, flitting against it harp-like. "I needed to gather my emotions in private."

"Me too," the human replied.

"I would offer to end them for you, but it's not my style, I'm afraid." Ambrose narrowed his eyes, offering a smile, surprised when he received the same.

"See, was that so hard?" the human asked. "Was it so hard to say you'd end *them*, instead of just assuming?" Their nostrils flared, a soft nose on a beautiful face, full lips and large teeth with a gap in the middle. "It's worse when they *know*, you know? And they know. I've never tried to hide who I am. And especially who I'm not. *What* I'm not."

Some long-forgotten organ inside Ambrose came to life. The human was like Jacques then, neither here nor there, perhaps in both places at once, perhaps not even on the same line of being as someone like him, someone who had ventured across a wall of brick, clawing it with the raw tips of his fingers. Marcel had given him a mallet. Jacques had held his waist while Ambrose swung. The three of them had crossed that line together, Marcel and Jacques holding Ambrose's hands through the hardest moments.

Did this human have anyone to give them a mallet?

"Did you die to get those teeth then?" they asked. When they tilted their head back, Ambrose spied fresh tears spilling from their eyes. "Is that too personal?"

"I did," Ambrose replied. He remembered having questions and nobody to answer them. He remembered binding himself to the point of pain because nobody had shown him how to do it safely. There *had* been nobody like him in his time, not that he knew of. The men would eat him with their eyes as he walked about the tables and served them drinks in his boyish garb, his hair gathered beneath a cap. They would grasp at the air and then a little closer, squeezing parts of him that made him round. Until he resolved to leave no roundness, to bind it all away, to carve out the rest with his hunger. He wished now he had tasted more food when his stomach could take it. Sometimes he wished he had never stepped foot in that place, that he had never met the man who'd followed him first with his eyes for weeks, then round the alley where Ambrose would die.

"Did it hurt?" The human closed their eyes, squeezed them shut. "It would be easier than living in this hell, I think. To live perceived as everything except..."

"It was the truest agony I've ever felt," Ambrose replied. He leaned forward, glancing at them through his eyebrows. "I would not recommend it."

"If you tasted me, would it make you feel better about your friend?" the human asked.

"Yes," Ambrose replied.

"Would... would it hurt?" The tremor in their voice was clear as day.

"A bit. Only at the start," Ambrose said. "It would feel good after that. I can make it feel good for you. I would."

"Will I become like you if I let you?" Their blue eyes searched Ambrose's gaze. Jacques had called his eyes diamonds once. Ambrose smiled as he recalled it.

"No," he replied.

"Will I still feel like this if I ever become like you?" Ambrose wished he could fill them with as much hope as rested on their question.

"Darling, you will only stop feeling like this if you surround yourself with people who understand you," Ambrose said. Instinctively, he reached out a hand. Marcel tucked his hair behind his ear every time he was upset.

You're not Marcel and this is not your charge.

Ambrose let his hand drop. "There's nothing wrong with who you are. I loved someone like you once. Still do."

"Will you tell me about them?" The human twisted to face him a little better, eyes wide with awe and expectation.

"Jacques was the second face I saw when I first opened my eyes, no longer human." Ambrose looked up at the night sky, knowing that should he extinguish every star, blot out the moon, it would never be dark enough to match the tresses flowing down Jacques's back that day they'd met, the intensity of their lovely narrow eyes. "They were enchanting. I was enchanted."

"Were they also..." The human curled their upper lip back, pressing their teeth into the soft flesh of the lower. "Vampy?"

A laugh trickled out of Ambrose, warming him better than any coat could have.

"Yes. As vampy as they come," Ambrose replied. "Jacques adored being as they were, relished the feed, and even with so terrible an education, they were gentle about it. Everything they did was beautiful."

"An education? Do you go to, like, a vampire school then? Do they teach you how to kill people?" The human's eyes widened. Ambrose wasn't sure whether it was fear or wonder, but judging from their heartbeat, he could assume it was a bit of both.

"No. Nothing like that. We're not supposed to kill people, anyway." Ambrose brushed his corset. "And Jacques never killed. Even when their Sire punished them, they did everything in their power to fight it."

Ambrose paused. It was more difficult than he'd assumed it would be, recalling the darkest moments of Jacques's past, remembering the stories whispered into his ear while Jacques braided his hair with fingers that would never hurt him.

"They sound... like you." The human looked away from Ambrose, fixing their eyes on a tall hedge. To be compared to Jacques was the greatest gift anyone could give him, and this human had done it unknowingly. It had come to them as easily as breathing.

"They were spectacular. It was a beautiful time—me, Jacques, Marcel. Everything was good and quiet and beautiful. There was dancing in the halls of our house, music and learning, love. So much love." Ambrose wished he could cry. "Jacques was the sun that lit up the darkness our condition binds us to."

"Was." Their voice had grown throaty and hoarse, thick with emotion. Ambrose could only nod. "I hope they loved you as well as you clearly love them."

"I think they loved me better," Ambrose replied.

Of course I did.

Ambrose bowed his head, relishing the memory of Jacques's voice, that deep low timbre crooning as they lulled him to rest after long nights roaming. "I think they loved beyond human comprehension. And the world can't take that much goodness."

"The world can, respectfully, go to hell." The human was frowning when Ambrose looked at them again. Their eyebrows were thick brown lines meeting over a wrinkled nose, genuine rage vibrating off their skin. This was the beautiful thing about humans; they felt everything with their bodies. "I'm sorry. It isn't fair."

"No, it isn't." Ambrose tucked his hair behind his ear. "But I didn't mean to make you feel worse. There *are* beautiful things about life, and the world isn't always a cruel place. We simply... had the misfortune."

The memory of Claude's face filled Ambrose with bitterness.

"Did Jacques like being this way? Being like me?"

"Jacques could be no other way. And they were the most beautiful person I've ever known." Ambrose glanced at the human through the corner of his eye, offering the softest smile a vampire could muster. "There is joy to be had in difference too. I was not always Ambrose. Well, I was, but I wasn't always known as Ambrose or seen as Ambrose. Now everyone I know only knows and sees me as myself. It's all a matter of being around the right people."

The human eased, sweeping their clump of curls away from their bare neck, a light brown that might have been Marcel's before he'd turned, before Ambrose had known him, before Claude had almost killed him, then relented because Marcel was just so beautiful. As though this could ever be a reason by which to determine whether someone lived or died.

"You seem very much like the right people. Go on. Dig in." The casualness of the human's invitation drew a laugh from Ambrose. It was not uncommon for humans to respond this calmly when they saw him. Jacques had always said there was a gentleness about Ambrose, a calming spirit that reached and touched these humans' souls, that promised them he'd keep them safe. Ambrose leaned in, calling his fangs. So many years after Ambrose's first bite, the odd sensation was no longer painful as they slid out. He swept back his hair, leaning in.

"It will only sting for a moment," Ambrose said. His hand wrapped around the human's neck, thumb gently rubbing the skin on the other side, comforting, soothing, trying to ease the hammering pulse he could both hear and feel. "You'll be fine, dear."

There were few things in the world as beautiful as sinking fangs into a neck. Flesh gave way to sharp teeth, splitting as gracefully as a ripped seam, coming apart for Ambrose. Blood pooled at the bite, filling his mouth, sustaining him, settling on his tongue—a glorious first gush.

All humans tasted different, each with their own little fingerprint—a scent, a taste, a texture. In his many years walking the earth, Ambrose had come to believe that this was where the human soul lingered, in the sanguine promise of life that rushed through their veins and arteries, keeping them warm, giving their heart its work, their kidneys, all the organs Ambrose didn't need anymore. Because Ambrose didn't *have* a soul.

Jacques had said that Ambrose must. That if anybody in the world did, then it had to be Ambrose. By that logic, Ambrose had said that if such a creature existed, then it must be Jacques.

The human gasped, easing as the initial stiffness melted away. They leaned into the bite, humming their pleasure, moaning, hands reaching out to grasp anything. Ambrose offered a hand. The human slid their fingers into it, gripping his cold knuckles, their warmth reminding him he had once been human too.

"Care to share?"

Ambrose pulled away just as the human sprang to the other side of the bench, their heart accelerating to the speed of a thousand horses, fear oozing out like sweat from their young supple skin.

"You're fine," Ambrose whispered, encircling their elbow with a hand. He looked up at Algernon, wishing to wipe the smirk right off his face, along with the fangs he kept flashing at the human. "You did not have to frighten them. You know that isn't my way."

"I only asked if you wanted to share." Algernon glanced at the human. "*You* seem comfortable. May I participate?"

"Why? So you can rip into them like your master taught you?" Ambrose stood, nostrils flaring, and stepped in front of the human, curling his nose at Algernon.

"I'm not a *dog*, Ambrose. I can handle myself," Algernon said. "Have you forgotten our hunts? Hmm?"

"I have not forgotten a single moment." Ambrose found Algernon's dark gaze. He expected it to be limned with mischief and play, but Algernon looked earnest, as far removed from smug, cruel Claude as any person could be. "I remember you bending to Claude's will like the stalk of a daisy caught in a hurricane."

"Claude is not *here* to impose his will." Algernon's entire face stiffened, giving up his discomfort. "You speak as though you have never had a drop yourself. I follow you and find you feeding. Has it even been a minute? Why is it that when I want to do the same, it's wrong? What makes Ambrose DeVoreur worthy of the moral pedestal and me and my clan no better than scum?"

"I am not beholden to that cockroach of a man. I have never pretended to be better than what I am, but at least I do not answer to a monster." Ambrose turned away, the sight of Algernon's evident pain crushing something in his chest.

"Why do you define me by something I had no control over, Ambrose?" It came out a whisper. "You should know b—"

Ambrose did not want to discuss this. He'd spoken plenty of the past already and going back even further was not something he wished to entertain. His softness turned sharp as fangs, clawing the viciousness right out of his bruised stomach.

"He treats humans like *table scraps*. And he teaches you to do the same. You know it's true. Marcel is—"

"*Perfect*, of course, since he's associated with you and your precious—"

"Say their name to my face." Ambrose met Algernon's eyes squarely. Algernon took a silent step forward, raising a hand. Ambrose corrected the distance between them, moving back. "Don't come here telling me you missed me only to spit Jacques at me."

"I wasn't..." Algernon closed his eyes. "Please."

"Please what?" Ambrose fixed his gaze on Algernon's mouth, watched the plea form on his tongue, circling those kissable lips that had never failed to ruin him.

"Listen, it's getting cold. Are you going to bite me or not?" Right. The human.

"May I?" Algernon asked. It took him a second to tear his eyes from Ambrose, but eventually he found the human's face, a far gentler smile on his lips than Ambrose was accustomed to seeing while they hunted.

"You do *not* have to accept," Ambrose murmured, stepping closer to them. "You can say no. Always."

"Will it feel the same if..." The human turned to Ambrose. "Will it be as good?"

"If Algernon agrees to be gentle, yes," Ambrose said, glaring at the other vampire through his brows. "If you hurt them, I will *end* you."

"So touchy over someone you must have only just met," Algernon said.

"Well, how dare you assume?" Ambrose crossed his arms over his corset. Algernon leaned against the tall bush behind him, his waistcoat gleaming crimson, flashing its dangerous light back at the moon.

"What's their name then?" Algernon's eyebrow popped up, lips twitching. Ambrose wished he wasn't so susceptible to his charms.

"Listen to that. Are all you people so considerate?" the human asked, turning to look at Ambrose, wide-eyed.

"Weren't you listening to our... squabble? Algernon is the least considerate asshole I've ever met," Ambrose said. "Acknowledging others without assumption is basic decency..." His voice faltered as he searched for a name he hadn't requested.

"River. I go by River," the human said, the corners of their lips curving up. They wore the name well too, their earthen hair and blue eyes calling as much of the forest to the hotel garden as their handsome moss-colored outfit. They glanced Algernon's way. "If you apologize for mentioning Jacques and upsetting Ambrose, then yes."

It was a kindness, and it was not lost on Ambrose.

Algernon found his eyes and held them. The moment lasted an eternity. The silence felt longer.

"I was about to," Algernon said. It would have to be enough. It was.

They sat on either side of River, who had since scooted back to the middle and tilted their head back. Ambrose's eyes drifted to their neck, where the evidence of his feasting had left a slow trickle. He leaned in, rolling his tongue up the line of rich thick red. River shuddered at the touch, stiffening as Algernon's fingers wrapped around their throat, resting at the dip, pressing where they swallowed. Ambrose glanced around them, found Algernon's large glistening fangs out and ready, remembered the feeling of being at their mercy, of wanting him.

Ambrose closed his eyes and bit. He felt Algernon's bite through River's neck, tasted their pleasure, their fear, their *aliveness*. If he could, Ambrose would never stop. He would drink and drink and drink until his stomach was past fullness, until there was so much blood in him it seeped from his pores, sprang forth from his eyes, gushed out his mouth. He had always had a greater desire for the taste. For the feed.

Perhaps this was another reason Claude had wanted to poach him off Marcel. Other than the obvious, other than the ugly history that tainted the relationship of Ambrose and Algernon's Sires. Yes, Claude had wanted Ambrose. And who wouldn't? What a beautiful monster to have; one that could not be satisfied, one that always yearned for more. For all of his accusations, Ambrose had to work twice as hard as anybody else to stop when he did. Claude would have feasted on his weakness, would have worked his strings like the puppet master that he was, would have turned Ambrose into a killing machine, into a man that would consume, consume, *consume* above all else.

But Ambrose was not a machine. Ambrose was still a man—a dead one, perhaps, but with more respect for life than he would have had if Marcel hadn't shielded him, if he hadn't taken blow after blow on Ambrose's behalf, guarding him like a delicate flower on a cliffside, swallowing the wind so it would not ruffle Ambrose's soft petals.

So Ambrose pulled away. River had started to ease, to give in, their grip on Ambrose's thigh slackening. Ambrose cradled their head, rubbing away the trickle of blood with his thumb. Algernon stopped, eyes rising to meet Ambrose's.

"I *can* control myself," Algernon said, rubbing the sides of his mouth with a thumb, "if I mean to."

"Do you call this control?! God, Algernon, you're incapable—God, *no*. I promised. I promised them." The maze garden was spinning. Ambrose cradled his temples, glancing at a delirious River, quickly slumping against the bushes, heart slowing, beat weakening. If Ambrose had a working heart, it would be racing right now. "I have to..." Ambrose turned his still dripping fangs onto the fair unblemished skin of his own wrist.

"Ambrose, no. It's too dangerous." Algernon stood, rubbing his face. "Leave it. You didn't *mean* to do this. *We* didn't. We didn't mean to hurt them."

"Yes, but we might have, Algernon. And I can't just leave it. I'm not *like* you. I don't like killing the people who sustain me. I know what it's like to be on the other end of that, to be destroyed at the whim of another. And it's not going to happen to River." Ambrose ground his teeth and looked at River, thought about the way their eyes had glimmered when he'd addressed them the way they preferred, thought about the hope in their eyes that things would get better if only they spent their time with people who understood them. Ambrose couldn't sit there and watch that fade away. He couldn't just stand up and leave River alone to die.

"Ambrose, *don't*." Terror darted across Algernon's eyes, hardened. Ambrose did. He raised his wrist to his mouth and *bit*. "*Ambrose*," Algernon hissed.

"You may report me if you wish," Ambrose said. He didn't wait for Algernon's response.

In a flash, his wrist was pressed to River's mouth, blood dripping in through their lips, flowing free and smooth. Ambrose watched their throat swallow reflexively, willed them to react, to latch on.

Come now, River. You've fought your whole life, haven't you? Fight now.

River's face contorted as the tangy rusty taste of Ambrose's blood hit their tastebuds, awareness grinding alive in the whirring cogs of a mind that would not succumb. A moment later, River latched on, fingers wrapping around Ambrose's wrist, mouth pressing harder around the bite, tongue lapping up every drop Ambrose could give. River's eyes snapped open, glancing left and right, like a hare in a field to the cock of a gun. They found Ambrose's face first, their eyes swiftly darting down to his wrist on their mouth, slowing to a stop as they pulled back. Ambrose's skin stitched itself shut.

"Feeling better?" he asked, offering them a smile.

"What..."

"Can you stand?" Ambrose rose to his feet, offering an arm. River took it, but stood without much effort, without swinging or swaggering back. "Dear, I need to compel you to forget this, what happened. Can I do that now?"

"You're not serious," Algernon hissed. "You don't need their consent for *that*, Ambrose. It's our sacred *law*." Ambrose cast Algernon a glare. "Though it looks like you're fine skirting around the laws now."

Ambrose shook his head, looking at River again. "You're going to be all right. Just... try not to die over the next three days, will you?"

"Am I free to die after that?" River grinned. It reminded Ambrose why he'd risked this. He cupped their face, hoping the touch was not overly familiar, but River seemed at ease with him.

"I wish you a very long, very fruitful life as yourself," Ambrose replied. "Can you promise me that before I make you forget what we shared? Can you promise me you'll rid yourself of the people who chain you?"

"Won't I forget my promise after?" River asked. *Mischief.* It brought Jacques to him now, Jacques and their playful eyes, Jacques and their free spirit that refused to adhere to any binary set by man.

"Not if you mean it." Ambrose inclined his head, meeting their eyes. "Just... be careful, all right? My blood will clear from your system in a few days and then everything will be normal again."

"I wish I didn't have to forget this," River replied. They pursed their lips. "But I know I do." Their blue eyes found Ambrose's. An eternity of affections passed between them—other lives that could have been lived in which Ambrose was born in this time and place, in which Ambrose was alive, in which Ambrose could age with a person like River, be friends with them.

Their expression altered, smile dropping and eyes going blank as Ambrose called his power. He had never much enjoyed compulsion; what an ugly, intrusive thing. What a necessary tool.

"Algernon and I were never here. You wandered to the garden for some space and left, knowing you needed to change some things about the people you surround yourself with, determined to put your happiness first, determined to stay safe." Ambrose leaned in and kissed them on the forehead. "Now go."

River blinked, eyes clearing. They looked right through Ambrose, as though he wasn't even there, and they turned and walked away. Ambrose watched until they were swallowed by the darkness.

There were no words. No sounds. Two long-dead people stood in a maze, a taut string of tension between them, ready to snap. Algernon shifted against the hedge, then straightened, approaching him.

"You think I would report you?" he asked.

"I think you would do whatever Claude tells you to do. I thought we had already established that," Ambrose replied. He met his eyes directly, unflinching. Ambrose had experienced the fear of men. It had slipped from him with his human life. Every fear Ambrose had possessed since then had come to pass. Every minute of his life, he pictured Jacques and the fingers that would never touch him again.

"And I thought we had established that Claude is not here." Algernon's fingers grazed Ambrose's cheek. "What if someone finds out what you did tonight, Ambrose?"

"How would anyone ever find out?" Ambrose asked. "Will you tell?"

"Ambrose, turning humans has been outlawed for more than two centuries. If something happens to that person—"

"River." Ambrose wanted to swat away Algernon's hand but didn't. "They have a name."

"If something happens to *River*, others will know there's a baby vampire on the loose. You know the signs. You remember."

"It's been well over six hundred years," Ambrose replied, arching an eyebrow.

"Not long enough." Algernon pressed his eyes closed. "Sometimes I still shudder when I think about that unquenchable thirst. Sometimes it gives me goosebumps, thoughts and plans for a rampage." He bowed his head. "Ambrose... I only get angry because I *do* care."

"That's funny." Ambrose's eyes slid away, fixing instead on the bush where River had slackened, where he and Algernon had almost killed a human who had offered them their blood. "We have not seen each other in a decade. And we are not friends."

"I like to think that you're my oldest friend." A thumb brushed Ambrose's jaw. "You're the one I shared every big moment with, Ambrose. We were turned almost at the same time. We were babies together. I remember you through every stage and every transformation. I remember you with Jacques and I remember you after."

"And I remember you ten years ago." Ambrose turned away, pacing to the tallest unencumbered bush. It was harsher than it looked, the needly leaves pricking the cold skin of his brow as he bent forward. He should walk away. He should trust that Algernon wouldn't report him.

"It isn't my fault." Vampires didn't exude warmth or body heat, didn't need to breathe, although many did, for the sake of comfort. They didn't have heartbeats. Still, Ambrose sensed Algernon's approach and did nothing to stop the palm of Algernon's hand from coming to rest on his shoulder. "I have to go where my Sire demands. It's different for me. Marcel does not command you, nor does he abuse the bond between you. Claude wields it like a leash."

"Yet you choose not to sever it." Ambrose twisted his neck, eyes resting on Algernon's hard knuckles. "You have that choice."

"He's all I know," Algernon said. "You should understand. You have not left Marcel."

"Marcel is not *cruel*." Ambrose whirled, flashing his fangs. There were many things he could spit out in Algernon's face, many things he wanted to say, things he had been desperate to share over the last ten years they had spent in different places. "Your Sire ruined everything."

"*Your* Sire ruined everything first. It's not our fault Marcel took Jacques from Claude. That spite should not be our inheritance, should not be our poison. Claude... is just angry sometimes. It says more about him than about you." Algernon reached for Ambrose, but Ambrose inched back.

He had you on and off for two centuries after it happened. Ambrose may not have known back then about Claude and what he had done, but now he did. And he was done giving Algernon time that had been stolen from him, from Jacques.

"You recoil as though my touch would burn you," Algernon said.

"I wouldn't want to take any chances," Ambrose replied. Even with his fangs locked away, he could be sharp. "Your clan is silver. And you... you might just be pure sunlight."

Algernon's jaw stiffened, his gaze betraying the bleeding wound Ambrose had torn into him.

Wounds heal. But my grief will never stop.

"There was a time you'd search for it, you said." Algernon's voice went soft, cotton candy at the fair, cutting his teeth with sugar that could make them fall. Why did he have to twist into Ambrose like this? Why did he have the power to wrap those long fingers around his heart and make it wish to beat? Even after all that had happened. "I remember..." Algernon leaned in. His brow felt somehow warmer than Ambrose's, perhaps because he hadn't just forced all the blood in his body to go to his wrist and feed a human he'd almost killed. Ambrose wanted to flinch away but didn't. "I remember you telling me about the cliffside with your parents and how you wished you could recall the feeling of the sun on your skin, its kiss."

Algernon pulled away and if Ambrose had still been human, his breath might have caught in his throat at the sight of that soft mouth again coming closer, pressing velvet into the satin of his cheek. A hand wrapped around his waist from behind.

"This is what it feels like... the sun on your skin." Algernon brushed his lips against Ambrose's jaw, feathering kisses down his neck, making him want to arch his back, to bend and break for him as he always had.

"You're a monster," Ambrose murmured. He'd never meant it as much before.

"Aren't we all?" Algernon didn't stop kissing around his neck, his soft curls brushing Ambrose's chin like down feathers.

"How can you touch me like this after..." Ambrose squeezed his eyes shut, faltering at the thought of repeating Jacques's name out loud to Algernon again, opening a door for the other vampire to coat his lover's name in venom.

"After what?" Algernon pulled away at last, his brown eyes fixed on Ambrose's gaze, focused and untrembling, his fangs freshly out and poised for a bite. A proper predator. Why did he have to be this beautiful? Why did Algernon look better monstrous?

"After Jacques." The words pushed out of Ambrose a whisper.

"Everything you ever do in your life will be after Jacques now." It didn't sound cruel falling off his lips. It sounded like a plea, like a soothing breeze on a summer's day, the glow of a campfire on deep winter nights, crackling logs.

"I don't want your pity," Ambrose said. What he wanted, he could never have.

"It wasn't my pity I wanted to give you tonight." Algernon's hand traveled further south, sliding over his backside, squeezing him close. If Ambrose thought about the rest of his body, he would feel Algernon's shape, his hip bone pressing into the planes of his stomach, his arm brushing his side. He looked up into Algernon's face. "Break for me, Ambrose," Algernon said.

It made him shudder, brought his *yes* to his mouth so quickly, he had to grit his teeth to swallow it. Ambrose's nose curled. "I hate you," he said.

"It's always better when you're angry." Algernon's smile was darker than the night itself, his scent pouring into Ambrose, musk covering up the smoke of the burning ruins of his life. He leaned in, nipping on Ambrose's earlobe before he spoke again. "Your rage is delicious."

Ambrose lunged first this time, two centuries' worth of grief spilling through the venom of his teeth, ten years' worth of anger cutting into Algernon like he was a slab of meat.

A growl rumbled in Algernon's throat, bubbling against Ambrose's mouth, thick blood sliding over his tongue. Burning burning burning him, filling his body until the taste of *Algernon* consumed his every thought.

His every feeling.

His every reluctance.

Until there was only Algernon.

Algernon.

Algernon.

Ambrose remembered with ease now why all those years before he'd sought him out, why the very sight of Algernon would fill his stomach with a joy unhindered. Unexplainable. They *were* good together. And Ambrose hated it. He hated that he had given in, that he had given Algernon what he wanted, that he had bent to his will yet again. More than anything, Ambrose hated that he had liked it. That he wanted to do it again.

And now Algernon was getting dressed, and who knew whether he'd be gone for another decade without word or warning, leaving him to simmer in this guilt of what they had done, in his dirty desire to be with a person whose family had—?

"This won't happen again," Ambrose said, turning to face him. "I am not your plaything to pick up and take whenever you deign to grace the city with your unwanted presence. I am not a *doll* to be dropped when you decide to leave without a word or warning."

"I never said you were." Algernon arched his eyebrows, buttoning up his shirt like a person, like he wasn't bound to the most brutal Sire their world had ever known. "And I have no plans to leave."

"When did you get back?" Ambrose asked, tucking a strand of hair behind his ear. His rage had boiled over, frothing over the lip of his pot while he faced the hedge, and now his grief simmered alone and endless, as before. He looked at Algernon, at his lips curving, his sidelong glance.

"I thought you didn't care about me." Algernon stretched to button up his pants at the curve of his hip. "I'll help you with that. Turn."

Ambrose liked the feeling of familiar fingers doing up his corset, pulling on the laces so it cinched him in and tightened around him, pressing into lungs that did not need to breathe. Algernon was swift in this as in all things. Ambrose despised himself for relishing his touch. He couldn't wait now to go home and curl into Marcel's side, pour out this ugly confession into ears that would not judge him.

"You haven't answered me," Ambrose said as Algernon tied the laces. His mouth was soft as it pressed into the long white column of Ambrose's neck.

"We've been out of the country, but all of us missed it." Algernon took a step back. "You're done, love."

Ambrose turned to face him again, compelled for whatever reason to button up his waistcoat for him. He closed the distance, fumbling with each button, focusing on the intricate carving in the gold.

"What did you miss most?" Ambrose asked. "The traffic?" Unlike Marcel and Ambrose, Claude and his clan lived in a large house in the center of the capital. It had once been a quieter place, although never the quietest. His lips quirked to the side as he glanced up at Algernon. He hadn't expected to find those eyes on him still, boring into him.

It was not new, Algernon's devotion. Ambrose remembered the way Algernon loved, the way he touched, the way he consumed. Everything was done with *reverence*. Worship. Except Ambrose had always supposed Algernon must be this way with every person he touched.

As his eyes burned through Ambrose's skin as surely as though they were the sun, Ambrose understood that while *he* had been consuming Algernon on as many casual nights as six hundred years of chance encounters could afford, Algernon had been making love to him, yearning to have him as only Jacques once had, watching him love another in the shadows. Because they had been friends. Ambrose had thought so. But Algernon had kept his clan's ugly secrets close and now Ambrose wouldn't venture any closer. If he did, he would impale himself on the cold hard blade of betrayal.

"May I court you?" The words spilled from Algernon's mouth like water over a soft round hillside, babbling into Ambrose's ear. "I do not seek to replace them, Ambrose. I can share your heart. Jacques was a good person. Despite my terrible behavior before, I respected them. I always will. And for all my horribly insensitive words, perhaps I was jealous and playing house with you is all I could ever want. All I could ever dream."

"I don't think people *court* each other anymore, Algernon." *All Algernon could dream.* The sentiment choked Ambrose, made his unbeating heart want to race. Ambrose stepped back, smoothing the fine fabric of Algernon's waistcoat. A breeze blew into the maze garden, ruffling his soft curls, billowing through Ambrose's thin ruffle shirt.

"Well, we're from a different time. I would very much like to do things as I might have back when I was human had our paths crossed." Algernon looked down at Ambrose in earnest, dropping into a crouch and inviting him to step into a boot.

"When we were human, your type would have made my type wear dresses and bear them children," Ambrose said. "And you never respected Jacques. Don't insult my intelligence."

"Then you didn't know my type because I never would have done that. Not then and not now and not ever." Algernon zipped up Ambrose's boot and reached for the other. "You forget that my type were not exactly beloved in our time either. There." Algernon rose, running long fingers through his curls. "And I would sooner drain you dry than insult you. What do you know of my feelings toward—"

A fierce wind cut through the maze then, bringing with it the smell of caramel that stuck to everything Marcel owned—his car, his clothes, his bedroom. Ambrose started like a meerkat standing up at being caught with Algernon, but Marcel barely glanced at the other man, eyes fixing on Ambrose and only Ambrose.

"We should go. There's been a fight in the ballroom and someone's died. Cracked their head on the floor. On their neck, they have..." Marcel paused, pressing his lips together and finally looking at Algernon. "Have either of you fed tonight?"

Ambrose's head snapped Algernon's way, their fixed gazes piecing together the puzzle. They took off in a run, zooming down the maze, past the hedges, turning each corner at the speed of a thousand cheetahs, Marcel running behind them, telling them to run the other way, to steer clear of this.

"They don't have your fingerprints on record. Any of ours. Let's go. Algernon, you can alert your clan to leave," Marcel said.

"My clan is not here." Ambrose's head whipped left. Had Algernon come alone? "I know you can't resist a ball." Algernon shrugged. "I had to chance it."

"And why are you running with us? You don't care about River," Ambrose said. *You don't care about anyone.*

"*You* care about River. And I care about you." Algernon halted, stopping Ambrose in his tracks and taking his hands, searching his eyes. "We'll say it was me. Claude will make it go away."

"No, Algernon." Ambrose tore his hands free, expression hardening. "What Claude would do is make *River* go away." Something dead softened. Because they *had* been friends, hadn't they? At least once upon a time. "Or you."

"What are we talking about?" Marcel looked from Ambrose to Algernon. "What's happened, then?"

"Uh... congratulations?" Ambrose stretched his mouth into an uncomfortable curve. "You're a grandfather?"

If Marcel could lose color, he would have. A hand rose to cover his mouth. He looked at Algernon, who shook his head, promising his silence, then at Ambrose. Marcel tilted his head back and looked up at the moon, as though it held all the wisdom of the world.

Perhaps realizing it didn't, Marcel let his shoulders drop and gave Ambrose a nod.

"It happens," he said. "Come on. We have a lot of compelling to do. Let's take our baby vampire home."

The heavy velvet drapes were drawn shut, barring the morning sunshine from entering. Ambrose had sat on the same armchair for hours and hours, pausing only to pace from one end of the room to the other. Marcel sat on the divan. Both of them had changed out of their outfits from the party and sat now in far more comfortable pants and loose cotton shirts. Ambrose had braided and unbraided his hair seven thousand times, anything to keep his fingers busy.

"They'll wake up soon. I remember this with you." Marcel pretended to leaf through his book, but Ambrose knew he could think of nothing else either, that he was only pretending to be calm for his benefit. "And when Jacques came too. I was the one Claude assigned to watch them."

"I really am sorry," Ambrose said, curling his legs in. His knees were hard and bony, but the gap between them cushioned his chin well enough. "I didn't mean to take so much, and I couldn't let them die. I know killing is not exactly against our law. I know it's just frowned upon. But..."

"But you did what you believed to be right and I'm very proud of you, Ambrose." Marcel's eyes slid to the right, to where River lay still in their party clothes in the bed Marcel had given them, a room away from Ambrose's. "I will not ask what's going on between you and Algernon, but I hope you know there is no need to walk around in the shadows.”

“I’m not about to walk around in the sunlight, gramps.” Ambrose flashed him a wry grin.

“Call me gramps again and I’ll put you out in the yard at noon.” Marcel narrowed his eyes, closing his book and giving up the pretense of doing anything other than wait. He stretched his legs over the other end of the divan and turned on his stomach, folding his arms beneath his chin. It was hard sometimes to remember that he was more than eight hundred years old. “You know what I mean. I know he’s one of Claude’s, but as long as he doesn’t hurt you, I won’t come between the two of you.”

“Him being of Claude should be enough to make him ineligible,” Ambrose said, picking at a thread of fabric on the armchair.

“Every person you love is of Claude, Ambrose. I’m of Claude. As was Jacques...” Marcel paused. “Don’t hinder yourself from living. We are not here to simply exist. You deserve some joy in your life.”

“I do have joy. I have *you*.” Ambrose shrugged. “And now we have River too.”

“Algernon would have taken the fall for you.” Marcel pressed his chin into his forearm. “I’m not the expert on love *or* sex, never having experienced either. Nor do I want to be. But I’ve read enough novels, seen enough films. And I’ve seen two people in love before. I see a person still in love every day.”

Ambrose found Marcel’s gaze fixed on him. He had no words, was glad for once his heart couldn’t give away his nervousness, that he couldn’t blush. In the end, he settled for a nod.

“Allowing yourself to love and be loved will not replace them, Ambrose.” Marcel shifted around again, stretching his legs up in the air. "And if he ever wants to leave that *clown*, there's space for him here, with us, too."

"You're entirely too forgiving sometimes, Marcel. Have you forgotten—"

"Not for a second." Marcel shook his head. "But Algernon is *not* Claude, Ambrose, and you must remember it."

"He says he wants to court me," Ambrose said.

"Then let him," Marcel replied.

Ambrose wasn't sure what to say, but then he didn't have to say anything. The temperature in the room shifted, the mood altering as the sheets twitched. He sprang out of his armchair, rushing to the bed, where River was slowly shifting awake. Their fangs hung over their lower lip. Ambrose waited for their eyes to open, for that blue to be even brighter than it used to be before.

River gasped without breath, a panicked noise climbing out of them. Ambrose remembered waking up, thinking he was still in that alley being stabbed, remembered everything rushing back, realizing how cold he felt and that it didn't bother him, how strong the strange dull pain had been, pulsing around his wound, different but there. He waited for River to do the same.

Their eyes fluttered open, cobalt on an ashy light brown face. Their gaze darted from side to side, landing on Ambrose, remembering him now that the compulsion had worn off.

"What..." they started to say.

"I think you took me a little too literally when I said you should stand up for yourself." Ambrose brushed a curl out of their brow. "Don't panic. You did die after all."

"I what?" River sat up, looking around the room. "Where am I?"

Ambrose's lips curled, recalling Marcel's first words to him after he'd woken up like this, the words that anchored him still, that would anchor him always. He felt them on his tongue, shaped them on his lips, took Marcel's gift and passed it now to one of his own.

"Home, River," Ambrose said. He met their eyes, watched hope sink into the blue. A surge of joy gave him life for a minute. "You're home."

Blood and Oil

by Mae Murray

It woke, disturbed first by seismic waves shattering millions of paper-thin layers of shale, radar penetrating thousands of feet below the earth's surface into a deep, black well. It stirred in the slurry like an infant jostled in the womb, a foot scraping along rock which bore the bones of ancestors. It did not stay quiet long after that.

Then came the sound of the drill, boring through the shale and thicker layers of sediment, a hole the size of God's fist coming down like a hammer. Many weeks like this, the sound of that distant drum growing closer day by day, and the whole of the Creature's world began to quake the nearer it drew.

When the drill pierced that blackest layer, the earth began to spit, as if shaming its disrupters. The Creature within felt a mighty heave, sucked up through the funnel in a rush of fluid. This was how it remembered it had hands, hands that grasped at the crumbling shale as its oil-slicked body rushed through the man-made birth canal. Nearing the surface, it clung to a petrified root jutting out of the soil, wrapping arms and legs around it until the pressure of the pull eased. It lay there with its cheek pressed to the root, mouth open and drawing in oxygen that sent a searing pain through its chest. The air above was cool on its exposed back as night fell. It finally lifted its head.

Through the hole above, it saw the off-set head of the drill, and beyond that, a sky with swathes of deep and shimmering indigo. The Creature took its hand, long claws that ended in straight, black-tipped points, and began to scale the remaining yards to the surface. It dragged itself onto the flat earth, using its knees to belly-crawl a dark trail through the rock dust. It gagged like a leper, crude oil expressed from its stomach, its black mouth dripping. It stood, oozing oil-like blood from a wound, dragging its feet as it staggered across a flat and empty plain.

And that was how it was born.

The crescent moon of Darling's nail cut into the clementine, a spray of orange juice misting across her lips. She peeled the rind away, her knees bent awkwardly as she sat on a neat stack of three cinder blocks. Four more clementines nestled in her lap like orange-dappled robin's eggs.

Once peeled, she began eating segments, prying them apart with her front teeth as her other hand scrolled through her phone. A black box appeared on her social media page that warned of a graphic video. The caption above it read, "WELP, THIS JUST HAPPENED! NEVER BEEN SO SCARED! EVERY-ONE IS OKAY!" It had been posted several hours ago.

She glanced around the industrial park, but she was alone, as she always was this time of night, eating dinner in the earliest hours of the morning. Every bite of the fruit's flesh was tinged with a sharp chemical taste that reminded her of cancer. She tapped to turn up the volume, then pressed "Watch Anyway."

She balanced the small screen on her knee and began to systematically take apart the clementine as the video played.

It was a shaky phone recording of a children's birthday party. A teenage girl's voice was in the background, speaking to the adults gathered around a pool where children were splashing and playing. Pink streamers lined the white painted fence, and a grill released plumes of smoke that wavered like a mirage in the summer heat.

Offscreen, a popping—like firecrackers—started distantly, then grew closer. Someone cut the music abruptly, and the partygoers looked around with unease. Wails from the children rose into a cacophony of cries while the parents, still holding their beers, began to frantically usher them from the pool. A man in coral-colored linen shorts and boat shoes scooped a baby up from a high-chair and ran toward a sliding door. Another series of pops, and the shaky camera suddenly whipped, the summer scene becoming a swirl of blues, greens, and browns as the teenage girl screamed, ran, panted into the phone.

"It's a fucking gun!" The pitch of her voice broke from the frantic force. "It's a gun, it's a gun! Mommy!"

The camera turned in a sweep, and there was a man in the trembling lens, staggering through the fence's gate, leaving the swipe of a bloodied handprint across the white paint. A piece of his scalp was detached from his skull, the blood glimmering briefly in the sun's ray. The children still in the pool clung to the sides, screaming as the man fell face first into the water, blood streaming like red smoke from the head wound. It all happened in a matter of seconds.

The recording stopped suddenly, with a prompt to watch again. Darling took it back and paused on the moment the man stumbled through the fence, zooming in on the head wound to try to see the bullet hole. She couldn't tell if the video was AI, couldn't recall if colors during the day were really that bright, or if families always looked so rich and healthy. She discarded the clementine peel and picked up the next, her sticky hands turning brown from the dust collecting on her fingertips.

Then she moved on, continuing to scroll, her feed increasingly filled with black boxes and prompts to watch. If the video started with an animal, she clicked away quickly, scrolling as if running from it. If it opened on a person, she watched until the anxiety it caused became unbearable. Eventually, she looked up from her phone and found herself down to the fifth clementine.

The smell of the industrial park clung to her clothes like a tick. The concrete dust floated in the air, a million toxic stars, and Darling breathed them in and out, in and out each night. She'd worked at the oil refinery for four years now. Or had it been longer? She couldn't remember exactly when she'd started, her night shift turning the days passing into nights, a dizzying kaleidoscope of misery, a void where time was lost entirely. She was only thirty-six, but she felt much older, clearing the dirt and caked makeup from the lines around her eyes each morning before falling into bed, only to start all over again the next night. Late last year, just after her father died, she had begun seven-day shifts, and she hadn't stopped since, squirreling away her wages and spending nothing. There was no time to spend and no daylight in which to spend it. It wasn't like in the movies, a montage where she watched her life pass her by. It was more like being suspended without movement in the darkness, and she couldn't even bring herself to feel unsatisfied.

She had considered taking her own life. Even now, sitting under the stars and the industrial plumes, which could look strangely beautiful at night, streaming into ozone, she was thinking of the end. She bit at the side of her thumbnail, pulling away a thread of skin. It began to bleed.

"Where you been at?" came a gruff voice and scuff of boots from behind Darling.

"Where I always been," she said, standing up from her seat on the cinderblocks and giving a languid, cat-like stretch and yawn. Her body ached, each segment of her spine popping as the stretch moved up her body. "I still got break left, Jitterbug."

"You're damn near late. Boss sent me out here to get you."

"Well, I got two minutes left."

"You know how he is."

Darling nodded, gathering up her long dark hair and twisting it into a quick bun at the nape of her neck. "Still, you didn't have to disrupt my peace."

"If I hadn't, then I'd be the one in the hot seat. And I much rather he pick on you than me." Jitterbug grinned, nudging the toe of his boot at the scattering of clementine peels. "Same supper every night, huh? It ain't much. Don't think I haven't noticed you been slimming down."

Darling shrugged. "What's it to you, anyway? See you inside."

It was listening.

It could hear the screams emanating across the plains, the sound like warm milk to its ears among the thundering of the concrete smoke stacks. It followed that sound, those piercing wails, weaving its way through a maze of steel blue pipes held together by bolts rusted red as blood.

It peered at Darling, the image of her reflected in the sclera of its black eye as she watched the flickering screen of her phone. Its nostrils flared, the scent of blood carried on the wind like a song as Jitterbug walked up behind her. The words they exchanged sounded to the creature like the warbling of those seismic waves that had awakened it, a sound as foreign as the idea of language itself. Darling walked away, back toward the large processing plant, placing a dark mask over her face and leaving Jitterbug behind. He pulled out a soft pack of cigarettes, tapping one halfway out, then seemed to remember something and put it away again. The creature watched all this intensely.

It was the moment he turned his back to look at the sky, the first signs of daylight bleeding through the darkness, that the creature made its move.

It tackled Jitterbug from behind, quick as a bullet, his breath rushing from his lungs as he hit the ground. He had no time to gather air before it was upon him, its mouth stretching to an impossible wideness, revealing a row of jagged teeth and two canine points glinting like diamonds. When it sank its fangs into his throat and tore, he felt every moment of it, the artery severing and spraying blood like a rubber hose, the tough sinew fraying. When Jitterbug parted his lips to scream, a gush of black blood erupted from his throat.

The creature took long, deep pulls of blood, its back arched and belly heaving with each drag of the wound. Jitterbug was subdued, his head lolling to the side as his cheek pressed to the ground, a clementine peel clinging to his temple.

It was the sound of Darling's footsteps that drew its attention away from its meal just before Jitterbug's heart ceased to beat. It turned its head slowly, rose from its crouch.

Darling stood there, taking it in, her breath shuddering from her nostrils, her mask clasped in her white-knuckled hands.

"Why?" The word left Darling's lips, the sound of her own voice like a stranger's. She was scared, and she wasn't often scared. Not of rattlesnakes nor scorpions nor the wandering eyes of lonely men.

The Creature was tall, standing on two legs at full height. It looked like a woman, its skin as black as water and shimmering colors without name. Galaxies were written across its skin, the testaments of dying stars. Its body looked soft and supple, well-fed and strong, hips sloped like a gentle wave. Its hair was ankle-length and wound around its limbs and torso, black and wet as the oil from which it was born. Blood dripped from its teeth and chin, its mouth hanging open. It panted and took a step toward Darling.

Darling took a step back in turn, but the thing drew closer. With each backward step she took, it quickened its pace, until Darling dropped her mask in the dirt and turned to run. She yelled, the sound foreign as it filled her head, the rigid soles of her steel-toed boots kicking up dust and gravel. She didn't dare look over her shoulder, but she was certain she could feel the Creature's breath on the back of her neck. The hot mist of blood came off its teeth as it chased her.

She reached a heavy iron door cracked with rust. In the factory beyond, her coworkers milled about, their hands permanently stained, unaware of Jitterbug's last gurgling breaths or the horror at her heels. It was just a wrought iron landing and spiral staircase, two heavy doors below that separated her from them. She gripped the handle, then an explosion of pain in her back rocketed her forward, into the inner stairwell that led down into the depths of the refinery. The machinery roared, heat rising from below.

The Creature was on her back now, and she screamed, turning over as it dropped to its knees in a straddle above her torso. Darling beat at its chest, at the large breasts, the soft fold of its stomach, as it leaned close to her face, spilling blood from its mouth all the while. It caught her hands and pinned them, making a soft sound with its black lips: *Shhhh.*

Darling went quiet, her hands still curled into fists as it gripped her wrists. She stared into its eyes, nearly forehead-to-forehead with the thing, lips still parted wide in a silent scream. The creature's jaw stretched wide, its black hair falling around Darling's face as it lowered itself closer. It made a soft gagging sound in the back of its throat, punctuated by a whimper, and then a torrent of blood and oil washed over its tongue, flowing into Darling's mouth. It locked its lips against hers, the rush of fluid coursing into her stomach. She tried to close her throat, to resist, but it surged past her uvula, drowning her groans.

They were locked in this position, in stillness. She could feel its heartbeat thrumming in its chest, the press of its breasts against her. Darling relaxed into the nebula of its eyes, their lashes so close they touched, her hands going limp. The Creature released her wrists, allowing her arms to drift to her sides.

From Darling's stiff denim jumpsuit came the muffled sound of voices and a trendy song. The Creature released her mouth and lifted itself up, its gaze moving down her body to the bright box of light illuminating the thinning pocket. It took a claw and tore the fabric, the cut swift as a surgeon's, and held Darling's phone in its palm.

Darling's social media was open and auto-scrolling through her suggested videos. A thin, pregnant woman making Oreos from scratch, her large brown eyes dead as she spooned dough from a mixing bowl. A fluffy kitten that had been thrown from a bridge into a churning river, miraculously still alive and being nursed back to health by a good Samaritan. A slideshow of pictures documenting one woman's story of domestic abuse, her plump and youthful face transforming into something barely recognizable—cut, bruised, and swollen, healing into a gaunt survivor.

The slam of a door snapped the Creature's attention away from the phone. The gravelly voice of Darling's boss, Monty, reverberated in the stairwell.

"Where the hell is that woman?" His heavy work boots started up the steps, the structure of the stairs trembling under the weight of his anger. "This generation, goddamn getting on my last nerve!"

Darling stared up at the Creature, her eyes still wide, breathing shallowly. It looked down at her, considering her a moment more. Its clawed hand caressed her paling cheek, leaving a fresh smear of Jitterbug's blood trailing through the viscous substance coating her skin. Then it turned and fled with the phone into the fading night.

When Monty found Darling, she was catatonic. He shook her by the shoulders and called her name, shouting spittle into her staring eyes. When that didn't work, he smacked her across her cheek with his palm, his wedding ring leaving a welt. He called 911 when he couldn't rouse her, and it was upon their arrival that Jitterbug's body was discovered, laying in a swirling puddle of blood and oil, thickening in the crisp morning air.

Darling's face was relaxed and staring, as if she were looking at a fixed point miles away. The report of a body in a town so rural drew the local paper to the scene almost immediately, the photographer snapping a photo of Darling being taken to the ambulance on a stretcher, sitting upright with her hands folded limply in her lap. Her haunting stare was in the foreground, a blurred image of Jitterbug's body covered in a darkly stained sheet in the background, and these words plastered in the headline: ONE DEAD IN FACTORY SLAYING, WOMAN SUSPECT OR SURVIVOR?

The Creature burrowed into the tough desert dirt, using its claws to create a cavern in which it bedded down like a dog. Curled in the dark, it watched the phone continue to auto-scroll through short videos, the blue light reflecting in its black eyes.

A car bumping over the bodies of protesters, leaving a dark smear across the asphalt. A red-faced politician, a bullet grazing his ear. A forest of felled trees. A starving man curled on the steps of a Wall Street brokerage, his thin hands waving at passersby. The strewn bodies of bombed children, identified by a freckle on the top of a foot, or by glittery nail polish on a tiny pinkie finger.

The Creature watched until the phone went dark.

Who killed Jitterbug? That was what they all wanted to know.

When Darling arrived at the hospital, her clothes were collected, bagged, and tagged. A sizable soak of blood had seeped into the fabric of her jumpsuit, and it was whisked away for DNA testing. The police left her with nothing but a thin gown and a white sheet tucked around her waist.

Her head lay on the pillow, eyes distant and rolling from side to side in her head as her eyelids fluttered. Her thin lips muttered feverish, inarticulate whispers like ghost chatter, hands white-knuckled in the sheets.

The detectives in the room discussed her as if she was absent—and in many ways she was. Had she witnessed an animal attack? There were unmistakable bite marks in the torn flesh of Jitterbug's neck, the wounds ravaged by sharp points and a powerful jaw. The blood on her clothes would make her their prime suspect, if not for the strange handprint with its elongated fingers, not quite human. It could be an alien, the detectives joked, sipping black coffee from little styrofoam cups. It *was* Texas, after all.

The Creature did not sleep, but it visited Darling in her drug-induced dreams. They were tethered together now, bonded by blood and the spirit of the land. It was not a lucid coupling, but an ecstatic dance in the liminal space between consciousness and dreaming; their bodies were nebulas spinning like tops through black space. That deep *thing* which thrummed beneath human perception, the thing which humans had forgotten, Darling had become that now, all from looking into the ancient thing's eyes and remembering. Remembering the common thread which united matter to matter and made all things and beings the same.

Darling could feel the Creature's fear and sadness, its longing to return to the cradle of the earth, to feed and be fed eternally. She could see the creature's many histories, an existence so old it could not be calculated by lifetimes, and how it had changed and continued to change as a liquid took the shape of its container.

In turn, the creature in its burrow saw Darling, her entire life, from her birth in Overton, Texas to the inevitability of her taking a job in the oil fields. It saw when Darling was three years old, the time she cut her big toe on a broken beer bottle, heard her wailing as her mother wrapped her little foot in a dish towel. It saw Darling's first fumbling kiss in the back of a 1984 Lincoln, the seats smelling of cigarettes and soda. It saw her failing exams in high school, dropping out, eventually taking a job at the oil refinery. It saw Darling holding her father's trembling hand as he took his last breath surrounded by beeping machines that no longer kept time with his heart. It saw Darling wishing for death.

It saw this and more, all the moments large and small that make up a human life, souring as time wears on a tired spirit.

It came for Darling when the moon was full, hanging round and heavy in the sky like a mother. It came for her, leaving a trail of blood and oil in its wake, smeared on white hospital walls and white hospital tiles and on Darling's thin sheets.

When Darling saw it, she leapt from the bed onto her knees, her over-sized hospital gown hanging from her body, her arms outstretched toward the ancient one with a crooked-toothed smile on her face, dark hair wild. She put her hands together in supplication, a soft choking sound in her throat as oil stained her lips.

The lone detective in the room stood, pulling his gun and firing two shots into the Creature's chest and belly, but it didn't so much as stagger before lifting his head from his shoulders, a fount of blood streaming down its body as it held his neck over its mouth and drank. Animated and eager, she placed her bare feet on the tile floor, crouching down over the twitching headless body and rummaging through his pockets until she found a soft pack of cigarettes, a BIC lighter straining inside the cellophane wrapper. Placing them in the breast pocket of the gown, she looked up at the radiant, earth-born Creature, its black skin slick and glittering under the fluorescent lights as it tossed the head aside. It turned its eyes, those infinite eyes, on Darling, who was not afraid.

The Creature carried Darling in its arms, her hospital gown fluttering like a bride's as distant lightning lit the sky purple across the desert. It looked down at her, the glint in its eye watery, seeping oil. As it strode toward the oil fields, it wept for the loneliness of this modern world, the flow of information which seemed endless, but was finite, like the river from which it had been pulled like a screaming infant. It found that in a short time, this world had filled it with such rage, and this Creature, which had never before desired to meddle in human affairs, now felt obligated to save at least one from itself.

"Don't cry," Darling whispered, moving her thumb to caress the tears away. "We ain't ever gonna be lonely again."

When the Creature came to the lip of the well, Darling reached into the pocket at her breast, taking out a soft pack of cigarettes. She placed one in her mouth, drew out the lighter, tossed the cigarettes to the side. She looked up into the Creature's eyes, into the stardust pattern that moved within the sclera like living things, and then flicked the lighter, awaking the flame.

It consumed them both in a burst of light, and the Creature gripped Darling tightly as their bodies toppled with purpose into the deep oil well.

Darling felt like Alice, weightless, the fire licking away her skin like a barbed cat tongue. They landed in a river of crude oil, the fire rocketing up the well walls and spreading throughout the underground tunnels to other drilling sites which stretched for miles across the desert, from Texas to Arkansas to Louisiana. The explosion sent all the bobbing pump-jacks flying like herons, their molten metal parts hailing across the desert. Such a fire would burn for thousands of years, until their furious love cracked the earth, and they would rise again.

Teeth Sharper than Moonlight

by U.M. Agoawike

The damsel fled from the beast under the full moon's sentinel eye.

The damsel was neither woman or man, and the beast more man than monster. Nor were they traversing the drear Gothic halls of a castle whose name time had long since forgotten. Instead, the two wound through alleys bathed in fog, a relentless barrier through which nothing living penetrated.

Gwyn ran through the backstreets of this midnight city, knowing that between getting lost and getting *caught*, one was much more appealing than the other. Their gaze darted around the blanketed path. In one hand, they clutched an electric torch. With the other, they tightened their hold on the hem of a diaphanous nightgown made of moonlight. It barely kept the chill at bay. The hair on their arms rose beneath their impractically long sleeves that one might think would lend themselves to warmth. Alas. If Gwyn had any thoughts beyond *"run"* and *"hide,"* they might have considered the ill-fitting nature of their attire.

Cold terror skittered down their spine as the growls of the beast grew louder. He hunted with the efficiency of a mountain lion, sinful and sinuous and savage.

The only other sounds were of Gwyn's staccato breathing, the hammer of their heart, and the slap of dirty bare feet on wet cobblestone.

Navigating with wild—and frankly reckless—abandon, they took a corner, then another in quick succession, hoping to lose the beast in the labyrinthine lanes. Gwyn's gaze, dilated by adrenaline, kept a vigilant scan. Left and right, above, below, and occasionally over a shoulder as unknown sounds shattered the night. What could have been a cackle or a cry became but a distant hum at the edge of their awareness.

Grit scraped away at Gwyn's heels until the skin was raw. Beneath the unstoppable rush of heated blood, was the haggard breathing of the beast. The sound curved over the points of Gwyn's ear.

A harried half-glance back confirmed to Gwyn they were still alone.

For now.

They yelped when their foot caught the wrong side of a puddle. Their ankle turned sharply inward, sending them into the nearest wall. The damnable ground was a dangerous mire. Should Gwyn have fallen the wrong way, a misplaced step might end in their blood spilling across uneven stones, joining the wet from a recent storm. It never really seemed to stop raining in the city; the sun never rose higher than a few inches above the horizon, never managed to pierce the ceaseless gloaming for longer than a few hours. The streets were slick with rainwater camouflaged by night, waiting to catch you unawares. Waiting until you were stumbling. Until you were falling. Until you were dead with a predator's teeth goring what was left of your corpse.

Gwyn would not be one of those sorry corpses. Not tonight.

They pulled free of the wall, hiding a wince as their sleeve ripped, the sound slicing the silence. The strip of fabric left behind resembled a fish, slit from belly to mouth with a smattering of blood like tiny rubies at the throat. Gwyn didn't cast it a second look, inhaling sharply and pushing ahead as brine filtered into their nose. It mingled with sweat and dust and moist spittle as a reminder—that they were being hunted.

It was the most alive they'd felt in ages.

From the night came a rumbling. A voice startled Gwyn back to the present, like cold needles prodding their brain. It thickened like molten honey, as warm and deliciously rotten as a steaming carcass beset by carrion birds.

In dulcet tones, the beast said, "You can't run forever."

"Watch me," Gwyn called, forcing the words out through a sprint-borne breathlessness. Then they remembered. *You're running for your life, dipshit.* If the beast didn't kill them first, their own tongue just might. "Actually wait, don't—"

Laughter was the beast's ominous reply. The sound sank into Gwyn's bones and reverberated through the marrow as though etching into the fabric of their being. Terrifying. Thrilling. *Delicious.*

Delirious amusement bubbled up Gwyn's throat, boiling out in a fit of manic giggles. Perhaps the rabbit was not what it seemed. Perhaps the ravenous wolf was not, in fact, pursuing a helpless quarry, but its own end.

Even as familiar with these streets as Gwyn was, hidden dangers made novices of masters. As with all accidents, it takes only one wrong step to begin a cascade—an unfortunate waterfall of disastrous proportions. Put simply: a mess.

Reynaud-pale fingers squeezed the torch, and the light shuddered. Shadows fled with the skittishness of prey. Darkness swallowed up the world outside the bubble of brightness.

Lost in their head, the next bend seemed to leap from the fog like lightning. They careened toward the end of the alley and lurched around the corner on a heel a second too late in their distraction.

Gwyn grunted as their arm scraped the wall, losing their breath and balance. The world swam.

Gwyn hissed as pain laced up their arm and snared their chest. It felt like there was a hot poker twisting between their ribs while someone dug an elbow into their stitched side as a cherry on top. Not to mention the temperature. Gwyn was always cold, but it was particularly nippy night and the water-thin gown did *not* help.

Hunger was in the air, thick at the back of Gwyn's throat like spit that had gone down the wrong pipe. It carried the scent of musk and sweat and petrichor. Iron sat on their tongue much like sugar would in more pleasant circumstances.

Chancing a glance back, their eyes widened at a pair of glowing spots much closer than expected. The beast's own eyes flashed retro-reflector red-ringed blue, locked on Gwyn with single-minded intent: *devour, devour, devour.*

They let out a choked yelp as the beast bounded forward, an unstoppable organic machine heralding delicious violence. If the beast caught them, *well...*

A frisson coiled in their gut at the thought. It sounded thrilling—were it not for the possibility of death.

They switched the torch to their other hand to examine the injury as they ran. Blood slithered down from their upper arm, soaking into the nightgown's ephemeral sleeve until the fabric was almost as black as the starless sky. For a moment, they watched the tiny red line, letting memory guide their feet. They let out a petulant whine. In response came a hint of laughter from the relentless beast.

Bare feet whipped below in a blur; raven black curls fell into straining eyes. The only thing keeping them moving was self-preservation and the vile need for victory.

Though need wasn't quite accurate. A certainty. *Yes.* Gwyn was as certain in this victory as all the others.

Footsteps. *There. Close.* Right behind them. The beast's pants sounded right next to and fathoms away from them; the illusory weight of the monster felt closer than he actually was. His slavering maw was inches from their ear, dripping with the filth of all that lingered in the unseen corners of night. Places where vermin that once shied from the poisonous radiance of churches now dwelled freely.

Gwyn pushed faster. They couldn't lose. Couldn't let the beast capture them. His presence was a suffocating embrace that would wrap around them, split them open from groin to gullet, and crawl inside to make a home among their organs, falling asleep to the metronome of their naked heart.

"I smell blood." The beast's voice warbled through the mists. "I hope you... don't mean to sully my prize." His tone had an odd wateriness, shaky as though it could tip over into concern.

A frown glanced across Gwyn's lips, and they stumbled as they searched for their beast.

The night turned his hulking shape into a smudge, limned in silver-blue and crowned with a signature vampiric crimson. Those red stars twinkled and narrowed, prompting the damsel to lift their chin sharply.

The chase—remember the chase. Remember the stakes. Remember the prize.

At that, Gwyn sped up seconds before a large hand snatched at the space where their head had been. Claws scraped the wall, sending rocks tumbling to the ground in a quiet rain. Four lines gouged brick, joining other scars that marked the struggle between this not-so-maiden and that not-quite-monster.

A startled gasp escaped them as the beast's fragrant breath warmed their nape, rustling the gentle curls that framed their attempt at a guileless expression. Demure certainly did *not* come naturally to them. Not that it was made easier by the split-second weaving in the city's tangled backstreets. Damsel-in-distressing was a dangerous game.

The dreadful beast closed in, and the damsel knew they had to think fast or lose soon. So Gwyn listened. Waited until they heard the beast's arm displace the air as he reached out. Then they ducked and darted forward. A risky move that nearly sent them face-first into another wall.

Truly graceful.

Since a rolled ankle spelled obvious disaster, they leaned into the motion and lunged around the corner.

Slipping away at the last second, they found themself emerging onto another road.

The way widened suddenly as a determined blade of light cleaved away the shadows. Warmth fell over Gwyn and the beast, noise rushing in like the waves that weathered the base of the cliff on which the city perched precariously.

From the dense fog, the pair barrelled through a night market lost in their deadly chase.

All over the city—on nights when the moon was ripe and bright—such markets sprang to life, makeshift assemblages of wagons and wooden stalls laden with trade from lands that knew no gods. Bell-shaped lights formed a cross hatched weave, strung from window to window of the buildings that boxed in the small but vibrant square. Awnings sagged with remnants of the last rainfall, a steady stream of water spilling down the side of the mossy green walls against which several stands rested. Fried oil, saffron, and the fragrance of mortified flowers filled Gwyn's too-sensitive nose.

But the bystanders paid little care to Gwyn's flight nor the beastly bulk pursuing them.

The market melted into a mass of colour as they leapt over tables in a fan of silk and rushed around vendors overburdened with wares. Faces blurred to pulsating smears, and through white noise they caught the tail end of a conversation pointed their way.

"*—not these dumbasses again—*"

Or perhaps their ears were playing tricks on them. The night was ever so dark and oh-so-full of illusions.

As suddenly as they had emerged, Gwyn re-entered the fog, the words soon forgotten. Diving back into the darkness felt like sinking into a lush bed of rose petals, satin tinged with the sharpness of decay.

"You're getting slow. And here I thought this was meant to be a chase," said the beast. They were tethered together by the nature of their roles. Maiden and their monster, beast and his beauty.

"Some of us have short legs," Gwyn retorted. "Although isn't it curious how mine have managed to outpace yours thus far?"

They struggled to keep the amusement from their face as they glanced over their shoulder, thrilled by the verbal exchange.

Something glinted in the corner of Gwyn's vision. The moon's light turned black iron into a rippling mirrored pool. In their distraction, Gwyn took a step—the *wrong* step—missing the low fence wrought in the shape of twisting, dancing bones.

They stumbled, tumbled, fell head-over-heels over the finials capping the spindly sentinels of the barrier, and collapsed into a cemetery. Miraculously, they only left behind a *little* bit of bloodstained silk, making their location all the more obvious. As if the scent wafting from their flesh wasn't enough already.

A piece of Gwyn's nightgown fluttered on the pinnacle in the breeze. Without pause, even for breath, they rolled across the dead wet grass and sprang back up.

The wild survival instinct of prey dragged Gwyn deeper into the cemetery.

A smile ghosted across their lips. The air seemed different here, as though they had stepped into another world. Fingers of mist rolled across the ground, wrapping around their ankles. Short stumps of stone jutted up like spectral fingers. As torchlight broke the fog, more wheeled in to take its place.

Death clung to the cemetery, a distinct *nothingness* that always accompanied places of rest. It was as if someone had taken the smell of rot and sick and buried it in an unmarked grave. A small part of Gwyn hoped it had been consecrated so the holy ground might slow the beast, but they knew from personal experience that faith bore no danger to the undead. Churches had died long ago, and the holy symbols sewn into the lining of their gown were merely adornments these days. In the lands beyond the city lay richly ornamented castles that had once been places of magnificent worship. But like a body without a heart, what was a cathedral without its congregation?

An expletive shattered the tension as Gwyn staggered over a rock, dropping their gown to catch themself. They heard a laugh and knew the beast was close.

Warmth bloomed across their face in a fluster. They shook their head and gathered the gown again before it could trip them.

Gwyn looked around. The beast was nowhere in sight. Nightgown fluttering in the wind alongside the untamed bob of their curls, they faintly wondered if some poor grave digger might think them a spectre. To say nothing of the shadow skulking through the cemetery just out of sight, surprisingly inconspicuous for someone of his stature.

They stepped onto the stalwart stone of an ancient grave ledger when something crunched behind them.

Their breath stilled but they knew better than to freeze. Let it be known that by virtue of their archetype, all damsels had an excellent sense of self-preservation. Acid burned in Gwyn's veins; they'd keel over if they stopped even for a moment.

A flare of warmth fanned the side of their face. Alert eyes widened at the potent scent of blood. The air shifted with the weight of a body shifting—but the beast caught nothing. His arms snatched empty air as they dodged, feet shuffling across the earth.

"Aww, too slow," Gwyn laughed before losing the beast in the mists again. "Don't tell me you've lost your touch. Where's the fun in that?"

The beast's chuckle was distant—and nearby. The cemetery warped sound like it was pressed directly into bone, seeding its way inside until you were more noise than person.

"The fear is the fun," the beast crooned in a voice deep as a velvet wrapped valley. "It will soak into your flesh. Taint the meat. And once you're marinated in the foul elegance of pain, terror—your blood shall taste of bliss when I sink my teeth in to drink you dry."

Gwyn was unable to quell the shiver that shook them. They pressed a bloody palm to their heart and inhaled.

"Scare me then."

Though he remained silent, the beast's smirk was palpable.

Cat and mouse stalked through the graveyard, but you might be hard pressed to tell which was which.

Guided by torchlight, Gwyn wove around gravestones. Each step, the beast matched. He reached out in heartrending, breathlessly close calls that Gwyn whirled away from.

Finally, a looming structure rose from the gray, and Gwyn knew they had won.

Ahead lay the mausoleum: a domed spectre aping the grandiloquence of churches with pillars carved to resemble serpents set on either side of the doors Gwyn had flung open before the chase had begun. The lintel was painted black and grey with a supine figure done in raised relief, a stake piercing its chest where an undead heart lay—once a warning, now a marker of salvation.

Gwyn darted up the steps, racing for the door. Moonlight spilled across the floor just past the threshold.

The gown fell from their grasp as they clambered up the last few steps to victory. They launched forward, one foot hovering at the precipice of the realm of the dead.

But the shadow caught them first.

His tall form peeled up from liquid darkness to shroud the frame. Gwyn only had a second to gasp, a startled half-sound, before the doors slammed shut and the world narrowed to the torch's beam. A pair of hands landed on their hips, engulfing them as they were pulled back. Cursing, they let the beast draw them close, lean in, and whisper.

"I win."

Gwyn groaned. "Damn you, Rodrigo."

His furry muzzle nosed at their pulse—hummingbird fast. He traced the two tiny holes on their neck with the tip of his tongue.

The gentle pressure of teasing fangs elicited a yelp from Gwyn. The sound melted into a breathless sigh when he crowded in.

Torchlight skittered across a ceiling draped in cobwebs and inlaid with bones. As Gwyn's vision adjusted, they found themself staring into the gaunt face of a jewel-eyed skull. The grave faces were set into the wall, sealed together by time and mortuary wax. An uncountable many; neither light nor sight could take them all in. Time and gravity had deformed the bones into a rippling wave of patterns.

Fleshless lips and naked teeth pressed along Gwyn's front. The nightgown did nothing to hide their anticipation as Rodrigo shoved their wrist against the wall. The torch tumbled free. It rolled to a stop against the far wall, casting the pair in its unbroken beam.

He buried his face in the seam where shoulder met neck. His inhale pimpled their skin with gooseflesh.

"You smell divine."

His tone was proud, rumbling through Gwyn like a gentle rockfall. He rubbed his face into their hair, breathed them in again before lowering his lips to their bleeding bicep.

Rodrigo dragged his scalding tongue down the injury. Spit irritated the cut and Gwyn's toes curled, eyes fluttering as their arm jerked from the resulting sting. Ostensibly, he was licking the wound clean, but from the motions of his tongue—up and down and around like a spell—Gwyn felt like they were being tasted. Savored.

"I—Gwyn wait..." Rodrigo stuttered. "You're *actually* hurt."

Gwyn waited. The corners of their mouth lowered when Rodrigo remained still. Huffing, they tipped their head back, rising onto the balls of their feet to nudge his shoulder. The chase may have ended, but the game wasn't over.

"*Prize*," they mumbled under their breath.

The lines had been a collaborative effort born of a wine-soaked evening, but the plan—the path through the city and thereafter—had been meticulously plotted by Gwyn all for this moment.

They felt him tense before the beast returned, slipping back hesitantly. Suave, sultry, he whispered: "You... should be more careful. I don't want my prize damaged *too* badly."

Gwyn laughed as the atmosphere thickened, pupils contracting at the scent of their blood in Rodrigo's mouth. There was a headiness to it, as if smelling too much for too long might intoxicate you.

Gwyn turned to take in the man in his entirety. White silvered his monstrous silhouette and bounced across the deep shadows that deepened the strong creases of his face. Atop his head, a pair of hirsute ears perked up—one had been bitten and the other looked to have been stitched back together crudely.

He grasped the back of their thighs and lifted them. It was instinctual for them to wrap their legs around the heft of his waist, which was softened by a generous layer of fat.

But as Gwyn eagerly leaned forward to capture his lips, Rodrigo's foot found an obstacle in the darkness. A loose stone, bone, or piece of wood—by the fallen torchlight it was unclear. What was clear, though, was the subsequent series of unfortunate events.

Rodrigo squealed as he tripped, losing his grip on Gwyn in the process. Two faces collided—in a far more unpleasant manner than Gwyn had hoped for. Their forehead connected with his jaw, the sound of something cracking lost beneath twin cries.

Rodrigo cursed, reaching for his mouth. Held up precariously by a single hand, Gwyn's balance wavered, and their head snapped back against the skeletal wall. Bone knocked on equally hollow bone with a dull *thunk*.

Wincing, they clutched their face. Tears beaded at the corners of their eyes, and Gwyn loosed a series of curses capped off by a poignant, but simple, "Shit, ow!"

Any semblance of thrill or anticipation fled, leaving an awkward cloud as the pair staggered apart.

With the mood officially ruined, Gwyn threw out a long-suffering groan. No longer even pretending at the guise of a damsel, they let the subtle glamour fall, teeth elongating to small tusk-like fangs and skin gaining a faintly grey-brown hue. They dragged a hand down their face and blinked, crimson eyes glowing as they scowled.

"We almost had it this time!"

A reedy whine rose, high as a stalk reaching for the sky. The source of said whine buried his face in his hands and sank to the floor, radiating pure embarrassment. His shoulders hunched as he brought his knees up in shame. His tail sagged sadly, whisking at the dust.

"I'm *so* sorry," came his muffled wail.

Gwyn blinked and looked down at him.

"What? No, absolutely not." They shook their head and pressed him into a seated position before dropping squarely onto his lap. So large was he that their legs only bracketed a single thigh. "No self-deprecation, Ruy. Remember?"

"B-but the scene—"

"Screw the scene!" They grabbed his muzzle and pressed their foreheads together. Eyes wide and wild, their scarlet gaze turned piercing as they poured every ounce of concern they could into him. "All that matters is how you feel."

He stared unblinking before looking aside. He dithered over his response with a familiar moue that made Gwyn's heart twitch.

"What do you need—water? Blood? Food? Space? More prep time?" Their eyes grew larger, and they squeezed his bearded cheeks, imagining all the possible ways to lift his spirits. "I'll give it to you, just tell me."

After scanning his face and cataloguing each minute shift in his expression, they leaned forward to capture his lips.

Keening, Rodrigo's body melted as he enthusiastically let them take the lead. Deepening the kiss, they pet his nape and twirled the downy fur, wondering if they should braid it. He purred and pushed closer as if trying to slip right through them. Gentle hands—more like big, fuck-off paws—caressed their thighs.

In the near darkness, you'd be hard pressed to tell where Rodrigo ended and Gwyn started, their bodies forming a shifting beast with two backs.

When they parted, Gwyn licked their lips. Rodrigo's gaze was dazed. With delicate touches, they guided him out of the floaty space to which he'd sunk, allowing the haze to dissipate.

The next few minutes were silent. Rodrigo's admiring gaze was locked on Gwyn as they groomed the fur on his face in the direction of the growth.

"Are you..." he began. An audible gulp, the apple in his throat working under the smaller vampire's ministrations. "Are you upset with me?"

Their fingers paused; they sighed. "Oh no, the shiny eyes. You know I'm weak."

"That's why I use it."

"Brat."

Their tiny fangs nipped his cheek, pressing indents around a mouthful of ruddy fur. Pulling away, they smoothed the spit-slicked patch with a pleased hum and moved to groom the rest of Rodrigo's doughy face.

A sombre blanket fell over the pair. In, out; Gwyn sank into the pattern of his involuntary breathing and waited until he was ready. Waited until his soft voice filled the mausoleum with the reverence of a lone organist in a shattered cathedral.

"I doubt I'll ever get it right, Wyn." Rodrigo muttered. "You're the dread vampire Gwynllyw, Harbinger of the Gloaming Age and the Impaler Reborn."

Oh. The Impaler Reborn. What a hopeless romantic.

"Incorrigible sap." Gwyn waved, failing to hide their flush. How he vexed them with sweet words.

His smile was a small sad thing. His ears twitched. "What use could a creature of insurmountable infamy have for a bumbling brute such as I?"

The words were a sword to their spine. Shooting up, Gwyn countered with well-honed steel. "Screw that—*you* are *thee* vrykolakas!

"Even when they disturbed your cist, stripped you of person-hood using all manner of atrocity—faith, stake, and flame—you persisted. They were terrified of you before I ever crawled from my grave," they said insistently, clutching his face, deter-mined to get through his lovely, but very thick, skull. "Nothing about that is unworthy of admiration. I may be the violence that heralded our new age, but you are a testament to what once was feared."

Shoulders slumping, their voice softened. "My darling bear... you *must* perish the thought you need feel shame about what you are. Who is left to judge us when churches are dead? You *are* a vampire. I don't care what you look like, only how your heart feels—the way it calls to mine."

The only consequence for spending their immortal afterlife in the arms of their lover was the loss of the sun.

Luckily, Gwyn loved the night. Loved the way the silken light of the moon revealed Rodrigo's truest self. When they placed their hand over Rodrigo's chest, they didn't need to feel a heartbeat to know he had one.

Overcome, they peppered kisses over his face, leaving no part of him untouched by their devotion: the pale star-shaped patch on his forehead that popped against his red fur, the bend of one ear and the bitten edge of the other, his wrinkled snout, both cheeks and the sides of his plush jowls.

"I don't need perfect—dead gods know *I'm* certainly not—" Gwyn rubbed their noses together. His wet and cool, theirs crooked, broken and improperly set a lifetime ago. "Right now, I just need you. No glamours, no scripts."

"You worked hard on that script."

"Dearest beat of my undead heart... we spent like half a night on it."

He shrugged, wearing the ghost of a smile.

Humming, Gwyn smoothed a hand up his chest to toy with his rosary. The necklace was done in a style that was old even when churches lived. Cherry wood beads slightly smaller than an eyeball, engraved in the symbols of an extinct faith with sacred knots that once might have burned vampires to the touch.

They knew they were abrasive, vain, demanding at the best of times and selfish at the worst. But they wanted their presence to be a comfort in this private enclave where they were the only two who existed. The only two who mattered.

"Shall we continue?" they asked tentatively after a beat.

Shyly, Rodrigo nodded.

Precious. Gwyn wanted to squeeze him tight and never let go. A grin split their mouth wide as he pressed his hands to the base of their spine, arching them forward. They gathered him in their arms and stroked his fur before connecting their lips in an embrace that was more teeth than kiss. Blood danced on their tongues. One of them had broken skin, but Gwyn couldn't find it in themself to care—not with the heart-aching way Rodrigo handled them. The depth of his want made them shiver. An all-encompassing desire burning for them alone.

Drawing back, they nuzzled Rodrigo and reached for his collar. "May I?"

He took their hand and led it to the buttons of his blouse, which was already open to the navel, doing nothing to hold in his straining chest. With each patch of fur and flesh revealed, Gwyn dragged their lips up his expectant throat.

"Now let's."

Pop.

"Get back."

Pop.

"To business."

Pop.

The blouse slipped down to pool at his elbows and Gwyn grinned as he tugged it the rest of the way off his stout frame.

Then his brow furrowed, and they went still. Warnings blared in their head—they'd done something wrong.

Rodrigo sighed. "I'm going to need a new blouse—someone seems to have stolen my buttons."

This man. They rolled their eyes. "What you *need* is to work on your jokes. You almost gave me a heart attack."

"Heart attack?" He raised a brow.

They swatted his chest, followed by a quick peck to his jaw. "Don't harsh my vibe, puppy."

Gwyn snickered at his pout—he had mastered the art of manipulating them with an expression. He knew how they hated seeing him anything less than delirious with happiness.

He fell silent for a moment, ears twitching in thought. He worked his lower lip with the fang that Gwyn's head had chipped earlier.

"I meant it when I said you were divine. I... I want to feast on the bitter marrow of your bones and lick grey matter from the inside of your skull. I want to eat you alive."

They looked aside in false irritation but could not hide the darkening of their cheeks and neck.

"You're disgustingly sweet."

As they cupped his face, Rodrigo leaned into the touch. He cradled the back of their hand as his lips ghosted their palm, the bend of each knuckle, their cracked and bitten nails. Thick tendons, necrotic varicose veins, numerous scars—he kissed them all as if each was more precious than gold.

The look in his eyes was soft as suffused light through a gossamer veil. It warmed their long dead body.

"It's how I was remade," he pressed the words into their wrist. "I don't know anything else but loving you, Wyn."

Dizzy with affection, Gwyn's breath caught. It was too much to hold in and the words fell out.

"I love you too, Ruy."

Once more they fell into each other. The beast lapped crimson from the damsel's lips. He kissed the blood from their mouth like a man in the desert and they relished him like a dedicated supplicant of the profane.

It tasted like love. It tasted like a promise. It tasted like eternity.

Suckr

by Austen Lee

The rain had just slunk back into the gutters, leaving Portland slick and glistening like a fresh kill. The city pulsed under a low ceiling of clouds, the stars smothered, the moon a ghost behind the haze. Jackson strutted like he owned the night—shoulders squared, boots polished, hunger coiled behind every step. The wet sidewalk reflected the glint of his watch, the sharp line of his jaw. He was dressed to kill: black suit, blood-red shirt, no tie. His kind didn't need to try, but he enjoyed the aesthetic.

Tonight, the hunt pulled him out of the house. It was out in the wild, warm and pulsing and just reckless enough to be fun.

Sky.

That was the name. Bright, hopeful. And deliciously stupid. Jackson smiled, the point of his fangs just barely showing. He loved when the names were sweet, icing on raw steak. Suckr, the app, had delivered again. Some men came begging, horny and trembling in his DMs. Not this one. Sky made him work for it. Sent pictures without his face. Said he'd meet at a bar, in public. Said he wanted to see Jackson in the flesh.

Consent, bless his heart.

Jackson paused under a flickering streetlight, pulled out his phone, and tapped a message with his black leather-gloved thumb.

"I'm nearing the bar."

The response came almost instantly.

"I'm inside." Winking emoji.

A thrill curled up Jackson's spine, tightening around his throat like a silk rope. He could taste the night—salt-sweat, vodka on breath, hot blood with a spike of pleasure and fear. The anticipation was intoxicating. Maybe he'd let Sky get off first, take the time to savor the experience. That always sweetened the meat. Endorphins were the oldest seasoning in the book.

He was grinning again when a crusted old street phantom with gloves and an outstretched hand appeared.

"Spare some change, mister?" The man's voice wind-whistled through broken teeth.

Jackson didn't break stride. "Get the fuck out of my way."

The man flinched back, his hands still up, cowed and trembling. Jackson hated to waste the gaze on vermin, but sometimes rats needed reminding

He leaned in close, his voice low and cold. "You're lucky I have plans tonight. Otherwise I'd rip your fucking head off and paint the sidewalk with what's left."

He let the man see his eyes then—just for a blink. Just enough.

The old thing shrank away, head down like rot vanishing into mist.

Jackson cracked his neck and resumed walking. There was real prey waiting—smooth skin, dumb smile, a heartbeat he couldn't wait to taste. Portland might sleep, but monsters? *We dress well, we fuck hard, and we never sleep.*

The bar had no name, just a cracked neon sign buzzing over the door that looked like it used to spell something. Now it was just a crimson red "O" like a marker on a blood donor card. The windows were painted over in matte black, sealing the place in permanent midnight. A bowl of rainbow condoms by the entrance sat beneath a faded cardboard sign: SAFETY FIRST in fading Sharpie. The door creaked when Jackson pushed through it, and the warmth inside hit him like a tongue—beer sweat, cologne, wet denim.

He smiled, teeth briefly on full display, and scanned the gloom.

There he was.

Sky.

Standing at the far end of the bar, bait on a hook. Short, compact, beautiful. Russet skin that shimmered under the amber light. A floral shirt unbuttoned halfway to reveal a smooth, sculpted chest, soft silk stretched over sin. Legs crossed, and... *God, the ass on him.* Jackson had drained movie stars, athletes, married CEOs, and none of them had a build that perfect.

He could hear Sky's heart from across the room.

Steady. Unafraid.

Interesting.

Jackson crossed the room like a man on a mission, hunger pacing behind his eyes. The stool beside Sky groaned under his weight.

"You're even more delicious in person," Jackson said.

Sky turned his head slowly, those ridiculous baby-blue eyes catching the light. His smile was pure sunshine. Well, fake sunshine. But Jackson was already halfway hard.

"You ain't too bad yourself," Sky said, his voice a little rough at the edges, gravel polished just enough to pass for charm.

Jackson felt something tighten in his throat, some deep pulse of animal instinct. He wanted to fuck this man raw, suck him dry, maybe even keep a piece. Maybe take him apart and build something new out of the beautiful leftovers. The blood would be wild with pleasure, soaked in lust and heat. Better than heroin. Better than heaven.

"So," Jackson said, sliding a little closer, letting his knee brush Sky's. "I'm not a psycho. Want to get out of here?"

"Ah, ah, ah," Sky wagged a finger. "I said I wanted a drink first."

The smile on Jackson's face didn't change, but a little fire sparked behind his eyes. He hated delays. Hated refusal. But the chase? The chase was sacred.

"I could always use a drink," he said, voice slick.

They ordered. Jackson faked interest in a lager, hating the sour fizz of it. He missed the old nights, the old drinks. Mulled blood with cloves and cinnamon, warm and red and thick on the tongue. But this was the new age. He had to 'blend.'

Sky asked for a vodka cranberry. "Usually just a splash of cranberry," he said, smiling. "But something tells me I want all my wits with you."

Jackson raised his glass. "To unforgettable nights."

They clinked.

Sky took a long sip, then paused. Just for a second. His smile didn't quite reach his eyes.

"Yeah," he said. "Unforgettable."

Jackson didn't drink. He watched instead. Watched the column of Sky's throat bob as he swallowed. Watched the pulse flutter in his neck. Listened to the music of it, the slow, strong beat that would soon belong to him.

Sky smacked his lips and giggled.

"You've got a stare like a starving wolf," he said. "Earth to Jackson."

"I see something I want," Jackson murmured, eyes low and hungry.

Sky tilted his head with mock innocence. "Maybe the feelings are mutual."

Then he turned toward the stool, knees brushing, gaze locked in.

Jackson drank him in—the curve of his smile, the slope of his collarbone, the perfect architecture of prey.

It would have been so easy to gaze him into submission. A flick of the eyes, and Sky would follow him into any alley, bed, or grave. But no, no, Jackson wanted it given, not taken. That made it taste better. That made it *sport*.

"You hook up on the app a lot?" Sky asked, breaking Jackson's reverie.

"Here and there," Jackson replied. "But I prefer flesh. Digital screens are too... sterile."

Sky grinned. "The name always cracks me up. Suckr. Like some designer came out of a coke coma and thought he was clever."

Jackson leaned in, voice low. "You ready to be fucked so hard you forget your name?"

"Sounds delightful," Sky purred, taking a long sip of his drink.

Jackson watched him drink. Watched him savor it. His own fantasies bloomed: taking Sky against the hotel mirror. Dragging his fangs across that golden skin. Tearing open that chest and drinking until Sky stopped begging and just went still. The thought pressed hot against his trousers.

"My, my," Sky said with a sly look. "Someone's excited."

"Images of things to come," Jackson replied smoothly.

Sky laughed again, draining the glass. "You've intrigued me."

Jackson slapped down two twenties—over-generous, but money was a game for the prey. A sharp *tap-tap-tap* rattled from the bar's ancient speaker system like cracked bone: "All right, freaks, monsters, and glorious degenerates—get your asses on the floor!" The DJ's voice was thick with static. "Let's see sweat, hips, goddamn movement!"

The beat dropped, a low and grinding bassline that rippled through the walls and pulsed in Jackson's chest like a second heartbeat. The center of the bar bloomed to life, a cracked checkerboard floor flashing sickly purples and reds. Laser lights sprayed across the ceiling like veins of electric fire.

Sky set down his glass. "Come on," he said, grabbing Jackson's hand. "Let's dance."

Jackson hesitated only a moment—watching a bead of condensation slide from the glass, curve around the rim, and vanish. Then Sky was tugging him into the pulse of the crowd, into the sweat-slick heat of bodies grinding under the lights.

They moved like animals in a pit, hips rolling, hands trailing skin, mouths parted, gasping. Jackson inhaled and caught everything. Sky was close, chest glistening, shirt unbuttoning further as he moved with a liquid rhythm that made Jackson's mouth water. He could hear the quickened thump-thump-thump of Sky's heart, now syncing with the beat of the music.

The boy slid up against him, thigh to thigh, and began to grind in slow, deliberate circles. Jackson's hands fell to Sky's waist without thinking.

He gave Sky a toothy death grin.

He was going to devour this man, fuck him until he collapsed, then drain every last drop from that smooth throat. But not yet. No. Jackson had learned to wait. To edge his hunger until it screamed. The longing for the moment of realization, that final flicker of terror in their eyes before the blood let go, that was his *true* climax. The peak. The rest was just foreplay.

Jackson licked his lips, lost in fantasy:

Sky, bent over the hotel bed.

Sky, twitching under him.

Sky, looking up, realizing he was dying.

God, it made him hard enough to bruise.

"Earth to Jackson," Sky said, leaning close. "You dance like a corpse."

"You're not wrong," Jackson replied with a sly smirk.

But he moved now, let his hips fall in line with Sky's. Their bodies began to mirror, slow, carnal. Jackson twirled him once, and Sky came back, his arms sliding over Jackson's shoulders, fingertips grazing the back of his neck. A shiver ran down Jackson's spine like a lit fuse.

He wanted to bite him. Right there. Tear through the club's rhythm and shred this human on the dance floor. But that would be messy. And wasteful. And above all, not his style.

"Patience," Jackson muttered.

"What?"

"Nothing. Just... excited."

Sky's hand slid down, casual, deliberate. He cupped Jackson's arousal.

"Well, hello," Sky said. "Someone's ready for dessert."

"You've got small hands, handsome."

"You just make them look small."

They moved together, tighter now, closer. Sky grinding back into Jackson's body and sliding down until his head nearly brushed Jackson's chest. His ass pressed tight, lifting, rubbing as if he could feel the beast underneath the skin. The tension coiled in Jackson's gut until it felt like barbed wire.

They danced like that—danced like they were fucking through cloth, teasing the violence with every shift.

Then, like it was nothing, Sky pulled away and glanced at the DJ.

"Yeah," he said. "Let me finish my drink. Then we can head to the hotel."

Jackson said nothing. His fangs had slid halfway from his gums, aching. He watched Sky drain the rest of his cranberry cocktail, lips red from the drink, neck bare and gleaming.

And then they were moving, arm in arm, toward the exit.

The rain had started again—just a light mist, a whisper of water hanging in the air—but the sidewalks still pulsed with life. Stragglers lingered. A group of punks laughed too loudly near a food cart. Someone shouted from a doorway. A woman cried into her phone.

Jackson walked beside Sky, hyper-aware of every pulse within earshot. Every heartbeat was a flavor. A temptation. But the one beside him? That was his chosen dish. He wanted to drag Sky into an alley, slam him against the bricks, fuck him until his voice cracked—and then rip out his throat. Dump what was left in a trash heap and walk off hard and satisfied.

But no. Not yet.

"You like the rain?" Sky asked.

"There's peace to it. But this haze? It's just annoying."

"This kind of mist always reminds me of New Orleans," Sky said. "My—uh, someone I knew used to call it 'ghost rain.'"

Jackson raised an eyebrow. "Boyfriend?"

Sky smiled. "Yeah. Something like that."

Jackson faked a laugh. "I have other assets."

"Oh, I know. I plan to explore all of them."

Jackson stopped and grabbed Sky without hesitation—hands firm on his hips, mouths crashing together like a firestorm. His tongue claimed Sky's mouth, tasting vodka and something citrus. They moved together like wolves, desperate and hungry and full of unspoken threats.

Sky moaned into the kiss, soft and breathy. Jackson pressed his hard-on against Sky's thigh and growled into his throat.

"You're going to take everything I give you."

"Yeah," Sky whispered. "I am."

They pulled apart, faces still inches away, breath warm in the mist.

Heart beats surrounded them. A couple were approaching down the street.

"Come on. The hotel's only one more block," Jackson said.

Sky rested his head on Jackson's shoulder as they walked.

Jackson's mind howled with lust and blood and hunger.

The hotel was the kind of place that didn't bother pretending. Fifteen rooms stacked like shoeboxes over cracked concrete. A flickering "VACANCY" sign buzzed above a paint-peeled door. Inside, the lobby smelled faintly of mold and cleaning chemicals. Jackson signed for the room with a fake name and let Sky press the elevator button.

Room twelve.

King bed.

Crimson blanket like a bloodstain stretched across it.

The window unit rattled in the wall like it was possessed. A cracked TV hung at an angle above a laminate dresser. The whole place was suspended in that too-quiet hush, like even the ghosts had checked out.

"It's cold as a grave in here," Sky said, toeing off his shoes.

Jackson said nothing. He crossed the room in three steps, grabbed Sky by the waist, and threw him onto the bed like a gift he was unwrapping.

"Oh," Sky said, smiling wide, bouncing once on the mattress. "Someone's eager."

"Clothes off," Jackson growled. "Or I'll do it for you."

Sky sat up slowly, lazy and languid, like he had all the time in the world. He didn't strip, not exactly—he *peeled*. Shirt first, the floral fabric slipping from his shoulders to reveal that smooth, defined chest. A soft sheen of sweat already painted the hollow of his throat. Jackson could hear the drumbeat of his heart, fast now, throbbing with heat and anticipation.

He'd never tasted a man this pretty.

Sky was halfway undressed, toying with his belt, when he tilted his head.

"Did you bring protection?" he asked, voice light.

Jackson blinked. "Did you?"

Sky reached into his pocket and pulled out a small plastic bag. Something brown inside, fine as dust. Not cocaine. Not quite.

Jackson's hunger twitched, annoyed. "What is that? Drugs?"

"Not particularly."

Sky brought the bag to his lips, blew softly.

The dust hit Jackson's face like fire.

The fuck!

He reeled backward, snarling, clutching at his eyes. The room flared white-hot, pain igniting like a match in his sinuses. His vision vanished. His skin sizzled.

Garlic. Pure. Refined. Weaponized.

"SHIT!" Jackson howled, stumbling. His claws extended instinctively as he raked the now empty mattress, shredding the crimson blanket like tissue paper. His breath came in furious bursts, marred vision pulsing white behind his lids.

"Where are you?!" he shouted. "Fucking coward—show yourself!"

A voice behind him, amused. Calm.

"Jackson Carter Cole. Born 1932, turned 1963. That makes you what—ninety this year?"

Jackson whipped around, blind and wild, claws slicing air. He slammed into the wall, plaster cracking behind him.

"I'm going to rip your goddamn head off, you smug little twink—"

"Cute," Sky said. "You know, you've killed more people than Ted Bundy. One a month, sometimes two. That's a *lot* of meat for one city, Jackson. You're not a monster. You're a dumb, horny *serial killer* with a god complex."

Jackson blinked through the haze, his vision slowly recovering. Just shadows at first. Then light. Then Sky, across the room, holding something glinting in one hand.

"Who the fuck are you?"

Sky smiled. Not the flirty smile. The real one. Cold. Focused.

"A vampire hunter."

Jackson's eyes cleared. He locked on Sky, smug and unaware. He would rip his head off.

"Submit!" Jackson used his charm gaze to control the hunter.

Sky's face went slack. His arms dropped.

"I was going to make it feel good. Now I'm going to rip your dick off and drink you slow."

Sky drew closer. Close enough to kiss.

Jackson grinned—

And then the stake slammed into his chest with a *wet crack*.

Jackson looked down to see a silver-tipped stake pierced through his ribs and just at the edge of his heart. Pain lanced up and down his body. Sky pushed the sharpened wood into the vampire's heart.

"How?" Jackson gasped.

The stake didn't kill him.

It froze him.

He hit the floor hard, paralyzed—his body a slab of stone. His eyes still moved. His mind still screamed. Pain exploded from his chest, lightning searing out from his heart like it was trying to burn its way free.

"See," Sky murmured, rolling him over with a grunt. "The stake doesn't end you. Not right away. Just takes the body of-fline. You still get to *watch*."

Jackson's mouth hung open in a silent snarl, jaw trembling, fangs bared to no one. His limbs were dead weight, frozen in lancing pain. Fire crackled from his chest, each pulse a jagged reminder that his body would not die.

It would only hold him.

A prisoner.

Caged in meat and horror.

Sky crouched beside him and held up something small and clear between two fingers.

"Fake contacts." He popped one out with a blink, revealing a black iris underneath. "Blocks the charm."

He stood. Reached into his pocket. Slipped them back into their case—carefully. Like a ritual.

"I'm married, asshole. Or was married. Until the night he swiped right on you."

Sky crossed to the window. Drew the curtains open.

The sky outside was already warming, indigo bleeding into orange on the horizon.

"We've got the room until sunrise," Sky said softly.

Jackson tried to scream.

Nothing came.

Sky sat back in the chair and watched the sky change, arms folded.

"I hope it hurts," he said. "You always made them watch."

Outside, the first blade of light broke over the city skyline, soft and golden, indifferent. Inside, Jackson's eyes began to sizzle, the delicate whites bubbling like egg in a skillet. Smoke coiled from his lips, thin and acrid, rising from beneath his collar. His skin puckered, blistered, then split, peeling away in wet curls as the sunlight touched more of him. He wanted to scream. To thrash. To claw his way into the shadow. But his body was a tomb, sealed and silent. Only his eyes moved, burning. Only his mind remained, awake and screaming, as the light kept coming—slow, creeping, final. And still, somehow, he never looked away.

The Girl in the Grove

by Andi Astra

The soft thud of her great horse's hooves across the forest
floor has long driven all thoughts from Alondra's mind.
Thaddeus has long been her most trusted steed, his black mane
and coat glimmering in the setting sun as he follows the now
familiar path, bearing his mistress to her destination.

The farther they get from the castle, the more Alondra's
mind settles, the tangles of day-to-day life drifting away. Now,
she is aware only of what surrounds her, the heaviness of the
thick cloak draped over her shoulders, the soft leather of the
saddle creaking underneath her, the metallic tinkling of her
jewelry. The sun has almost set in the distance, and although
they are shielded from its burning rays by the arms of the
forest, Alondra's mind quiets further still as the shadows
deepen around them.

She has ruled these sprawling lands for longer than any
recorded history. She has seen the rise and fall of empires, of
kingdoms, of a thousand lives and loves scattered like ash to
the wind. Now she is a shadow. A remnant of a dying world, a
race of things that no longer have a place among the living.

Alondra has been called many things through the ages.
None of them have ever pleased her. *Strix, upyr, strigoi.* Many
words, all meaning the same thing: creature of the night,
drinker of blood. The mortals whisper them with reverence,

with fear, as if naming her might summon her from the darkness. As if anything could.

Tonight, like every full moon, she rides upon Thaddeus's back to the edge of her land, where the forest is thickest and untouched. Hidden deep within is a grove unlike any other, her most secret of places. She has been coming to it for nearly two hundred years. There, at the center of seven towering pine trees, she will stay through the night, her saddlebags heavy with books and journals. It is there that she escapes—if only briefly—from the madness of her castle, from the endless hunger of her daughters, from the screams of servants who never seem to last long in the presence of monsters. There, beneath the silver canopy of ancient trees, she can exist as something other than what she is.

But as she approaches the end of the familiar path, a ripple of unease sparks down her spine. Thaddeus tenses beneath her, his massive frame taut with apprehension. He does not spook easily. His ears push forward, and he stills. The forest swells around them.

A breath later, she hears it—voices. Men.

The scent of them carries on the wind. A sickness curdles in her stomach, instinct setting her body alight. Before she even has to nudge him forward, Thaddeus surges into a gallop, hooves devouring the path. Shadows streak past, the now silver-lit forest a blur as she leans into his speed. Laughter reaches her ears, the heavy thud of axes, the sickening crack of splitting wood.

The grove appears before her, and her breath halts in her throat. The humans have torn through it like beasts, leaving ruin in their wake. Half of the trees—her trees, sacred and ancient—lie severed, their pale trunks spilling sap like open wounds. The ground is littered with splintered wood, footprints trampling the once-pristine clearing.

Thaddeus bursts into the clearing, snorting with fury, the huge horse just as much a creature of the night as his mistress. Alondra is off his back before he fully stops. Rage ignites inside her like a funeral pyre. Shadows curl around her, her limbs lengthening, fangs aching in her skull, claws sharpening like curved daggers. The men barely have time to turn before she is upon them.

Alondra is twice the size of the men, death incarnate. The first one dies before he can even scream, ribs crushed in her grip. The second stumbles backward, mouth open in a plea he never gets to finish. His bones snap like dry twigs. The others try to fight, lifting their pitiful axes as if steel could save them. They fall one by one, their cries silenced by the wet rip of tearing throats, the sputter of lifeblood spilling onto the ground.

When the last is still, she moves methodically, her mind blank with the edges of anger and grief, tying their bodies to their horses, sending them back toward the village like an omen, like the specter of death knocking at their door. But it does not fix what has been done. It does not undo the ruin of her most special place.

The silence that follows is unbearable. She stands in the wreckage, breath heavy, the wind stirring the broken leaves at her feet. The ache inside her is deep, the grief of centuries pressing down on her all at once. Then, movement—a flutter of something tucked against the great stone at the center of the grove. A body. Small and pale, it's smell distinctly inhuman, sweet and sour.

Fae.

Alondra stills. She hasn't seen one in nearly a century, not in flesh, not like this. They are nothing but stories now, forgotten spirits lingering in the wild places, slipping between the cracks of the world. But here one lies broken at her feet. Blood stains the delicate curve of her throat, pooling at her collarbone. A cut, blunt but not deep enough to kill.

Alondra steps closer, kneeling beside her.

Gently, she presses her fingers against the fae's throat. Warm. Alive. Barely. The wound is deep, but not fatal if tended to.

She is nearly glowing in the moonlight, although the dark stain of blood marks the translucence of her skin, her white hair matted with it. She is beautiful, in the way untamed things are—ethereal, delicate, a being of root and river. Alondra should leave her. She should return back to her estate, grieve what was lost. But her hands are already moving, tearing a strip of silk from her sleeve, pressing it to the wound at her throat.

After so much destruction she cannot bear to let another part of the old world slip away like this.

She gathers the fae into her arms, weightless as a breath of wind, and lifts her onto Thaddeus's saddle. She does not look back at the ruined grove. There is nothing left to protect.

But this fading creature in her arms—perhaps it is something she can save.

She arrives at the castle just as the first blush of dawn brushes over the horizon, pale light catching on the jagged rooftops, gilding the edges of towers and casting long shadows over the gray stone walls. The gargoyles watch from their perches, their sightless eyes turned toward the east, their mouths forever twisted into silent snarls.

Alondra is no longer the sole mistress of the castle. By her own design. She cannot stand loneliness. For several centuries, she has shared this place with her five daughters, creatures carved from darkness and sharpened into something lethal.

They are hers, made by her own hand, and they have lived together long enough that time no longer matters.

She slides from Thaddeus's back, dragging the fae's limp body with her. The horse does not linger—he knows the way to the stables, and it will not be the first time the stable hands have scrubbed blood from his saddle.

Beyond the threshold, the castle yawns open to receive her. The doors groan as she steps inside, the stone beneath her boots smooth and worn by centuries of passage.

She shifts the girl in her arms, glancing down. White hair spills over the fae's ruined throat, a river of silk matted with blood. Her ears are long and pointed, almost rabbit-like, too sharp and fine to belong to anything human. Yet her face, with its large, heavy-lidded eyes and slight, tapering chin, is deceptively close.

She carries the fae up the grand staircase, through halls lined with cold candlelight. The maids follow at a respectful distance, whispering behind their hands, their hushed voices weaving through the air like threads of spider silk. But she does not stop until she reaches the guest chambers nearest her own. She lowers the girl onto the great bed, where dark plum fabrics all but swallow her whole.

Alondra does not think of the girl again until the following evening, when Ryanna, the most trusted of Alondra's maids, bursts into the sitting room, breathless and pale. The door slams against the stone, rattling the chandelier overhead, startling both Alondra and Dana, the eldest of Alondra's five daughters, who were deep in discussion.

"My Lady! The girl... she's—" Ryanna catches herself, glancing nervously at Dana before stiffening her spine. "May I speak with you privately?"

Alondra does not bother to excuse herself. She simply rises, setting her half-empty glass of wine aside, and sweeps toward the door, ignoring Dana's narrowed eyes.

Out in the hall, Ryanna grips her hands together, whispering furiously, "The girl you brought in yesterday—she's awake. She... she is not in her rooms."

The air seems to go sharp. "What?" Alondra's voice is dangerous. She seizes Ryanna's arm. "Where is she?"

"I—I don't know," Ryanna stammers. "She must have woken up when we weren't looking. And... escaped."

"Escaped?" Alondra repeats, her fingers tightening. "When you weren't looking?" Her voice turns to cutting silk. "Tell me, Ryanna, what exactly were you doing?"

Ryanna opens her mouth to explain, but Alondra silences her with a flick of her hand. This is already an inconvenience. She grabs a candelabra from the wall beside her and moves deeper into the castle.

She wanders the halls, dwelling on the futility of the search. It is doubtful the fae would survive long at all if she turned down any of these passageways, with their traps and cellars and monsters lurking in the shadows.

But then, at the edge of her vision, lit by the moonlight streaming in through the window, movement.

She turns, eyes catching on a pale figure. There, barely visible in the flickering torchlight, stands the fae. She is draped in a dressing gown, thin and too large, slipping awkwardly from one shoulder. Her hair, now clean, is impossibly long, cascading past her waist, pooling at her feet in silken waves. In the dim light, she does not look even close to mortal.

Alondra hesitates. Call out, and the girl might flee deeper into the labyrinth of corridors.

But if she stays silent, if she lets her slip too far—who knows what will find her first?

"I would not wander these halls alone if I were you, little spirit," her voice echoes against the stone.

The fae stops. Her head jerks toward Alondra, eyes flashing like struck gold. Though the space between them gapes wide, Alondra can hear the hitch in her breath, the quickening pace of her heart.

Then, before Alonda can even register the movement, the fae begins to run.

But not away. Not into the dark, the safety of the unknown. She runs toward her.

Alondra stiffens, stunned into inaction as the fae races to her, her bare feet making no sound against the long carpet as she moves down the hall with impossible grace. Her hair flows behind her, a ghostly river, and the silk of the dressing gown flutters loose, baring pale shoulders, the delicate curve of her throat.

Before she can fully comprehend what is happening, the girl leaps.

Instinct jolts through Alondra's limbs as the fae throws herself into her arms, scrambling upward, her arms locking around Alondra's neck as if she means to climb her like a tree.

Startled, Alondra drops the candelabra. It clatters to the ground, snuffing out with a soft hiss. Her hands move of their own accord, one circling the girl's waist, the other bracing her back as the fae clings to her, pressing herself flush against Alondra's body.

Then, the fae exhales. A deep, halting breath against Alondra's throat, warm, relieved. Alondra cannot move. Cannot think. The girl's scent overwhelms her—cool earth, damp leaves, something wild and green, the breath of the forest itself. Her hair spills over Alondra's arms, draping them both in silver. The steady pound of her heartbeat thrums against Alondra's chest, alive and frantic.

"Are—are you—" Alondra tries to speak, but her voice falters. It is rare that she is rendered speechless. She does not even know what she means to ask.

Nothing touches her like this. Nothing would dare.

The fae shifts, pulling back just enough to meet her gaze. Her face is so close Alondra can see the flecks of gold in her eyes, can see the way her lips curl—not in fear, but in something like... glee.

It makes no sense. Nothing about this makes sense. The girl opens her mouth as if to speak, but almost immediately, a wince overtakes her features. Her fingers fly to her throat, touching the neat bandage wrapped there.

"You were struck," Alondra murmurs, still holding her absurdly in her arms, watching her curiously. "Your throat was cut. By—"

The girl interrupts her with a sharp, clear motion. *Woodcutters.* She presses a hand flat against Alondra's chest, her gaze narrowing. Then she makes a biting gesture, her nails pressing slightly into Alondra's skin—a question.

One Alondra understands clearly.

"Yes. I... killed them."

The fae nods, seemingly satisfied. Approving. Then her expression shifts. She lifts her hand again, holds up seven fingers, then folds some of them down. The trees. Another question.

Alondra hesitates. For reasons she does not fully understand, she does not want to answer.

"They... cut down most of the grove," she says finally. "Four of the pines, destroyed."

The girl inhales sharply, eyes going wide with sudden, visceral pain.

She shakes her head, mouthing the word, *No.*

"Yes," Alondra says quietly. "I did not stop them in time."

The fae makes a soft, wounded sound, then crumples further into her arms, her weight sinking against Alondra's chest. Something startles to life in Alondra's ribcage. Sympathy, perhaps. She knows something of what the spirit feels. She too will mourn the destruction of the grove—another thing torn apart by man's careless hands. Another thing lost. She shifts the fae's weight so she is cradled properly in her arms.

"Let me take you to your rooms, little spirit," she says softly. "It is not safe here during the night, alone."

The girl does not resist as Alondra carries her away, her pale arms still looped loosely around her neck, her breath soft and steady against her skin.

Alondra sleeps during the day, though the curtains that shroud every chamber of the castle are thick and dark enough that she and her kin may walk the halls at any hour without ever fearing the sun's cruel touch. It is a world of her own making, one she has been shaping for centuries. Ornate chandeliers hang from vaulted ceilings, their candlelight dancing against silks and tapestries that smother the cold stone walls, swallowing their sterility in opulence and warmth.

The castle has become her world, and at the center of that world are her private chambers, a sanctuary carved from the endless march of time. The heart of these rooms is her bedchamber, vast and quiet, the high-arching ceilings and immense stone hearth making it feel more like a temple than a place of rest. A great four-poster bed stands at its center, draped in heavy, layered fabrics, the rugs beneath overlapping in a tapestry of muted golds and deep crimsons, spilling from the bedchamber into the adjacent study.

Aside from the grove, this is her refuge. The one place where time can pass unnoticed, where she can exist as she pleases, undisturbed.

She steps out of her gown, folding it carefully before placing it in one of the great wardrobes that line the walls. The faint glow of dawn is beginning to creep at the edges of her senses, a heaviness settling into her limbs.

After leaving the fae in Ryanna's care, she returned to Dana in the sitting room to finish their discussion.

It did not go well.

Dana, the eldest of her daughters, is growing restless. More than restless—impatient. Reckless. She is young, in the way only an immortal can be, still riding the high of her fledgling years, still convinced of her own invincibility. She does not yet have the wisdom to understand restraint, nor the patience to learn it. The estate and the village below are no longer enough to satiate her; she wants more—more power, more conquest, more indulgence. She has no sense of the long game. Each year, she becomes more petulant, her hunger sharper, her urges harder to control. She pushes boundaries, provokes where she should not, leaves bodies where she should not.

And Alondra finds it tiresome.

She has spent centuries ensuring that this castle remains undisturbed. She knows how to be a monster without sending the mortals into a panic, without torches at her gates and would-be hunters storming the halls. There are ways to take without drawing too much notice, ways to hunt that do not invite ruin. Dana does not yet care for such calculations. None of her daughters do. They still think themselves untouchable.

They are foolish.

Alondra slips a silk nightgown over her head, the fabric slipping cool against her skin. Perhaps she should send them away for a time—to one of her other estates, farther south, where they can indulge their impulses without turning the surrounding villages into a wasteland of missing people. It will keep them occupied. Give her time to think.

She eases onto the great bed, sinking into the weight of the layered blankets, the mattress soft yet firm beneath her. Sleep is already calling her, pulling her downward, wrapping her in its slow, quiet gravity. The last thought she has before darkness claims her is not of her daughters, nor of the village below.

It is of the fae. Of how strange it was to hold something warm in her arms.

When she wakes, the study door is ajar. She sits up, startled as her gaze falls across the crack of light. In the flickering candlelight beyond, the girl sits on the floor, surrounded by a sea of books. The fae does not look up. Her long fingers move absently across the page she is reading, tracing the ink like she is learning the words by touch alone.

Alondra watches her for a moment, at first unaware if she is somehow dreaming—her vision untrustworthy in that moment between sleep and waking. But she is here. Alondra can smell the sweetness of her blood through the thin air. Alondra frowns, sweeping her legs over the side of her bed. Her feet press against the cold floor, reminding her of the unyielding reality of the castle, of herself.

Her eyes slide again to the fae, her white hair spilling over her shoulders though the slightly open door. It makes no sense for the creature to be here at all, much less to have sought out Alondra's rooms of her own volition. There is no explanation as to why she would sit in the study with such ease, as though her presence was something usual, expected. What could the girl possibly be searching for in the pages of her many texts? What could she possibly want here—in the den of a predator? Alondra lets her eyes linger and she frowns, shaking her head before pulling her dressing gown over her shoulders.

The sound of fabric shifting catches the fae's attention, but still, she does not react. Not until Alondra steps into the room. Then, she lifts her head and smiles. It is bright, eager, as if she has been waiting for this moment. She gestures to the books beside her with both hands, as though presenting a gift.

Alondra frowns as she moves closer. The books surrounding the girl are among her most beloved—volumes so old they have been rebound countless times over, their spines softened by centuries of turning hands. But the one the girl holds is different. It is from Alondra's desk. Again, Alondra falters—she has never known the spirit folk to read.

"What are you?"

The fae's expression falters. Just slightly. Something flickers across her face—not fear, but something close to it. A hesitation, an unease. And then, slowly, she raises her hands.

She gestures, pointing at Alondra, bringing a hand to her lips. *Yours. Your secret.*

Alondra's frown deepens. She crosses her arms, shifting her weight. "What do you mean?"

The fae gestures again, slower this time. *Your secret. The grove. The trees, the stone. All this time.*

Her eyes are steady, as she holds Alondra's gaze, waiting for something to register.

Alondra stares at her, lost. Her expression hardens. "If you do not wish to tell me what you are, then so be it. Keep your secret, little fae."

The girl's smile fades completely. She blinks once, twice—disbelief coloring her face, something stricken and sharp cutting through the gleam of her golden eyes. She shakes her head.

No.

Alondra raises a brow.

"No?"

Her hands move again, slower this time, as if forcing her to understand. *Your secret. The trees, the grove.* She presses her hand to her own chest. *Me.*

Alondra exhales sharply. "I do not understand. The grove, the trees are a secret?"

The fae's shoulders drop. A breath of frustration escapes her lips, and she lifts her hands again—but then, something shifts. She stops. She watches Alondra carefully, something thoughtful in her gaze. And then she nods. Alondra studies her, wary, unsure what to make of this strange little creature who has curled herself into her space so effortlessly.

"Secret, then," she murmurs at last.

The girl's expression softens.

A knock at the door startles them both, and Alondra looks at the girl for a long moment before wrapping the dressing gown more tightly around herself and moving toward the door.

Ryanna is there, anxiety written in the tight purse of her lips, the restless wringing of her hands. "My Lady," she starts. "The girl—"

"She's here." Alondra cuts her off.

Ryanna visibly relaxes, her shoulders slumping. "My apologies, my Lady. It has been difficult to... tend to her."

"How do you mean?"

"She is... quite vicious. Like some wild creature. She does not let us get close." Ryanna hesitates, then adds, "She nearly killed Lucinda last night."

"Is that so?" Alondra raises an eyebrow, almost amused.

Ryanna hesitates, wringing her hands tighter. "Forgive me, but... what is she?"

Alondra does not answer, preferring to ignore her maid's curiosity instead of punishing it.

Instead, she exhales sharply, tired already. "She will stay here. I will tend to her myself."

Later, as the dawn began to paint the sky outside the window with lavender petals, the girl, Secret, slips into bed beside her. The pile of blankets Alondra left for her on the chaise lounge in the study is still neatly folded, ignored. Alondra watches her in the dim light, the smell of her sweetly overwhelming.

The fae moves as if it is expected, as if she has always done this, pressing her warm, bare skin against Alondra's side without hesitation. Nestling under her arm, she rests her head near Alondra's shoulder, her breath slow and steady against the curve of her throat.

Alondra exhales slowly. She can feel so much of her. The wild thing refuses to keep clothes on, and now, in the darkness of her bed, she is a blur of softness and warmth, her skin impossibly smooth against Alondra's own. Then, as if to test the limits of her own brazenness, the fae sighs contentedly and throws a leg over Alondra's bare thigh, draping herself across her.

Alondra swallows hard. Reckless, reckless thing. She shifts slightly, unconsciously, and in doing so, presses her thigh between Secret's legs. The reaction is immediate. Secret arches into her, a breath catching sharply against her shoulder, her body tensing before melting into the sensation.

Alondra's mind goes blank.

She does it again. This time, not out of absentminded movement but with purpose, shifting against the girl to draw another sound from her, to hear that soft, breathless gasp again.

Secret shudders in silent permission, pressing her body closer, pressing her lips to Alondra's cold skin.

Without thinking, Alondra's hand slips beneath the blanket, finding the curve of Secret's waist, drawing her in even closer. Is this what she wants?

This is something Alondra can understand.

It is not the first time she has had a beautiful thing like her in her bed. She has known pleasure before, taken it when she wanted, discarded it when she was finished. Why should this be any different?

But somewhere, at the edge of her thoughts, a voice whispers: *Because she is different. She is a wild thing. A myth. Magic.*

Alondra ignores it.

Secret's arms curl around her neck, light but certain, as if she already knows how Alondra will hold her in return. Her breath skims over Alondra's ear, lips brushing along her jaw, then lower, pressing a soft kiss to her throat.

The scent of her hair—forest and moonlight, deep roots and old magic—surrounds Alondra, dizzying, drowning her. A sound, hungry, possessive, hums low in Alondra's chest as she adjusts, shifting to hold Secret more firmly.

She has not allowed herself to linger on the fae's form. She has tried to give her space, to treat her with respect. But now Secret moves her hands, asking for more—and Alondra can indulge herself.

She leans forward, licking Secret's neck and kissing the column of her throat, excitement twisting inside her.

Perhaps this is all Alondra has wanted as well. Perhaps that is all this is.

She shifts, her other hand coming up to palm the warm weight of Secret's breasts, squeezing at the soft flesh. The girl gasps at the pressure, looking at Alondra, her eyes wide.

There is a thrill in this. A wicked, decadent pleasure in knowing she will be the one to ruin something so untouched. That her hands, her mouth, will mark Secret's perfect form, will drag those breathless sounds from her lips. She touches her, feels the girl shiver against her—but Secret does not shrink away. She pursues.

Her mouth is hot against Alondra's throat, fierce, demanding, her body yielding in all the right ways but still with a will of its own. She does not know submission, only desire—a hunger that made her reckless, a hunger that Alondra could ruin her with.

Alondra tightens her grip, drawing her in, her hands running slowly along her body.

"Do you like that, little fae?" Her voice is low, deliberate, laced with something dark and knowing. She grazes sharp teeth over the girl's ear, letting the words settle deep into her skin. "Have you ever been touched like this before?"

Secret makes a soft sound, her breath shuddering against Alondra's throat. But it is not innocence—there is something else in the sound. Something eager.

She does not answer. She only reacts—arching into Alondra's grip, chasing sensation, her gasps catching on her lips as if she can't help herself. Secret drags her tongue over a spot underneath Alondra's jaw and she hisses, almost angry for a reason she can't quite place.

Because this is what she does, isn't it? She destroys. She ruins. She takes. And perhaps that's where all this is heading anyway, because she isn't fool enough to think the girl will last long. Not with her, not anywhere else in the cold, cruel, mortal world.

So she indulges herself, like she always does, and tells herself she will just take the girl, and ruin her, and move on.

She wakes with the girl wrapped around her, and their bodies are sticky with sweat, blood, and the remnants of their joining—over and over again throughout the night.

Alondra carefully untangles herself, rising from the bed and ringing for the servants to fill the bath. Her body aches—her hips, her legs, her arms, even her fingers—sore from losing herself in the fae, attending to her body as many times as she did.

By the time the bath is ready and the night begins to stretch around them, she parts the curtains to let in the moonlight. Then, she turns back to the bed, brushing a thumb over Secret's cheek, waking her with a soft touch.

"Come bathe with me, my pet. Can you get up?"

Secret smiles, warm and drowsy, reaching her arms around Alondra's neck. An unspoken request. Alondra scoops her up effortlessly, carrying her from the bed, and something unexpected blooms in her chest at the trust in the gesture. Even now, despite the bruises and scratches littering Secret's hips and neck, she clings to her so easily.

In the bath, Alondra tends to her as best she can, brushing through the long, silken strands of her hair, untangling them, weaving them into a thick, wet braid.

"I must go tonight, out into the forest," she murmurs as she finishes the task. Secret's ears twitch slightly, and she lifts her head, alert and eager.

"My daughters have seen men lingering at the edge of my land." Alondra's voice darkens. "Woodcutters. Like the ones who destroyed the grove. They need to be reminded whose lands these are."

Secret whirls on her in the water, her skin flushed pink from the heat. Her golden eyes darken, that feral, animalistic expression flickering over her face once more.

She is already moving before she speaks, her hands gesturing sharply—pointing to herself, then to Alondra. *I want to come.*

Alondra didn't expected that. But perhaps she should have.

A laugh escapes her, quiet but amused, as she reaches to brush the bandage at Secret's throat.

"I would say you need to rest, but clearly, you're healing quickly, if last night's antics were no issue for you."

The wildness fades from Secret's face, and in its place, a pleased, unashamed smile.

She leans in, pressing a kiss to Alondra's cheek, before slipping from the bath, water cascading from her body. She bends slightly, squeezing the water from her braid, the length of it hanging sleek and heavy down her back.

Alondra watches her. Lingers. Something about the sight of her—her ease, her defiance, her impossible, ethereal beauty—feels so out of place, like none of this should be happening.

Like she's in a dream.

"You—" Alondra stops, then exhales. Her voice is quieter now, soft in a way she doesn't recognize.

"You are so lovely, Secret."

Secret pauses, then turns her head slightly, looking back at her. And for the first time a faint blush touches her cheeks. She leaves the room without a word, leaving Alondra alone with her thoughts, alone with a strange disorientation.

As they step into the cold night air, Alondra can feel the shift in Secret's energy. When they reach the forest, beneath the vast stretch of moonlight, something about the girl settles.

She exhales, and it is as if the air breathes with her. The glow beneath her skin grows stronger, her presence more tangible, more ancient. As the trees swallow them, she unfastens her cloak and leaps from Thaddeus's back with inhuman grace, disappearing into the arms of the trees. Alondra does not see her again for some time, but she feels her.

Secret follows them toward the farthest edges of the wood, flickering between shapes—a great white owl, wings silent against the sky; a glowing stag, weaving through the trees like moonlight made flesh; a shifting shimmer in the air itself, dissolving into the mist.

Alondra watches, eyes tracking the shifting figures, a rare and quiet wonder curling in her chest. There is something sacred in witnessing this, the fae stepping further away from the human world, dissolving the boundaries of what is real. It is a feeling she has not had in centuries.

The forest used to feel like this always. Eyes in the darkness, watching. Unnatural, beautiful creatures fading in and out of the night. The pull of something older than her own kind, something vast and unknowable. To see it again, even for a moment, feels like a gift.

At the farthest reach of her lands, they find what they are looking for. Evidence of a human camp.

Alondra reins Thaddeus to a stop, her gaze sweeping over the crude site—makeshift shelters, the large fire pit now full of ash, discarded tools scattered in the dirt. It is not a temporary stop. It is a base. A place meant for return. A foothold into her land.

A quiet rage settles deep in her bones. She grips the reins tighter, already calculating what must be done—but before she can move, Secret is there.

The fae appears at the edge of the campsite, emerging from the shadows like a ghost given form. Her shape is lost to her shifting forms, her braid undone, silver hair tumbling down her back like strands of moonlight. She is no longer entirely human-shaped.

Her eyes burn brighter, sharper. Her nails lengthen into claws, her teeth glint in the dark, pointed and wicked. She does not hesitate. With a feral, breathless snarl, she lunges forward, tearing apart the shelters, ripping wood from its bindings, scattering nails and rope into the brush.

Alondra watches her for a moment, stoic, calculating. Then, without a word, she dismounts Thaddeus and joins her. She works silently, dragging the stones from the fire pit, scattering the pieces of their camp across the forest floor. She does not share in the fae's wild, animalistic fervor, but her movements are just as precise, just as final.

When the last of the wood is splintered and discarded, the last of the campsite nothing but trampled earth, Alondra steps back, pressing a steady hand to Thaddeus's dark flank.

Satisfying as it is, this will not be enough. The men will return. They will rebuild. And the battle will continue forever until the day comes when Alondra will no longer be able to keep up with their destruction.

Secret stands beside her, breath coming fast, her chest rising and falling with sharp inhales. She hisses, a sound that is neither entirely human nor animal, then strides to the center of the clearing, where the firepit's ashes still stain the earth. She kneels, pressing her hand to the dirt.

For a moment—nothing. Then, something flickers. Alondra watches as silver grass begins to curl from the dirt, spreading outward in delicate tendrils. Vines slither and coil, rising from the broken earth, twisting around the scattered debris, swallowing the remains of the human structures. The firepit, the footprints, the destruction—all of it disappears beneath the thick, growing tangle of new life. Within seconds, the site is no longer a camp. It is simply forest once more.

Secret stands, stepping back, satisfaction settling in her features as she returns to Alondra's side. Alondra stares at the growth, then at the girl beside her.

"Well done, my pet." She turns her gaze toward the open woods beyond them. "Do you think we will find them this night, the men who did this?"

Secret shakes her head, gesturing toward where the firepit once was, now long buried beneath the vines.

"Yes," Alondra murmurs. "They are a few days gone. All we can do now is hope they do not return."

Secret's ears twitch, her gaze flickering toward the darkened treeline. She hisses softly, shoulders tense.

Alondra smirks. "Or if they do, that they do so when we are here."

Secret meets her gaze and smiles wickedly, something dark glinting in her eyes.

Alondra has never shared a bed before. Not really. She has taken lovers to it, drawn them into the silk and velvet decadence of her world, bled them near dry, kissed their throats clean, and then sent their trembling, exhausted bodies back to their own rooms, their own worlds.

But Secret has never left.

And it should unnerve Alondra. It does unnerve her. But it also soothes her in a way she cannot name. It is an ache—this strange, unbearable thing. A hunger unlike any she has ever known. One that does not still after nights of pleasure, that is not slaked by feeding. She wants the fae with her, beneath her, beside her. She cannot get enough, chasing the moonlit corners of the forest in her skin.

So Secret stays as the days turn into weeks. And Alondra, who has never asked for such things, finds herself allowing it. Encouraging it.

The fire burns low in her chambers, licking at the logs like a creature at rest. Shadows flicker against the stone walls, dancing in the hush between them. Secret sits curled on the floor beside the hearth, legs folded beneath her, a book spread open across her lap.

Alondra watches from her chair, draped lazily, as though unbothered. A lie. She is always watching.

It is dangerous, this feeling. To have her attention held so entirely by another being.

Suddenly, Secret bolts upright so sharply that the book tumbles from her lap. Alondra straightens, startled, irritation flickering through the haze of her thoughts. But before she can demand an explanation, Secret is shoving the fallen book into her hands.

Alondra scowls. "What has gotten into you—"

Secret stabs a finger at the passage, her whole body rigid with something like urgency.

No, more than urgency. Desperation.

Alondra's frown deepens, but she looks down, the firelight casting a dull glow across the old, yellowed pages. It isn't even a proper book—more a collection of letters and half-translated notes, hand-bound and ink-smudged, written by scholars long dead. She collected it centuries ago, little more than scattered observations on the fae and the spirits of the land. But now Secret is pointing, insistent.

Alondra sighs and leans into the light to read.

"There are places where the old world still lingers, places where the land itself is alive. A sacred grove, an untouched river, a great ancient wood—some are so steeped in magic that they are more than mere places. They are beings. If such a

spirit is strong enough, it may manifest beyond its roots, beyond its water, beyond its soil. It may take form. But beware—if a spirit is harmed, if its sanctuary is destroyed, it risks becoming bound in flesh, severed from its heart. It may walk the earth as mortal, unable to return, unless the wound is healed... if it ever can be."

She reads it once. Then again. And again.

Her fingers tighten against the spine of the book, the parchment crinkling beneath her grip. The way Thaddeus took to Secret immediately. The books she somehow knew before she ever opened them. The wound on her neck—an echo of the axe marks on the birches the night Alondra found her.

Slowly, she lifts her gaze from the book, lips parted, a question forming in the hollow of her throat.

Secret is already watching her. Already waiting, fingers curling around her arms as if holding herself back.

Alondra swallows. "Is this..." she hesitates, the words fragile, dangerous. "True?"

Secret does not move.

Alondra's breath catches. "Are you..." She licks her lips, her voice dropping to a whisper. "The spirit of the grove itself?"

The very act of giving voice to the question makes her feel unsteady, as if the ground beneath her has shifted. But the final piece is already falling into place.

Her voice, hoarse and barely audible, cracks with something unraveling. "You are... ?"

Secret, haltingly, signs the words she has been saying for weeks. *Your secret.*

The realization hits her. Alondra's secret place. The greeting she always whispered when she and Thaddeus arrived. *My secret place*, she would say, laying an offering at the center of the clearing. *Thank you for holding me.* A ritual. A prayer. A devotion. And it didn't go unheard.

Alondra is disoriented. For two hundred years, she treated the grove like a friend. She laid offerings at its stones, prayed in between the seven trees. She slept in its safety, shaded from the sun. She read her favorite books, laying with Thaddeus in the soft grass under the full moon. She always felt the magic of it. Like the spirit of the place looked down upon her fondly. She always felt welcomed into the grove as if gathered into the arms of the forest itself. And now...

She has heard legends. Stories. Spirits of the rivers, trees, walking the world. Taking human form, human lovers, siring half-fae children that grew up to be witches and wizards, strange humans with golden eyes. Could it really be that Secret is the spirit of the grove?

She looks at Secret, at her wide golden eyes, her fair hair, her perfect form.

Alondra closes her eyes. In the stillness, she can smell the forest on Secret's skin. She can feel the calm of the two centuries spent in the forest. She opens her eyes.

Secret has known her for centuries.

Silent, relentless Secret has never known her as a monster. Only as she is in the quiet moments no one else has ever been allowed to witness. She has watched Alondra read, listened as Alondra recited old verses in low, amused tones. She has sat beside her in the great, endless night, sharing nothing but breath and the turn of pages. Never deterred. Never afraid. Secret has only ever known her in stillness, in solitude. Not in blood. Not in ruin. Not as the thing she is.

She wondered at the strange closeness between them, but now Alondra realizes Secret might already know her better than anyone ever has, seen her at her most herself, her most intimate moments. She almost laughs.

She reaches out a shaky hand to cup the fae's cheek.

"Have you... ever taken this form before?" Her thoughts spin.

She kissed her. Held her. Pressed her down into the silk sheets, drawn cries from her lips with hands that already knew her, in a different form. She whispered devotion into her skin without ever knowing who she was, what she was. A spirit of the dying world. And she is here.

Secret leans into her touch and shakes her head slowly. *I didn't know I could,* she signs. She looks down and her cheeks turn slightly pink. *I would have done so sooner.*

Alondra smiles at her, surprised. Her thumb brushes Secret's cheek. "You've always... cared for me?"

Secret's eyes glow with embarrassed affection, but there is a weight to her gaze that Alondra notices for the first time.

Alondra has spent centuries believing she is the last of something. That no one else remains who remembers the world before men carved it up and buried its magic beneath iron and stone. But now, wrapped in a fragile human body, is something—someone—who has lived as long as she has. If not longer.

Alondra gathers the fae into her arms, overcome. "How I long to hear you speak, my Secret." Her throat chokes in frustration. "If this is true, then we—we have long been companions, you and I. We have much to discuss."

Her fingers brush against the girl's throat. It is nearly healed. The angry wound that once marred the delicate skin of her neck has faded, leaving behind a faint scar—a ghost of pain now passed. She no longer needs the bandage. Alondra removed it herself, her fingers tracing over the smooth, unbroken flesh, satisfied by the body's quiet resilience.

She aches to hear her. In the golden pools of candlelight where they sit reading, where Secret curls into the furs with her latest book, her expression shifting with every turn of the page. But more than that—more than letters and history and musings on the past—she wants to hear her speak in the darkness, when they are wrapped in each other.

She wants to hear her voice whisper Alondra's name with need, with something that is only meant for her. She wants to hear it tangled in pleasure, in breathless surrender, wants to feel it pressed against her lips in the dark.

Alondra swallows, pulling Secret's small form closer, burying her face in the wild tangle of her hair. The scent of her—earth and sky, the hush of untouched places—wraps around her, grounding her in the present, keeping her from being consumed by longing.

Patience, she reminds herself. It will come. And when it does, she will devour it whole.

The moment Alondra steps inside the castle, she feels it.

She was called away again, something that never bothered her before she had something to return to, some spark of warmth waiting for her in her rooms. But now she has returned, the end of a long night, and something is wrong.

The torches burn low, casting flickering shadows that creep and stretch along the stone walls. The scent of blood lingers, rich and thick—not hers. Not any of her daughters' either.

She finds them in the great hall, lounging like cats that have gorged themselves, draped across the velvet cushions and marble steps, their bodies slack with indulgence. They are waiting for her.

Dana, ever the proudest, leans against the balustrade, head tilted, her lip curved in amusement—but her face is marred with scratches, thin trails of red stark against her porcelain skin. Deep. Violent. Not the playful wounds of a shared hunt.

Alondra stops at the threshold. Her eyes, colder than winter's edge, settle on Dana.

"What happened to you?" she asks. "I've never seen you let anything mark you like that."

Dana does not answer, scowling. Marisella, curled at her feet, smirks instead. Mocking. Careless. Drunk on something other than wine.

"It was your fae, Mother," Marisella says lightly, stretching like a cat. "She fought back more than we expected."

The very air in the hall stills. Alondra's hands flex at her sides, her nails, sharp as claws, dig into her palms.

"Fought back?" she repeats, sharp as the edge of a dagger. Marisella sits up now, sensing the shift, but she is too bold, too young to realize she is in real danger.

"She wanders the halls like she belongs here. Like she is yours, immune to the danger of the castle," she says, smile still curving her lips. "So we thought we'd remind her—what she is. But don't worry—we did not spoil her completely. We let most of her be for you."

The breath leaves Alondra's lungs too slowly, as if her body refuses to move with the horror clawing at her ribs. She stares at them. At her daughters, her creations, her wolves in silk and lace. They are laughing. They are mocking her.

They do not understand what they have done.

The rage does not rise—it erupts. Dana barely has time to move before Alondra strikes, claws catching her across the cheek, sending her sprawling to the floor with a cry. Marisella screams, but Alondra is faster, slamming her against the stone with enough force to crack the marble beneath them.

"She is mine. And you should know better than to touch what is mine, daughter," Alondra breathes, fangs bared, voice barely human. Marisella gasps, claws scrambling at her grip, but Alondra does not let go.

"She is nothing," Dana chokes out from the floor, her own fangs flashing now, defiant even in her wounded state. "She is prey."

Alondra releases Marisella with a snarl, shoving her away like the dirt beneath her feet. The weight of her rage is a physical thing, pressing down on the room, making the very air thick with something dark and ancient.

"You fools." Her eyes burn as she looks down at them, her creations, her disappointments. "I thought I raised you better. You think she is beneath us?" She laughs, cold and humorless, shaking her head. "She is not prey, you naïve things. She is like us. She is your sister in the old magic, a dying breed. And when she dies, she will take something far greater with her. The old world will bleed dry, and you will laugh until you realize you have helped snuff it out."

Dana glares, wiping the blood from her mouth, defiant as ever. Marisella scoffs from where she has fallen, spitting at Alondra's feet. Dana smiles, but there is an edge to it now, a false bravado masking the creeping realization beneath her skin.

"You speak as if the fae are not our enemies, Mother," she says, still trying, still pushing. "Shall we ally with unicorns and angels next? Shall we bend our knees to elves and forgotten gods?"

Alondra does not hesitate. In a single movement, she snatches Dana by the throat, lifting her clean off the ground. Dana gasps, her fingers scrambling at Alondra's wrist, legs kicking uselessly in the air. Her eyes, wide and panicked now, reflect the candlelight in twin golden rings.

Alondra tightens her grip just enough.

"Tell me, child," she murmurs, almost softly, almost affectionately, but there is nothing kind in it. "Have you ever seen such creatures in your time? Have you seen a unicorn? Have you seen gods walking among men?"

Dana tries to shake her head, but she cannot move, cannot even breathe. Her lips part, her nails dig into Alondra's skin, but it is useless.

Alondra leans in, her voice a whisper of dark amusement against her ear. "No?"

She lets go, dropping Dana like a discarded thing. The girl hits the marble floor hard, coughing, gasping, her hands flying to her throat. The air is electric now. The entire castle seems to hold its breath. Alondra lifts her chin, surveying her daughters with a gaze that sees through them, that judges them and finds them lacking.

"Then do not speak to me of them."

The shadows tremble. The great hall shudders beneath the force of her fury. The very walls seem to bend toward her, toward their maker, their Queen, as if they, too, understand what her daughters do not.

"We are entering a time where the only allegiances that matter are those of the old world versus the new," she continues, her voice no longer raised, no longer needing to be. "Magic versus mortal. And you, my foolish, short-sighted daughters, know nothing of what is coming."

Alondra takes the stairs two at a time, moving fast. The scent of blood drags her forward, Secret's blood, cloying and metallic, a violation that burns through her veins like fire. Her daughters have always been wild, reckless—but this is something else. This is sacrilege.

Secret sits curled in the window seat, knees drawn to her chest, arms wrapped around herself. She doesn't look up when Alondra enters. Her white hair falls over her shoulders in tangled sheets, and there—there—along her throat, her collarbone, her thighs—the bite marks.

Wounds Alondra has never inflicted. Her stomach drops, a chasm opening beneath her. The blood on Secret's throat has barely dried. The wound is fresh, reopened, so close to healing, so close to breaking that delicate thread of silence and hearing her voice—and now... Now there are marks on her thighs. On her breasts.

Alondra's mind is clouded with rage, sadness, hurt. Twice now she has seen her grove desecrated... and this time by her own kind.

"Oh, my pet." The words spill out before she can stop them, broken at the edges. She crosses the room in three long strides. Secret flinches. It is the smallest movement, but it stings all the same.

Alondra drops to her knees before her, hands reaching, desperate, but stopping short. She can't touch her. Not yet. Not when Secret looks so—so wounded. So small.

Her little ghost, her wild thing, who climbed into her lap, into her bed, touched her as though she were someone rather than something—now sits curled in on herself, arms tight around her ribs as if she fears they might splinter apart.

Alondra's hands hover. Inches away. Useless. She doesn't know what to do. Doesn't know how to fix this. She has never had to fix anything before. Never had to make something right like this. After all this time, she finds she only remembers how to destroy.

Her voice is unsteady with regret. "I should not have left you."

Secret squeezes her eyes shut, fingers curling into her skin. Alondra swallows against the burn in her throat. She reaches again, slower this time, gentler. When Secret doesn't pull away, Alondra touches her. She traces her hands up her arms, over her shoulders, up to cradle her face. Secret exhales, a soft, shuddering breath. Her fingers tighten in the folds of Alondra's cloak.

"They should not have touched you like this," Alondra whispers.

Secret makes a small sound—half a sob, half a breath—and collapses into her.

Alondra catches her, pulls her tight, tight, tight against her chest. Secret's arms curl around her neck, clutching her as though she might disappear. Alondra presses her lips to her temple, willing herself to be calm. They have defiled something sacred. For that, there will be no mercy.

"I will make this right," she murmurs, stroking a hand down the girl's spine. "I swear it." She kisses the top of her head, fierce and reverent, then gathers her into her arms, lifting her effortlessly. Secret doesn't resist. Doesn't pull away. She only buries herself deeper.

Alondra's heart clenches, sharp and aching. She carries her to the bed to the warmth, to anything that might soothe her.

When the maids arrive, Alondra gives them a single, quiet order: "See to her."

She lingers, watching as they help Secret towards the bath, whisper soft reassurances, hands careful, movements measured. Alondra's gaze stays fixed on the curve of Secret's throat, the marred skin, the marks that do not belong. Her fingers twitch at her sides.

She turns sharply on her heel and leaves the room. She has punishment to deliver.

The villagers came in the night with fire and weapons, as they do from time to time.

As if they could do anything at all. As if she hasn't ruled this land for centuries, watching empires rise and fall, watching men wither and rot while she remains.

After four days and nights locked away in the darkest of her cellars, her daughters were grateful for the slaughter, for the permission. They had shrieked and swore when she had finally descended into the darkness to free them, but Alondra remained indifferent, directing their fury towards the sharp cries of the angry men waiting outside the castle walls. She herself was only vaguely irritated at the disruption, watching her daughters tear apart the humans with a vague disinterest, until a pitchfork lodged itself in her shoulder, driven deep between the ribs, the force of it sending her stumbling back for the first time in ages. Rage overtook her like flame. She tore it out easily enough, turned on her attacker with a fury so absolute she barely tasted his throat before ripping it open. The bodies lay in the fields now in the small hours before dawn, strewn like discarded offerings to a goddess who has long since stopped listening.

The castle is still dark when Alondra returns. The great iron doors groan as she pushes them open, stepping inside, her breath heaving in the silence. Blood drips from her fingertips, smeared across the torn fabric of her sleeves. Her cloak hangs heavy from her shoulders, damp with rain and the stench of iron. Her daughters are still out dancing in the carnage like the children of the night she raised them to be. Part of her wonders why she would ever expect them to be anything else.

But Alondra is too exhausted to think more of it, to think clearly as a thick current of anger and pain burns in her mind. The great hall is empty when she enters, her boots tracking blood along the stone. The remnants of her rage cling to her like a second skin, burning, simmering beneath the surface.

She wants to destroy something. Instead, she climbs the stairs. Her limbs ache. She is used to battle, to violence, but there is a different weight to her now. Something heavier.

It has been mere weeks since the fae arrived in her life, but somehow it seems that everything has changed in a way it hasn't in a thousand years. Alondra is slipping more quickly, grasping at the pleasure she used to find in the tearing of flesh, in the twisted discipline of her daughters. She used to revel in the sinking, solitary darkness of her life, comforted by the familiarity of her own monstrosity.

But everything—everything—feels different now. She is unsettled. Even tonight's killings were messy, weak. She wanted it over with, the villagers subdued quickly. In the back of her mind now, the fae is always there, waiting for her to return. Showing her a type of joy she forgot existed. Forgot she could want.

But she doesn't want it. She doesn't want to remember what it feels like to thaw the cold bars around the shadow of her heart. She doesn't want to remember that other type of pain, not the ripping of flesh, but the tearing of spirit, of heartbreak when the source of that joy is torn from you.

No, Alondra has long been a monster and a monster she must stay. She must not allow the fae to distract her from what she has built. She cannot allow herself to get too caught up in the tenderness of her touch, the sweetness in her golden eyes. She needs to remember herself.

What she is.

She reaches her chambers with steely determination, pushing open the doors, hoping for silence, for nothing.

Instead, of course, Secret is waiting.

She sits near the hearth, wrapped in one of Alondra's robes, her pale legs tucked beneath her. The moment Alondra enters, she rises, eyes widening in alarm.

Alondra suddenly hates how attentive the fae is—how much she dotes on Alondra, as if Alondra deserves it. She lets the anger simmer, lets it consume, burning all other feelings away into something simple.

You're hurt, Secret signs, stepping forward quickly, hands reaching for her.

Alondra exhales sharply, not looking at her. She turns away, moving to unfasten her cloak, but her fingers fumble with the clasp. The torn fabric is soaked through, sticking to her skin, and her patience snaps, a spark igniting.

Secret reaches for her again, her touch gentle. Doting.

It sends a current of fury across Alondra's skin.

"Stop," Alondra growls. "Leave me alone, fae." She jerks away. Too fast. Her claws scrape against skin.

Secret flinches. A sharp breath. A tiny gasp. And then—blood.

A thin red line blooms across Secret's cheek.

Alondra freezes. Something in her chest tightens, something awful, sick, unbearable... but then anger rises again, overtaking the feeling, turning it into flame.

Secret lifts her fingers to her cheek, blinking, startled.

Alondra inhales, sharp and ragged, and snarls. Her hand shoots out, gripping the girl by the throat.

Secret gasps.

Alondra pulls her close, so close their breaths mingle, and licks the blood from her cheek. It is mocking, almost violent and sensual. She feels Secret shudder, fear rippling off her in waves. A part of her revels in it—*this is who you are. Who you have always been. Who they expect you to be.*

Alondra's grip tightens. "Everyone around me cowers in fear," she hisses, her voice dark velvet. "But still, you are here. Why?"

Secret makes a small sound, eyes wide and searching, hands grasping at Alondra's wrist. Alondra snarls.

"Why?" she demands.

Secret's lips part, her brow furrowing. *Stop.*

She's begging Alondra with her eyes, with her very spirit, but Alondra is lost to something else now.

"Don't you know what I am?" she hisses. "There is nothing but pain for you here! Nothing but death!"

And then—without thought—Alondra throws her.

Secret hits the floor hard, a cry catching in her throat as her head knocks against the stone. She gasps, clutching at herself as blood drips from her nose.

The silence that follows is deafening.

Secret lifts trembling fingers to her face, wiping at the smear of red, staring at it like she doesn't quite believe it. Then, slowly, she looks at Alondra.

And for the first time—she looks afraid. It is there in her eyes, flickering like tattered moth wings. Distrust.

Alondra feels it like a physical blow. It is what she wanted isn't it? She wanted to remind Secret—to remind herself—what she is.

But now, their eyes meet in some sort of tragedy, and the spell cast by Alondra's anger is shattered like glass.

"No," she breathes, stepping forward, reaching for her. "I didn't—"

The moment cracks through her like ice splintering underfoot. Secret stumbles back, breath uneven, a hand pressing to the blood welling at her nose. She looks back at Alondra, her eyes wide, disbelieving.

No, no, wait—"Secret!"

She reaches for her, too late. Secret bolts, knocking into the bed as she turns, fleeing into the study. The doors slam shut between them, and the sound cracks through Alondra's ribs. The lock slides into place.

She stands frozen, breath caught in her throat, as if stillness might rewrite the past, might pull back the words, the wounds, the ruin she has wrought. But time does not listen. It never has.

Once again, Alondra is off balance, grasping for something known to prop herself up. This was never meant to happen. None of it. She is not meant for tenderness, not shaped for kindness or care. She is a creature of blood and shadow, born of hunger, built for destruction. She does not protect. She does not keep. And yet—yet Secret looked at her as if she was something more. As if there was something in her worth trusting, worth staying for.

Secret should have known better than to press so close, than to think she could exist beside a thing like Alondra and remain untouched. She should have seen the warning in the sharpness of Alondra's teeth, in the cold weight of her touch. Should have understood that no one, nothing, survives her for long.

Alondra does not think of herself as the type to panic. But the next night, as she returns from her hunt and steps into her chambers, she feels the absence before she sees it.

Something shifts—wrong, hollow, cold. The air itself is empty, as if it holds its breath.

The moment stretches, slow and sickening, as her eyes scan the familiar space, waiting, unwilling to believe. The wardrobe stands open, emptied of a pile of dresses and the small cloak. The bed is untouched. The sheets remain smooth, undisturbed. She has not slept here.

Alondra turns sharply, the movement fluid. She strides from the room, her steps echoing down the long corridor, sending whispers skittering through the rafters. The night staff flinches from her path, shrinking against the walls. She does not slow.

The first servant she finds stiffens under the weight of her gaze. Alondra speaks low, dangerously calm.

"Where is she?"

The girl startles, hands twisting into the folds of her apron. The scent of fear rolls off her.

"M-my Lady—"

"Where?"

The girl swallows hard. "She... she moved."

Alondra's mind rejects the words. *Moved?*

"She requested to be moved back to the guest suite."

The guest suite. That first place. The room where she was left, small and broken, a nameless thing.

Alondra's jaw tightens. Her voice is ice. "Why?"

The maid hesitates, then, softly, "She told us it was your wish."

Her hands curl into fists. The anger rises, curling, twisting into something dark, unbearable. Had she truly made the girl think that? Was she so cruel?

The answer waits in the space between the maid's words.

Alondra exhales slowly. A single hallway stretches between them now. One corridor. One door. She could go to her. She could fix this. Alondra's gaze flicks toward the path she should take. But she does not move. Instead, she turns on her heel, stalking back to her chambers.

The door slams behind her, rattling the walls.

Let the girl have her distance. Let her think this is what she wants. Let her suffer for it.

The truth that claws at her, that twists in her gut with something dangerously close to regret, is far worse.

It has been two weeks.

Alondra does not go to her.

Instead, she lingers at the edges of the girl's absence, circling it like a wolf too proud to return to the den it abandoned. The maids are her only connection, their whispered reports drifting through the walls of her self-imposed exile. She tells herself she does not care. That it is only curiosity that compels her to listen. But she waits for the updates nonetheless, dreading them and craving them in equal measure.

Alondra never asks for these details. Ryanna gives them anyway. At sunset, Ryanna enters as she always does. But tonight, something is different.

There's a charge in the air, a barely restrained energy in the way she moves, her hands quick but uncertain as she places fresh linens in the closet. She lingers, hovering, stealing glances in Alondra's direction, as if she is holding something on the tip of her tongue, waiting for permission to speak.

Alondra notices but does not acknowledge it. She sits at her vanity, methodically pulling a brush through her dark hair, twisting it into a sleek knot at the base of her skull. Finally, she can take the human's tension in the air no more.

"Speak, human," she says, voice smooth, indifferent. "What is it?"

Ryanna hesitates, then, "The girl..."

Alondra stills, her grip tightening on the brush. "What of her?"

"She speaks."

Alondra places the brush down with slow, careful precision, but her chest constricts, something curling tight and sharp inside her.

"What?" The word is barely a breath.

Ryanna does not back away when Alondra rises so swiftly that the chair scrapes against the wooden floor, an unnatural sound in the heavy quiet.

"Her voice," Ryanna says, firmer this time, and for the first time in weeks, there is something like warmth in her eyes. "It has returned."

Alondra clenches her jaw.

Ryanna tilts her head, watching her carefully. "It is... lovely, my Lady. You should see her. She has been possessed of late, studying maps and ledgers. She... wishes to leave."

Alondra exhales slowly, pressing her palms flat against the vanity, staring at her own reflection in the mirror.

Secret's voice has returned, and it is lovely.

And she wishes to leave.

Alondra stands outside the door, lingering like a coward. The flickering candlelight spills beneath the crack, shadows shifting inside, proof that Secret is awake.

She should turn away, let the girl have her words, her books. But instead, she reaches for the handle, cool metal biting into her palm.

Secret stands by the fire, poring over maps. She does not turn at Alondra's entrance. She does not flinch. She knows she is there.

Alondra moves toward the table, gaze sweeping over the inked parchment, the foreign paths and strange markings.

"You cannot leave," she says sharply. "I do not know what foolishness you're planning."

At last, Secret looks up. Her eyes burn in the firelight, unreadable. She looks different—her hair shorter, neatly braided. There is no amusement, no quiet indulgence, just concentration.

"Why not?" Secret asks, her voice smooth as water rushing over stones. She glances back at her maps. "What concern is it of yours?"

The sound of her voice—soft, sure, as if she was never silenced—makes Alondra stumble. She wants to close the distance between them, to take the fae in her arms, to feel the truth of her presence. Instead, she steps forward, towering over her, her shadows curling at the edges of the room.

"You live under my roof. You do not leave without my permission."

Secret laughs, but it is sharp, cutting—nothing like the sound she once made, breathless and pleased, tangled in Alondra's sheets. "Your permission? You cannot keep me prisoner here."

The word makes Alondra recoil. *Prisoner?*

She does not understand. Was this not the same girl who all but forced herself into Alondra's bed, who draped herself over every corner of Alondra's life, filled the empty spaces of her world without being asked?

"You don't understand the dangers of the world outside these walls, fae."

Secret looks at her then, gaze steady, unyielding. "And you think I am safe inside them?"

The words strike sharper than Alondra expects. She flinches before she can stop herself. The silence between them stretches, thick.

Then, despite herself, Alondra steps forward, fingers finding Secret's chin, tilting it up, forcing her to meet her gaze.

She has missed her. The past weeks have been too long without her, and now, standing here, speaking, it feels impossible that they have ever been apart. And now she can speak!

"Your voice—" The words come like an exhale. "I did not think these would be the first words I heard you speak, my pet."

Secret stiffens but does not pull away. She meets her eyes, golden and knowing. "I wish they were not."

Her eyes say what her lips do not—*I hoped they would not be.*

Alondra's grip falters, and she releases her. Secret turns immediately, her focus snapping back to the map spread before her, the moment vanishing as if it never existed.

Alondra watches her too long, lingers when she should leave. Then, finally, she says, "You should come back to my chambers."

"No."

A flicker of something cold twists inside her.

"I am"—Alondra hesitates, swallowing something thick in her throat—"sorry. For the way I hurt you."

That makes Secret pause. She does not look up, but her fingers still against the parchment.

Alondra presses on. "I was wrong in what I said to you. There is more for you here than darkness." Her voice dips, almost uncertain. "I do not want this distance between us. I want—" She hesitates again, as if saying it aloud will make it real. "I want things to return to how they were."

Secret remains motionless, frozen.

Alondra leans closer, her breath cool against Secret's cheek. "Say my name, darling. I've so longed to hear you say it."

Secret looks at her, and in her eyes, Alondra reads everything she is trying to hide—hurt, heartbreak, longing that so echoes her own. When she finally speaks, her voice is barely a whisper.

"Alondra—"

She never finishes.

Alondra claims her mouth in a sudden, forceful kiss, stealing the rest of her breath, swallowing any remaining words. Secret gasps but does not hesitate—she presses back just as eagerly, fingers threading into Alondra's hair, pulling her closer, deeper. She is relentless, insatiable in the way she always is, and by all the old gods, Alondra has missed this.

With a low growl, Alondra lifts her, sweeping her onto the table. Maps and papers crumple beneath them, ink scattering in dark, careless splashes. Secret makes a soft, delighted sound at the destruction, arching under Alondra's touch, and this—this—is the wild creature she knows.

Her claws tangle in Secret's hair, gripping close to the scalp, pulling her head back just enough to bare the delicate line of her throat. Alondra's lips brush there, lingering, savoring. Secret moans under her touch, the sound sending a spike of hunger through her.

"Yes," Alondra purrs, her grip tightening. "I want to hear you, pet." She pulls again, exposing that soft, delicate skin, her pulse thrumming beneath it, quickened, wanting. "I have been waiting for this."

She kisses the column of her throat, teeth grazing along the flesh, teasing, tempting fate.

"Oh, yes," Secret gasps, hands curling into Alondra's hair, pulling her impossibly closer.

Alondra exhales sharply, pressing her mouth against Secret's throat, drinking in the warmth, the scent, the pulse that beats just beneath her lips. And then she turns and devours her, kissing her recklessly, dangerously. Her hands wander, pushing aside fabric, dragging across bare skin.

Secret sighs against her mouth, surrendering, and Alondra does what she does best—

She takes.

After they are done, Alondra holds her close, maybe closer than she ever has before.

"Come back to my rooms, come stay with me."

Secret, panting, pulls back, pressing a hand against Alondra's chest. "No. I cannot—this—this changes nothing. I must leave. You must let me."

Her voice is barely above a whisper, but it cuts between them like a knife.

Alondra's hands twitch around her, aching to keep her, to stop this before it begins. She has allowed the distance between them, tolerated the space Secret has carved for herself within the castle, but this—the very idea is intolerable.

"No," she says, dark and absolute, her voice the whisper of a storm before it breaks.

Secret swallows hard but does not waver. "This cannot be what you want it to be."

Alondra inhales sharply, something knotting itself inside her chest. She lets her gaze travel over Secret, committing her to memory—flushed and breathing, alive.

The only warmth in this cursed place. Her hair, disheveled from Alondra's hands, her lips still parted. *My Secret*, the thought curls inside her. Her fingers twitch again. She will not let her go. Her grip tightens, nails pressing into the curve of Secret's waist.

"Don't be ridiculous." She dips closer, her lips grazing the pulse in Secret's throat, that warm, fluttering thing that calls to her like a siren's song.

Secret gasps, barely more than a breath. "Alondra—you cannot have me like this!"

The way her name falls from her lips makes Alondra's hunger coil tighter.

"I must have you like this." Her voice is almost a growl now, her fangs grazing skin. "It was fate that brought you to me. Fate that keeps you in my arms. You wanted this, too, only a short time ago. Has so much changed?"

"Yes!" Secret wrenches herself away with startling force, shoving against Alondra's shoulders.

Alondra stumbles back a step, caught off guard.

Secret is changed. For a flickering moment, her features darken—her eyes blacker than midnight, teeth sharper, something dark and otherworldly surfacing beneath her skin. But it is gone just as quickly, replaced by something feral, something furious. "I have learned!"

Alondra stares, stunned, as Secret's chest rises and falls with heavy breaths. The girl who was so soft, so willing in her arms, now looks at her with glittering fierceness.

Alondra straightens slowly.

"You have learned?" Her voice is cool, measured, but her fingers curl at her sides. "And what, exactly, have you learned, my pet?"

Secret's mouth twists, her hands clenching into fists. "That fate is not enough! In the forest, you are the Alondra I know... but here..." She shakes her head, looking away. "Here, in this castle, you are something else. Something I do not want to believe in. I do not wish to remain here, among your monsters and pets. I will not be your plaything, only to be fed to your wolves when you tire of me."

Alondra's jaw tenses, something vicious flickering behind her eyes. "You are different," she growls, beginning to pace like a caged animal, her frustration barely contained.

Her fist slams against the table, rattling the ink bottles and maps Secret has been studying. The candlelight flickers violently, the castle itself shudders beneath the weight of her wrath.

Secret's voice drops, quiet now, laced with something deeper. "You think you have hurt me less than the rest of them? You think you are so different from the townsfolk? The woodcutters? From your daughters—who took what they wanted from me under this very roof?"

Alondra stills. Her eyes catch on the jagged scar at the base of Secret's throat, still raw, still healing. The mark of her failure. The proof of what she has allowed to happen.

Alondra feels it before she fully understands it—the loss, creeping in like the first cold breath of winter. The decision, the finality of it, has already been made.

A pause. A heartbeat. A chance for Alondra to say something, anything.

"I will return," Secret says, quieter this time.

Alondra hesitates. She can still fix this. She can make the girl understand, make her stay. "You are not leaving me."

Secret's expression changes. She looks at her with something close to understanding. Something heartbreaking. She has never looked at her like that before. Like she is something to be pitied.

Alondra doesn't know which is worse. The weight of it—Secret's silence, her eyes wide, shimmering with something fragile, something shattered—sinks into her chest like a blade. The girl does not cower, does not recoil, does not run. She just stares.

"You disappoint me, Alondra." When it comes, Secret's voice is soft, ruinous. "For two hundred years I have watched you pore over your books and records, mourning a world you thought lost, when it sat right in front of you."

Alondra stills, her mind suddenly blank.

"You confine yourself to this castle, to your own dying world. But you do not have to resign yourself to this fate." She moves a hand to Alondra's cheek. "Come with me." she whispers. "Into the mountains. Where the magic runs deep. You, me, and Thaddeus. Let us leave this place, your insatiable daughters, these cold walls. Look for others of our kind. Let us make life an endless hunt."

Alondra stares at her, emotion tearing through her chest. Leave her estates... ? She could not imagine untangling herself from the threads of her life here. But the girl isn't suggesting she make arrangements. She is suggesting they run off into the night, like the creatures of light and shadow that they are.

Alondra sneers, stepping forward, her voice a low hiss.

"You are ignorant, Secret. You do not know of what you speak. You have spent the last millennia rooted in one spot just as much as I have. You think you know more of the world than I do? That you have seen more?"

Secret does not flinch. Instead, she grows—her form shadowing, her presence swelling, the air crackling around her.

"You mistake me for something small." Her eyes glitter, sharp. "I am not like you, Alondra. I do not wither in the darkness. I do not cling to stone and solitude. I am the breath of a thousand winds, the whisper of roots threading through the earth. I have listened to the voices of men, of beasts, of the stars themselves. You are one being. But I—I am the forest."

Alondra feels almost afraid of her then. Afraid of many things, perhaps, but mostly of how apparent it is: Secret does not need her. Has never needed her.

And worse, she may be right.

All she can do is force the words out again, sharp and desperate. "You will not leave."

Secret looks at her for a long moment.

"You do not get to decide that."

Alondra feels it slip away—the moment, the chance, the promise of something softer.

That night, she is gone. She takes Thaddeus. Alondra lets her go, locking herself in her chambers, poring over her work. Going to bed when the sun comes up without checking to see if she has remained.

But she feels it the moment she wakes, the absence. The air in the castle is different, hollow. The scent of the girl, of earth and moonlight and something wilder than anything that should be tamed, has already begun to fade.

Alondra searches. At first, it is methodical. She checks the rooms. The corridors. The stables. She follows every lingering trace of scent, every shift in the wind. But there is nothing.

Something sharp and awful snaps inside her.

The scream that rips from her throat is inhuman, rattling through the stone walls like a beast set loose from its cage. And then she tears through the castle.

Everything shatters. Everything. Glass splinters beneath her hands, mirrors crack beneath the force of her fury, furniture breaks as she throws it against the walls. She destroys the place she has called home for centuries, ruins the halls she has walked a thousand times over, leaves nothing untouched by her wrath.

And when that is not enough—when the rage inside her has nowhere else to go—she turns it outward.

The night is endless, and it is hers to ruin.

She hunts recklessly, mindless. She kills without care, without reason, without restraint.

The village below feels her rage before they ever see her, their fear bleeding into the air like the scent of prey long before the first body drops.

She is merciless.

Because she had her.

And she let her go.

When the Day Met the Night

by Anna McG

In the last three centuries, people have come up with a *lot* of supposed facts about vampires. In Aileen Belisama's opinion, the "myth" of vampires being killed by garlic was particularly circumstantial, especially when the majority of the victims were the town vagrants.

The smell may not be enough to kill me, but it's enough to ruin my fucking day, she thought to herself as the man's weight finally went dead in her arms. For the last two weeks he'd stained the neighborhood's sidewalks, harassing guests as they came and went from the bar.

The Black Moon was the bar Aileen had bought for a pittance when she'd first rolled into town. It saw many creeps. However, they were never around for long, and the sleepy little town never seemed to question why. Nobody knew they had their very own vampiric vigilante to thank for the lack of real crime in the area—in part, thanks to her friend Mason's help in *cleaning house,* so to speak. As the county coroner, it wasn't much work for him to pass an extra body or two through the retort chamber every now and then. In exchange, he ate and drank for free—and Aileen didn't cut power to the karaoke system when he had one drink too many and hogged the stage with endless Cher numbers.

Shifting the corpse's weight onto her hip, much like a parent might carry a small child, Aileen walked down the alleyway behind the bar to the hatch she'd installed on the side of the building. The dumpster covered the opening easily enough until she had use for it. She tossed the body in and shut it behind her. Mason would be there within the hour to take care of things for her, driving off with him in the back of the county coroner van, the town none the wiser. Brushing herself off, she went back inside to finish up duties for the night.

While gluttony and pride were common sins, Aileen lived a life free of many others. However, sometimes one cannot help but fall victim to lust. Under the glow of the neon beer signs, the auburn hair of Black Moon's newest server seemed to be lit by flame. Veronica Taylor had blown through the door like a hurricane only days earlier, and Aileen's slow beating heart had yet to recover. Freckles spilled across her face like the stars in the sky, her wide brown eyes haunted by something Aileen couldn't name—but wanted to.

In her long life, she had been taught one thing above all else: time moves differently for vampires. Getting attached to humans would not end well. And yet, something about this fragile human had her questioning everything.

Veronica appeared to be in a world of her own, humming softly to herself as she polished the glassware, her body language showing a rare moment of peace. Often, she curled in on herself, speaking softly and keeping to herself despite the locals trying to bring her into the fold. While Aileen was no stranger to solitude, she couldn't help but wish to slowly unravel the complexities of Veronica's personality. She imagined it would bring the same sort of relief that came with finally memorizing a complex musical piece—she had whittled away many of the late nights into early mornings these last few weeks playing every song that reminded her of the shy woman.

Knowing she was easily startled, Aileen made a point of dragging her heel as she walked through the back door. Veronica still jumped as she wheeled around to face her. Her delicate face stained burgundy, to Aileen's simultaneous pleasure and torture.

Her scent was like nothing Aileen had experienced before, a heady combination of honeysuckle and campfire smoke. Her luscious curls curved through the air like a blade, throwing the bouquet further across the room.

"I didn't want to startle you," Aileen said, attempting a gentle smile beneath her makeup. "Just coming back in from taking out the trash." She resisted a chuckle at the double entendre.

While she did not need to feed often, and was fully capable of eating and drinking like humans, she did indulge every so often when a particularly despicable soul crossed her threshold. If she was going to be around for a while, she may as well be useful.

Still painted with that gorgeous blush, Veronica smiled at her. "I—I should have known it was you, sorry, I'm almost done here—I'll be out of your way in no time!"

Her willowy silhouette made its way back around the bar. She often hid herself beneath a large cardigan, but Aileen could never stop her gaze from tracing up and down those long, long legs.

Aileen cleared her throat roughly, trying to maintain composure. "Not a problem at all, you know you can stay as long as you like—I'll be in the back working on inventory, if you need me," she said, stepping back toward her office, ready to flee before she bounded across the room and took Veronica into her arms and did something she could never recover from.

Breathing deeply, leaning against the door of the office, Aileen had to admit the problem was only worsening. Every day, the desire to get to know the woman grew stronger. The need to be close to her, intense. The base instinct to indulge in her blood, overwhelming. It was impossible to ignore, and yet, Aileen did not have the strength to give in to something that at best would be as fleeting as the seasons of a single year. When you live for some version of forever, how can you tie yourself to something—or someone—so fragile? And yet, that knowledge seemed to be slipping further from her control each day.

All she wanted was to know the taste of Veronica's lips. The bar buzzed with the voices of regulars and the jukebox roaring loudly as Aileen reentered the fray. It had been such a surprise to her how quickly the small farming town had moved past the addition of a reclusive alternative woman to their community. Aileen was very much *not* the sort of woman you'd expect to meet in a rural mountain town. Long, inky black hair flowed down nearly to her hips, heavy black eye makeup framing her piercing grey eyes. She had always been pale and lacked proper circulation, but the decreased circulatory rate of immortals had comedically heightened those qualities. Tonight, she had her curtain of hair twisted into a series of intricate braids, which grazed her forearms gently as she leaned over the bar to hear what Mason was saying.

"But tonight, I want something *different*," he complained.

Aileen rolled her eyes. "Look at the menu all you want—you *know* you're going to ask me for a Dirty Shirley. Please spare me and let me pour you your silly little spiked cherry ginger ale." She was already reaching for the ingredients, secretly fond of the banter they shared. This was the closest she had let herself get to a human in this non-life of hers. She had been playing piano after closing one night when she'd heard the sound of a struggle.

Mason was being harassed outside his truck by an out-of-towner, who had soon found himself pinned by his throat to the ground by a very angry woman. Aileen had always been the kind of woman who stuck up for people, and seeing that sweet young man's face bloodied up had stirred more than just bloodlust inside her. It had reminded her of the very night she was turned by the monster who created her—the very kind who caused her to spend whatever time she had left on Earth hunting what vermin she could. Her rage had boiled over, and without thinking of the consequences of it, she'd drained the man where he lay. When she came back to herself, she carried the body off to its hiding place and then brought a stupefied Mason inside. While she cleaned him up, she told him her story, hoping against all odds that he would believe she was doing her best not to be a monster. And then, for the first time since her immortal life started, she had someone she could trust.

Mason smirked and toasted with his cherry-garnished glass, leaning forward on his barstool to speak quietly to her. "I took care of your *friend* for you, by the way. Just let me know when you need me."

She reached out with one cold finger and poked him on the nose. "Always can count on you, can't I?"

She looked around the room to make sure everything was still running smoothly, and made the mistake of letting her gaze fall on the woman she needed to spend less time thinking about.

Veronica was across the room, bringing a fresh round of drinks to a group of women, her hair pulled into a bun, curls slipping out to frame her face. It allowed Aileen a rare glimpse at the delicate column of her throat, her porcelain skin luminous and ever-tempting. The siren song of the blood rushing beneath the slope of her neck was mouthwatering, and Aileen shook her head to gather herself, unable to stop herself from watching as Veronica walked back toward them, blushing when she looked up and saw she was being watched. She stumbled slightly, tipping forward just as she made it around to the back of the bar.

Unthinkingly, Aileen reached forward and caught Veronica around the waist, pulling her upright and bringing the two of them nose to nose. Veronica's eyes were so much more than brown—they swirled with flecks of gold and amber, and pulled her in like quicksand. Aileen wanted to spend hours finding every hue they held, tracing constellations in the freckles spread across her delicate nose. She was so warm, eclipsing everything in their surroundings like the sun. She seemed to radiate an inner light, and Aileen was drawn in like a common moth. She realized the moment had gone on for too long, long enough for human senses, when Veronica's breathing stuttered and her blush deepened. She quickly removed her hands from Veronica's waist, already missing the warmth, and felt she could blush too as she realized Mason was very much watching the interaction play out with a knowing smirk.

"So sorry, I'm so clumsy sometimes," Veronica said in a rush, reaching up to tuck a piece of hair behind her ear. "I just wanted to check to see if this was an okay time for my break?" She was looking anywhere but at Aileen, probably uncomfortable.

Aileen nodded, clearing her throat in a nervous habit. "Yeah, of course, the back room's all yours—I'll keep things running out here." Veronica fled around the corner as Mason's smirk dissolved into chuckling, and Aileen groaned, resting her head on the counter.

"You're so awkward with her, it's hilarious!" he said, still laughing.

"I am such an idiot." Aileen said, dropping her forehead to the counter repeatedly to emphasize her words. "I'm too *old* for this!"

She was absolutely mortified with herself—what kind of life would this be for someone so special to resign themselves to? How could she ask such a sacrifice of someone so young and beautiful? Surely she had dreams that extended beyond this sleepy town. The city was less than an hour away, where there were far more exciting things to be found. Aileen was doomed to orbit a real human life like the moon around the Earth, stealing glances at the sun that was this woman who had captivated her entirely.

Aileen resigned herself to her work, trying to ignore her friend's pleading for her to be more open. "You never know, Ale, she could be interested in you too. Let your cold, dead heart warm up a little!" Mason said, popping one of the cherries from his drink into his mouth and chewing thoughtfully.

"That, my friend, is a reductionist stereotype—and I'm not a beer, I'm a person. So shut up and let me refill you."

The crowd cleared out within the next hour, and it was only as she was polishing the glasses in the same spot as Veronica the night before that Aileen finally snapped out of her customer service stupor enough to realize Veronica had never come back from her break. Double checking the front and back doors had been locked, she went towards the office, her concern growing with every step. What she saw when she opened the door took her breath away. Veronica was curled up like a kitten on the old velvet settee, her head resting on an open textbook, hair fanning out around her like flames. Her face in sleep was so youthful and angelic that it was almost painful to look at her for too long. Not knowing if she would ever be able to steal a moment like this again, Aileen leaned down and brushed an errant curl away from the bridge of Veronica's nose, her heart clenching in her chest at the innocence of the other woman's beauty.

"Veronica?" she whispered gently, half-hoping she was too quiet to hear, wishing they were waking up in her bed together, where Veronica's heat could make her feel almost human again. Veronica stirred and then startled, so quickly that their heads connected with a sharp thunk, and Aileen groaned at the universe's cruelty. As she stood back up, Veronica scrambled to a seated position on the settee, eyes flitting and breaths rapid. She seemed to be stuck somewhere between dream and reality, startled out of a sleep that Aileen was starting to suspect had not been pleasant.

Aileen moved forward slowly and sat on the opposite end, as if she was trying not to frighten a wild animal. "Veronica, it's just me. Everything is okay. You fell asleep at work," she said softly, watching the other woman's delicate frame vibrate like a scared deer. She reached out tentatively, offering her upturned palm to Veronica, who grasped at it like it was the only thing holding her to the planet.

"I—I'm so sorry, I didn't mean to, please—" she gasped out brokenly, eyes watering, chest heaving.

Aileen's throat constricted at the sight of her tears, and she began to rub soothing circles onto the back of Veronica's hand. "You're safe, everything is okay, *please* don't cry. What can I do? Please tell me how to help." It was causing her an unfathomable amount of pain to be unable to comfort this woman, who she absolutely should not be moving closer to. Whose heat radiated off of her like the sun's rays even as she pulled herself back from the precipice of hysteria.

"Will... will you..." Veronica seemed unable to say the words, so Aileen turned toward her and nodded, holding her hands out. Shakily, Veronica reached out to meet her, and pulled Aileen's cold hands toward her chest, pushing them into her sternum. Aileen began to rub firm circles into her chest and talked her through her breathing for a few quiet moments.

It was almost too easy to slip into the role of protector for this woman, who had somehow worked her way into every cobwebbed corner of Aileen's heart without giving away anything of herself. In that moment, she knew she would carry Veronica in her heart for the rest of her so-called life.

As her breathing slowed, she started to deflate, and Aileen allowed Veronica to slowly slide against her side, trying to ignore the ever-alluring honeysuckle scent permeating off her pale, freckled skin. She moved her hands away from Veronica's chest and gathered her hair back up into a bun for her as she composed herself. Knowing they might never have a moment like this again, she tried to soak in every square inch their bodies were connected by.

"Please don't apologize, really—there is *nothing* for you to be sorry about. How do you feel? Do you need anything?" Veronica shook her head, trying to stand but her face drained again and then she fell back toward Aileen. "Don't rush yourself. Here."

Aileen helped Veronica lay back down, then moved around to the other side of the room to grab a slightly moth-eaten blanket. She covered Veronica, who was still shaking slightly. "I need you to know—you're *safe* with me. I mean... you're safe working here. I'll look out for you, trust me." Aileen looked intently into Veronica's beautiful flecked brown eyes and did her best to keep control of her emotions. It hurt to see the suffering in Veronica's eyes, which made no sense considering how little they knew of each other, today notwithstanding. It felt like it was her sole duty in this life to shield this woman from any further harm, that she would tear apart anyone who tried to get in the way of Veronica's happiness.

Aileen found herself reaching out to hold Veronica's face in her hands, locking eyes as she leaned forward. At this distance, that dangerously tempting honeysuckle and smoke scent wafting across Aileen's face, Veronica's breathing picking up again—but not in fear. Her eyes seemed to glaze over like frost on glass, and she nodded slightly, breath shaking.

Suddenly, there wasn't a single reason in Aileen's head as to why they shouldn't do this. Every wall she had built up between herself and this beautiful, resilient woman crumbled away in the face of this quiet moment. She closed the distance between them and dared to brush her lips against Veronica's. They were as fiery as the red in her hair, the sweet source of her delectable scent. They were satin-soft, and suddenly pressing into hers with a passion. Veronica gasped and molded her body to Aileen's, her hands anchoring in her braids.

Time, reason, every bit of rationale left them both. They gasped into their kisses, Aileen desperate to give in to the sensory overload of this lustful interlude. Her heart had not beat so fast, her skin had never been so warm. She was ablaze, her entire being consumed by Veronica and her sweet scent. She found herself pressing forward with a new urgency, toppling them over to lay on the old settee, which creaked and groaned under their reverie. Her hands, still cradling Veronica's face, moved downward to take hold of the delicate neck she had spent too many hours pining over. She traced her thumb down the graceful column of her throat, letting it settle in the spot between her collarbones, feeling Veronica shiver beneath her and moan, her hands tightening in Aileen's hair before coming down to grasp her shoulders tightly. Their legs tangled together, and the resounding thump of the textbooks at the end of the settee falling to the ground pulled them sharply back to reality.

They jumped apart, startled, and Aileen looked wildly at the scattered books before turning to Veronica, searching her eyes for any sign of what she was feeling. Her cheeks were a sinful shade of scarlet, hair askew and eyes still burning with heat.

It was the most beautiful sight Aileen had ever been afforded. Veronica clapped a hand over her mouth and let out a tinkling giggle, leaning into Aileen as they both began to laugh. The lust of the previous moment began to shift, and Aileen worried that she had taken advantage of a vulnerable moment.

"I hope that wasn't too forward, I wasn't planning on—" before she could finish, she was shocked to once again feel the warmth of Veronica's lips against hers, feeling a smile that matched her own.

They pulled back, and Veronica touched her forehead to Aileen's. "Don't apologize. I've wanted this practically since the first time I saw you, I just... didn't think you would ever think of me that way." Aileen felt like she was basking in the glow of a warm summer day, swimming in the clearest blue waters. It was almost comical to imagine a world in which she was capable of feeling any sort of ambivalence toward this woman who stirred up emotions she had never experienced before.

Aileen chuckled softly, bringing her hand up to cup Veronica's warm, blushing cheek in her moon-pale palm. "I would venture to say I have never thought of *anyone* but you in this way—I've thought about you every day since you came to town." It was a relief to finally give voice to the infatuation that had plagued her. She knew it was a risk beyond what she could imagine, to open her life and her heart to a human woman, but she couldn't find it in her to care at the moment.

Veronica's blush deepened further, and Aileen swallowed with some difficulty, forcing herself not to notice how easy it would be to lean back into her sweet-smelling neck and sink her fangs into it.

"Well, I'm glad to know I wasn't the only one pining," Veronica said, leaning her weight and warmth back into Aileen, resting her head on her shoulder. "If we could move on from the pining, I would really love to take you out sometime."

Aileen pulled her from the settee into a standing position, holding her hands and appreciating the contrast of their interlaced fingers. "Well, there's no time like the present—and frankly, I feel I've waited for you long enough. Do you want to go on a date with me right now?"

Veronica's smile spread across her face like the sunrise on the horizon, and she nodded enthusiastically. They went out into the bar together and finished up closing tasks, stealing glances at each other and smiling like fools. When they were done, Aileen pulled Veronica into her beat-up, black Chevrolet truck, the engine roaring to life in the silence of a small town evening. The only place open at this hour was the twenty-four seven diner, of which Aileen was a frequent visitor. They spent the next several hours sitting in a sticky red vinyl booth, nursing cups of stale diner coffee and discussing every subject under the sun.

Veronica spoke animatedly about the degree in Library Sciences she had been working on since moving out here—she was especially fond of the Brontë sisters and Jane Austen, and they spent a fair amount of time ranking all their favorite classic love interests. She was a vegetarian and would eat Indian food every night if she could, which was unfortunate considering that their sleepy little town had nothing even close. While she couldn't share *everything* about herself, Aileen was more open with her than she had ever been since starting her new life. They talked for a long time about her passion for music, and she promised to play for Veronica after her next shift, when they could appreciate classical music instead of being jeered by the bar patrons for playing "Claire de Lune" instead of "Piano Man." She had always been fond of cooking and baking, and often spent her days trying to come up with new recipes, which she usually brought to Mason as she was awake to create more recipes than she could feasibly eat her way through. She was already planning a drive into the city to go shopping for ingredients to make Veronica the most authentic and romantic Indian meal she possibly could.

As the day met the night, they strolled hand in hand back to the truck, and Aileen came to the realization that the feeling in her chest had not depleted over the course of their conversation. It had only grown stronger. Aileen had not known much love in either version of her life, so all she had had to go on up until this point was the way great authors described love in their novels. The pining, the miscommunication, and the suffering they pontificated on for chapters upon chapters was suddenly no longer as relatable to her as it had been since she first met Veronica. Love felt as warm and comfortable as the cardigan Aileen now knew her beloved had made herself. Love lit up her heart with flames the color of Veronica's hair, as the sunrise crested the mountaintops and passed over the planes of her face. Love was rich like the chocolate brown of the depthless gaze she found herself trapped in, but unwilling to be saved from.

She kept this information to herself because, while the details had yet to reveal themselves, it was clear that Veronica had experienced something deeply traumatic. The last thing Aileen wanted to do was to scare her. She resolved to do everything in her power to make this beautiful woman feel safe, and special—because she was.

The next evening, Aileen took advantage of being her own boss and closed The Black Moon for one lazy Sunday. She was planning the date of a lifetime for them that evening: she drove into the city and purchased everything she would need to make

Veronica all her favorite foods, and on the way home, an idea started to take shape for the songs she would play on the piano. She wanted to tell Veronica about her life and her emotions the only way she knew how: through the piano. It went without saying that pursuing something as potentially notable as a musical career wasn't something that had been possible for Aileen, but she found immense pleasure in the secondhand piano she had bought when she took over the bar. Since vampires really didn't need much rest if they were well-fed, and sunlight was more of an inconvenience than a threat to her life, she spent many of the early mornings into afternoons, when the bar was closed, lost in music. It soothed the roughened edges of her lonely heart—she could pour her frustrations with immortal life and mortal sin into the beautiful instrument, giving herself purpose outside of her self-imposed heroic duties. The idea of sharing the first love of her life with Veronica brought a wave of emotion, and she reveled in the change that just one day could make in a life.

It was much easier to cook in the bar's kitchen when her ideas got away from her, and she started to build their meal while she waited for Veronica to arrive. Her car soon came down the road and into the parking lot, and Aileen went to greet her at the entrance. She leaned against the doorway, the afternoon sun a stark contrast to her ever-dark clothing. In an effort to dress up, she had unearthed one of her favorite pieces—a deep crimson silk skirt with cobweb black lace falling smoothly over top. She had paired it with a black velvet bustier and her signature black platform boots. Her indigo-black hair was secured with a silver hair pin shaped like a stake. Since she was going to live forever, she'd learned to appreciate the irony.

Veronica exited the car with a shy smile on her face—Aileen was *so* pleased to see she had chosen to wear her glasses. She wore them on a beautiful golden chain that threw the light into her auburn hair, and the reflection of the sun brought out all the golden flecks in her eyes. As Veronica approached, she blushed and waved at Aileen, who soon caught her by the wrist to pull her closer for a kiss. As their lips touched, electricity coursed through her veins. She wrapped her free hand into the hair at the base of Veronica's neck, who sighed and leaned further into their embrace. They spent a few moments appreciating the view of the sun setting over the mountains before Aileen led Veronica into the bar, keeping her hand resting on the back of her neck. She found that she wanted to keep as little space between them as possible.

As they walked inside, Aileen watched Veronica's reaction in her periphery. She had rearranged the assortment of tables and chairs that normally filled the main floor, stacked away toward the booths, to make space to roll the piano out into the open. The settee that had started this new chapter for them was pulled up alongside it, and in front was a picnic setup with the foods that Veronica had bemoaned missing at the diner—vegetarian entrees like palak paneer and tikka masala, fresh naan and mango lassi, samosas still steaming. Votive candles scattered the area, leftover from some special event or other. The jukebox was given respite for the evening, and instead Aileen had used the small speaker she usually reserved for blasting Depeche Mode during her kitchen frenzies to play a series of songs she had collected over the past few months in her pining for the beautiful future librarian.

As Veronica took in her environment, her eyes began to well up with tears, and she looked at Aileen with wonder. "You did all this for me? I can't believe-did you *make* all of this? Aileen..." She seemed at a loss for words, but pulled at the other woman's waist, bringing them once more into each other's arms. Their kisses were awkward at best, interrupted by their wide smiles, and then they were laughing together.

"I can't have you going without your favorite meal. And maybe after dinner, I could play you something?" Aileen's tone turned sheepish towards the end, fearing maybe she wasn't doing so well with revealing her feelings slowly. But Veronica seemed touched as she walked toward the setup, looking around excitedly. Aileen took a moment to appreciate her statuesque profile, finally noticing the black velvet dress that hugged every delicate curve, and the delightful slit that showed off one golden, freckled thigh. She fought to keep control over her fangs, which practically throbbed with their need to extend and *bite*—

She shook her head and moved to join Veronica, who had taken a seat with their meal and was looking at Aileen like she might very well understand the maelstrom of emotions that she experienced in their passage from acquaintances into... something decidedly more. Certainly, more joy, more passion, more *anything* than she had ever expected when she'd said goodbye to the normal passage of time. They sat together in companionable silence as Aileen watched Veronica sample the meal. She hadn't considered the way it might make her feel to watch Veronica's plump lips wrap around her fingers as she ate, the moan of appreciation she let out in response, making Aileen's mind wander down a very different path than she had intended for this evening.

Determined to put more effort into romancing the woman before absolutely ravaging her, Aileen began to feed bites of their meal to Veronica, kissing away the sauce around the corners of her mouth and chatting with her about the week. It felt sometimes as though they had always known each other, like Aileen could finally see why she'd spent decades alone. She had been waiting patiently for someone who could fit perfectly into her life, like the final piece of a puzzle she wasn't aware she had been trying to solve.

"This is incredible, all of this, really. I can't thank you enough for this." Veronica said, laying her head in Aileen's lap, her hair fanning out like the rays of the sun.

"I was happy to do it, sweetheart. I like seeing you smile." She twirled a piece of Veronica's hair around her finger as she smiled down at her, and Veronica twisted slightly to bring them closer together. The clink of a falling glass caused Veronica to jump up. Her hip had bumped into her wine glass, spilling it across the blankets.

Her face paled and she began to tremble "I—I'm so sorry, I didn't mean to, please—" Her voice shook, and Aileen's heart clenched. She had no idea who had programmed this kind of panic response in Veronica, but if she ever found them, they would suffer beyond imagination.

Slowly, she lifted onto her knees and placed her hands gently on Veronica's thighs. "Everything is okay, V. You didn't do anything wrong. Breathe for me, sweetheart. You're safe, I'm not upset, it was just a little spill." She continued to take dramatic breaths in and out with Veronica until she calmed. As they sat together, Aileen resolved to herself that she would do everything in her power to make sure that Veronica never had cause to feel this unsafe ever again. She couldn't change the past, but she could put her love and devotion to Veronica into her every word and action. For as long as they were together, Veronica would only know what it was to be cherished.

They sat for some time, holding each other, drawing strength from their loving embrace. Knowing it was the only way she could express herself at the moment, Aileen pulled Veronica's hands to her mouth to kiss them reverently before pulling away to take a seat at the piano bench.

"I was hoping I could play something for you, if you're okay with it?" She felt suddenly shy, but the smile that spread across Veronica's face, like the sunshine after a rainstorm, was all the encouragement she needed. Taking a deep breath, she began to play, trying to use the eighty-eight keys to communicate everything she was still too scared to say aloud. The music built around them, wrapping them in a lover's embrace. The song had taken shape in her mind slowly, starting out with the melancholy of the months of pining, with a crescendo into the night everything changed between them, then into something gentler, reminiscent of how the sunrise broke across the sky as lovers as opposite as the sun and moon started to achieve harmony. It was the sort of thing that might play at the end of one of their favorite period films.

As the final notes drifted through the air, Veronica sniffled. Aileen hardly had time to turn her face before she was overwhelmed with the scent of honeysuckle and campfire as Veronica threw herself into her arms. "That was the most beautiful... the most incredible... you *wrote that?*" she asked, pulling back to stare at Aileen with watering eyes.

"I was hoping you'd like it, considering"—Aileen took a deep breath—"it's about you. Well, us." Aileen pushed an errant curl out of Veronica's face, stroking her cheekbone, memorizing every facet of her features. Apparently too overcome for words, Veronica kissed Aileen like it was the only thing left in the world to be done. They kissed like they could consume each other, like the world was ending, and this was the last act left. Aileen pushed back from the bench, lifting them up. Veronica wrapped her svelte legs around Aileen's waist as she walked them towards the stairs that lead to the loft.

As the upstairs door pushed open, Aileen broke away from their embrace, the both of them gasping for air. "I don't want to do anything you're uncomfortable with," she said, her voice husky. "But I am absolutely crazy about you, and I desperately want to touch you. Will you show me what's okay?"

Nodding fervently, Veronica lifted a hand and with one swift motion, pulled the silver stake from Aileen's hair, her gaze darkening as she tangled her fingers through the silky tresses, and kissed Aileen with abandon. They stumbled backwards towards her four-poster bed in a slow but pleasurable introduction to a whole new facet of their budding relationship.

The next several weeks passed in a blissful haze—the nights the lovers worked together, they shared glances across the bar all night (usually while enduring endless commentary from Mason about how *adorable* they were), and after the bar closed for the night, Veronica often made her way upstairs with Aileen. They would share a late-night meal and cups of tea while lounging in Aileen's bubble-filled clawfoot tub, listening to their favorite music and exchanging lingering kisses, with interludes of a lust so powerful it almost overrode bloodlust. On the days Veronica went into the city for classes, Aileen often went with her. They had spent so much time apart wishing for each other that finally giving in felt like the gasp of air after emerging from the depths of the ocean. They showed their devotion in the way they fed each other—Aileen, with food and music, and Veronica with the words of great writers, and her willingness to be vulnerable after the horrors of her past.

Aileen knew that she was cradling something in her hands as fragile as a soap bubble, and the joy would inevitably burst. How could they truly be together if she could not be honest about who she really was? She had not fed in quite some time, and thankfully the town hadn't seen any issues pass through, so there was no guilt associated with her avoidance. However, she could only go so long, and she was terrified her sin would stain her hands and soul so clearly that Veronica would see. She had allowed herself to do the very thing she had always sworn to avoid: fallen so deeply in love with a woman who was too bound to the light to ever be condemned to an eternity of secrets and shadows.

That evening, Mason came into the bar as usual for dinner after work. He ducked through the doorway, brown curls flopping into his eyes, and nodded for Aileen to meet him in the back. She held the door aloft for him, then shut out the din of the Thursday night crowd. He carried a cooler backpack, inconspicuous enough.

He passed it to her, gaze intense. "I don't think I can get away with doing this again, but I think I got you enough for a few weeks if you ration it out."

She nodded tightly, throat constricting from the muted bouquet that emitted from the cracks in the zipper of the bag. Inside were several blood-donation pouches that Mason had squirrelled away from the county blood drive—she couldn't bring herself to go hunting right now. Though she made every effort to take the lives of those who would take that of others, it brought no less strain to her psyche to be reminded of her lack of humanity.

"Thank you, really. I know I ask a lot of you, and believe me, I wish I didn't have to." She had never meant to make her affliction anyone else's burden, but these past few weeks had really shown her all over again how lucky she was to know Mason Hughes. She stepped forward shyly and gave him a hug, suddenly rather emotional. He tucked her head under his chin and wrapped his arms around her shoulders, giving her a light squeeze.

"It's an honor to serve a badass like you—sort of like I'm the Robin to your Batman, no?" he joked, and they both laughed lightly before stepping apart. If anyone's eyes looked a bit watery in the glint of the office lamps, it didn't warrant discussion. The two of them knew every important thing they could possibly say already, somehow.

"I don't think you need to worry so much, you know. Your little bookworm loves gothic horror, and you're like something straight out of *The Horla*."

Aileen socked Mason in the arm, rolling her eyes as he chuckled at his own joke.

She put the bag into her personal fridge in the back office, locking it and tucking her keys into one of the many pockets on her black cargo pants. She shooed Mason back out to the main bar area, throwing together his signature Dirty Shirley before heading to the kitchen to start a grilled cheese for him. She was greeted by mile-long legs as Veronica emerged from the walk-in with fresh citrus wedges for the bar garnish trays. They made eye contact, and that adorable signature blush painted Veronica's cheeks as Aileen leaned in to kiss her gently. Veronica continued out to the bar, a gentle smile playing on her lips that Aileen would think about all night, until they were alone, and she could claim them again.

Aileen stared, watching the way Veronica's braided hair fell over her exquisite shoulders, how the plaiting of her hair showed off the smooth, flowing curve of her neck. Their connection was overwhelming even in the smallest of touches, and when they came together, it felt cataclysmic. She dreaded the hours between feeling Veronica's breath on her skin, tasting the addictive nectar of her honeysuckle flesh. They'd have the entire rest of the evening together, and then a long weekend; it was the start of holiday break for Veronica, and they intended to make the extra time together count. There was a beautiful hot spring not too far away. Aileen got through the final few hours of her shift fantasizing about the possibilities of a secluded, warm pool in the mountains.

As the night continued on, their casual touches fanned the ever-roaring flames of desire that lived in their glances toward each other. She saw the promise of carnal delights in the evening ahead with every swivel of Veronica's hips as she walked trays of drinks through the room, and by the time closing rolled around, anticipation boiled hot and fast beneath her skin. She worked quickly, moving perhaps a bit faster than the average person as she cleaned chairs and flipped tables. Veronica had finished restocking the coolers and wells and was bundling up the trash for the dumpsters. Aileen rushed to check that the walk-in was in proper order so they could *finally* head upstairs for their nightly routine. She couldn't wait to rub the lavender body oil she'd found over every inch of Veronica's golden, freckled skin.

A blood-curdling scream cut through the night. Feeling frigid from the inside out, Aileen rushed toward the back door.

A voice whispered, slurring slightly. "Did you really think there was anywhere you could run to escape me? That I wouldn't find you, you *stupid, lying bitch*—stop squirming or I'll knock those pretty fuckin' teeth down your throat."

Aileen heard Veronica's panicked whimper, and the distinct swishing of the opening of a switchblade. Beyond rational thought, she kicked down the back door with enough force to shake the doorframe.

The back alley of The Black Moon was lit dimly by the twinkle lights lining the building's exterior, but Aileen's eyesight was far superior to a mortal's. Veronica was frozen, eyes wide, blade glinting at her throat. Holding it against her, his other hand fisted in her hair, was a man Aileen had never seen before. He was quite tall, as tall as her, with dark hair that fell over his heavy brow. His bloodshot eyes jumped from Veronica's tear-soaked face to Aileen's murderous one, and he cackled, swaying slightly. He reeked of alcohol and stale cigarettes.

"Fuckin' idiots in this town didn't do a damn thing to keep you safe, oh wife of mine," he said in a singsong sort of voice, dragging the tip of his knife up the side of the neck Aileen loved so much. Veronica let out another whine. "The people I met at the diner were only too happy to tell me to find you here when I told them I was a long-lost friend from back home. Told me *all* about you and this"—He jerked his head toward Aileen, whose vision had gone as red as the blood she was going to drain from this man's throat—"little bitch over here. First you try to *poison* your own husband, and now you're fucking around with some bartender in fuckin' clown paint? How long did you think you could live in sin before I came to take you back to where you belong? Be a smart girl, Ronnie. Stop fighting, and *come with me*." He spit the last few words, his knuckles whitening as they gripped the blade.

In the last four decades, Aileen had come across more than enough motivation in the actions of her victims to mark them as such. She could become the basest version of herself, surrendering to her instincts and doing as biology told her. But she did not take great pleasure in the loss of life, however justified it may be.

Remorse would not be found in this dark alleyway tonight, for she had never been more prepared to rip someone to shreds.

Her fangs descended as her muscles coiled in anticipation, and her vision went red. "Get your fucking hands *off of her.*"

Aileen struck like a snake, grabbing him by his wrist and slamming it into the brick side of the building. She heard the unmistakable crunch of bone, and he yelled, trying to lash out with a kick. She met his shin with her steel toed boot, and the resounding *crack* echoed down the hallway in harmony with his screams.

"You stupid fucking—how dare you—she belongs to ME!" Spittle flew from his mouth, his eyes bulging out as he tried to collapse to the ground.

Aileen grabbed him by his throat and dragged him up the wall, relishing in the sound of his garbled breathing. Memories of the early weeks of her relationship with Veronica flashed across her mind—the nightmares, the panic attacks, the scars she had uncovered the first time she'd seen Veronica's body. She remembered the silent promise she'd made as she stared into Veronica's eyes when she awoke panicked in the back office. I will never let anyone harm you again.

She had failed to keep her promise—but she would make sure that she never did so again.

Aileen threw the pathetic excuse for a man to the ground and pounced, pinning him down.

"What... are you?" He gurgled, coughing up a spot of blood.

Aileen smiled, and her fangs shone in the moonlight. "Your worst fucking nightmare."

With that, she sank her fangs into his neck and took a deep pull. He tasted as sour and stale as he smelled, and yet, it was the most refreshing drink she had ever consumed. Feeling the life drain from him was intoxicating, and it fueled the possessive beast that roared in her chest for her to *destroy him.* To wipe him from existence, so she knew he could never lay a finger on the woman she loved ever again. She lost all concept of time, drunk on blood and power, an avenging angel, and eventually he ran dry.

She sat back, chest heaving, and came to the horrible realization that Veronica had not run back into the building after the man had released her.

Veronica was on her hands and knees just on the other side of the dumpster, staring at the mangled corpse. Aileen had known that it was only a matter of time before all her secrets caught up with her, but she never could have imagined that *this* would be the way their relationship fell apart. She wiped her hand across her face, hoping somehow that Veronica was in too deep a state of shock to process what she had seen.

"It's okay, V, it's over now. He's not going to get back up. I need you to do something for me, nod if you can hear me." Her head bobbed before Aileen could finish her sentence, and she swallowed painfully before continuing, knowing it was only a matter of moments before she ran off screaming. "Can you go inside and use my cell phone on the desk in the office to call Mason? Tell him to come as soon as he can. Okay, love? Can you do that for me?"

Veronica nodded again, and scrambled to her feet, whipping the door open and disappearing inside.

Aileen stood slowly, brushing off her band t-shirt and ripped skinny jeans—while her clothes bore no evidence of the turn their evening had taken, she couldn't help but feel like Lady Macbeth. Her hands hadn't been clean before, but they felt forever tarnished by her choices this evening. And yet, she couldn't regret what she had done—because Veronica was safe, and that was all that truly mattered. Moving on muscle memory alone, Aileen opened the hatch on the side of the building and tossed the man inside. She rolled the dumpster back into place and walked inside, a prisoner headed to the execution block.

She found Veronica sitting on the settee in the office, wrapped in the moth-eaten blanket Aileen had covered her with on the night of their first kiss. Unlike that evening, she sat still as a statue, eyes fixed on the phone that sat in her palm. Aileen sank to her knees in front of Veronica, willing her to look up.

"Mason will be here in a few minutes," she whispered, looking up through her lashes with glassy eyes at Aileen, who nodded in reply, trying to soak in every detail of her beloved's face. As she desperately searched the corners of her mind for *anything* reasonable to say, the tension in the room threatened to asphyxiate her. She never could have predicted what Veronica would say next.

"Is... is it really over? He can't come back again?" Her voice was trembling, but the look in her eyes was hopeful as she reached forward with a steady hand to push Aileen's hair out of her face.

Aileen's entire body threatened to cave under the relief of that single touch, tangible proof that the woman she loved beyond all reason truly was safe. Not only safe, but not running away in terror from the monster Aileen had revealed herself to be. She couldn't believe that Veronica was still here, touching her. "He can't come back again. I promise. Did he hurt you? Do you need anything?"

Veronica shook her head, pulling Aileen forward to sit with her, and drew the blanket around them both. "I don't know what I did to deserve you, Aileen. I can't believe you saved me. I thought... I thought..." Her voice broke, and she threw her arms around Aileen, the tears finally overflowing. They held each other tightly, and for a few moments, all she could do was offer what comfort she could to Veronica.

"I don't want to be pushy given what you just witnessed, but... who was that piece of shit? And why was he calling you his wife? I can't imagine how you feel right now, but I promise you're safe with me."

Veronica lowered to her knees to put them at eye level, her warm hands cupping Aileen's cheeks as she stared intently into her eyes. "I know I'm safe with you. I'm the safest I've ever been... it's just... hard to accept. And harder to forget the past. But you deserve to know." She exhaled shakily, and Aileen pulled Veronica in as close as physically possible, trying to offer her silent support while she gathered her strength.

"When I was in high school ..., I started seeing this boy. He was popular, charming, and very intelligent. Everyone loved him—other guys wanted to be him, every girl wanted to date him. And then there was me, the bookworm who hid in the background and just tried to survive. When Th-Theodore showed interest in me, it was like something out of a movie. The all-star jock wanting to date the wallflower? I was enthralled—I was more popular than I had ever been, and he was so adoring. My family thought it was the best thing that had ever happened to me. We were the prom king and queen, I went to all the coolest parties. Everything was perfect. But then...

"A few weeks before graduation, my parents were killed in a car accident. Suddenly, Theo was all I had. We eloped shortly after the funeral, and we sold everything I had left of my parents to get our first home. That's... that's when things changed. Or, I guess, when he finally let his true colors start to show. It started with little comments about my hair, my glasses, my outfits. Then it became regular arguments about how I was too friendly with others, how I should really just give up on the idea of college, his temper flaring if I so much as looked at another person too long. When he started drinking... that's when he started hitting me. For spilling things, for not cooking well enough, reading too much, you name it. I had nowhere to go, Aileen. I had no family left. So, I did the only thing I could think to do. I started a separate bank account, under my maiden name, and saved everything I could in cash tips from my shitty diner job. I pawned family jewelry I had hidden in Theo's crusade to sell all my parents belongings. And I bided my time.

"One night, after a particularly violent fight, I had enough. I crushed up some sleeping pills and put them into his whiskey, and when he fell asleep, I took what I could and ran. I drove a few towns over and traded in my car for something he never would have thought suitable for me. I drained my bank account and shut it., and I still live on cash to make myself as untraceable as possible. But somehow, I always knew he would come for me

"When I took this job, all I expected was to find an easy job that paid cash, and helped me stay hidden. But I took one look at you, and felt something I never had with Theo. It was so much more than infatuation, I am in *awe* of you, Aileen. You're so strong in your silence, I can tell you don't miss a thing. I guess now I understand why. I found myself watching you in every quiet moment, trying to work out what was going on in that beautiful mind. I was terrified to let myself feel this way about anyone ever again, but it was impossible to ignore after the first time you comforted me in the office. Every time something sets me off, it just reminds me that I could never feel truly safe—I've just been waiting for Theo to hunt me down. I've been running for so long, I didn't know how to stop long enough to tell you the truth. I just enjoyed every moment for what it was, knowing some day, it would all be ripped away from me."

Her eyes filled with tears once more, her chin wobbling as she buried her face against Aileen and cried softly. Aileen rocked them back and forth, attempting to remain calm with this onslaught of information. The only comfort she could find was that she had been the one responsible for the death of the pathetic excuse for a man who had instilled so much fear in the woman she loved.

After a while, Veronica spoke softly into Aileen's neck. "You don't need to be afraid. I'm not going to start screaming, or try and attack you with holy water. Your secret is safe with me."

Aileen flinched and pulled back to once again look Veronica in the eyes. "I don't know where to start…"

The overwhelming sense of deja vu came over her, flashing back to when she had revealed herself in front of Mason all those years ago. How resilient he had been in the face of the realization that the creatures from scary Halloween stories and ancient myths walked among mankind.

It was now or never. Aileen drew in a deep breath, and began to speak.

"In my first life, I wanted nothing more than to pursue my passion for music. But the world made no space for women in anything but the kitchen then. So, I disguised myself as a man and went in search of any work I could find, playing in taverns or at local gatherings. I didn't have much of an eye for anything in life outside of my own interests. I kept to myself a lot, and I guess that's how I missed the signs. It's ironic in a way, how much danger you can put yourself in while trying desperately to keep a secret.

"There was a patron who always stayed the whole night when I was playing, all the way until close. He wasn't particularly talkative, so he wasn't really on my radar. One night, I was helping the staff and I was there a bit later than usual. I thought he had left—turned out, he was just biding his time. I was just starting my walk home when he found me. He was faster and stronger than I ever could have believed—he ripped away the cap I wore to hide my hair. He mocked me, asked me if I really thought that I could hide who I really was. Then, the world went dark. He took more than just my mortality that night. He took *everything* from me

"He convinced himself I was his possession, and he kept me *caged*. My body, my voice—they felt like they didn't belong to me anymore. I was a vessel for his ego-driven madness, his pleasure, his most monstrous desires. Every day, I hoped he would finally kill me. There was no point to an eternal life when I couldn't even live for myself. Music was no longer a form of self-expression, it was a shield to keep the abuse at bay. Time moves differently when you have no autonomy—the days sometimes felt like years, and there were long periods where I just... shut down. It was easier to pretend I wasn't even a person than to acknowledge how grim my circumstances were."

Aileen's breathing turned ragged as long-buried memories flashed across her mind. The smell of decay, the dampness of stones beneath her feet as her prayers for mercy fell on deaf ears. She had spent every moment since her escape building a wall between her most horrible memories and her continued existence; if she buried it all deep enough, it couldn't hurt her anymore. If she continued to cleanse the world of filth, she would no longer feel so haunted by events centuries past. She would stop thinking about the power that men wielded like the sharpest blade to take from women. She had been given so much strength, and yet, this moment of remembrance seemed to seep all of it from her very bones. She felt small and defenseless, and she started to waver.

A warm, delicate hand on her cheek brought her back to the present, and she looked into Veronica's glassy eyes. A quiet understanding reflected back at her, the gaze of a woman who had also seen all of the worst things the world had to offer and still found a way to carry on. Her normally slow-beating heart banged at her ribcage, overwhelmed by adrenaline and fear, starting to calm. She leaned a little further into Veronica, and carried on.

"It took longer than I care to admit—but eventually, I figured out his weakness. And I exploited it. I pretended to want it, just once. And when he was stupid enough to let his guard down, I ripped him to pieces. I watched the light leave his eyes, and I *promised* myself at that moment that I would spend the rest of my days stopping monsters like him from getting their way. I'm just sorry I was almost too late this time."

Veronica pulled herself into Aileen's lap, wrapping herself around the other woman's frame so completely that it felt like the whole world began and ended with her. "You are so much stronger than I could have imagined. I'm so sorry, more than I can say. But I'm kind of glad every road we travelled brought us to where we are now, because I wouldn't trade you for anything."

Veronica's face was suddenly awash with a gentle pink blush, restoring some life to her complexion. "I knew there was... something different about you. I thought perhaps I just read too much fiction, but there was a feeling I couldn't shake." She leaned into Aileen's side. "After our first night together, after you played my song for me... I knew then I loved you too much for it to matter how different we are. Or who you really are, even. All that mattered was getting to spend whatever portion of your life I could with you."

For the first time in longer than she could remember, tears fell from Aileen's eyes. Veronica shushed her, wiping them away. She peppered kisses across Veronica's face, whispering affirmations of her love and devotion.

"I love you, I love you, I'm so sorry, I love you," she gasped, holding Veronica as tightly as she dared.

She had never allowed herself to imagine a reality in which she showed the darkest parts of herself and was embraced by the light. Somehow, the universe had brought her to the only kind of heaven that a child of the damned would ever know.

Slowly, Veronica pulled back from their embrace, looking at Aileen with determination in her eyes. "I love you, Aileen. I've wanted to tell you for so long now—I love you, and I will love you until my heart stops beating, and maybe after that as well."

Their kiss felt holy, a vow made in a church of their own making. The consecrated ground created by a love that felt as inevitable as the morning meeting the evening.

As they held each other, a knock sounded at the door. They walked hand in hand to greet Mason. "So, the cat's out of the bag, huh?" Never one to pass up an opportunity to inject some levity into a situation, Mason gave the two women a gentle squeeze, confirming that nobody was injured before jogging back over to his work van, driving it back into the alleyway to secure the body. As Aileen carried the corpse over and bagged him up to make his final journey, Veronica stepped up beside her, looking down with a blank expression. Then, she laced her fingers through Aileen's and nodded to Mason to take the body away. As his taillights faded down the alleyway, her weight pressed more fully into Aileen's side.

"Come on, love, let me take you upstairs." Aileen said, and Veronica nodded, putting her arms around Aileen's neck. She scooped her up easily and carried her up to the apartment. They undressed quietly, and slipped into a scalding hot bath. As they washed each other, Aileen shared the pieces of her life she had withheld, feeling an ancient weight fall off her. Since opening her eyes to her immortal life, she had operated under the assumption that she was never meant to share it with another. But somehow, beyond all logic and reason, there existed a person so loving and pure that it eclipsed her sinful ways. She had bared every inch of her blackened heart and soul, and found it cared for with a tenderness reserved for something precious.

As the lovers twined themselves together beneath the light of the moon, Aileen realized that she no longer needed to hide in the shadows.

Life, whether you are mortal or immortal, is rife with trials and tribulations. But if you're lucky enough, you will be afforded the luxury of a love so transcendent that all obstacles seem to crumble to dust. A love that is warm, and patient, and absolving of sin. Darkness always passes, and the light of the morning brings the promise of a new day. A new life, filled with love and possibilities.

Still, We Rot.

by L.A. Barron

"*H*emoTech *International, here when you need us most!*"

The television set crackled and sang as the screen flickered. Clinton's West Side never got good reception. All the towering brick buildings ate it up, half-starved like the people who lived inside.

Star Thomas turned over her shoulder to watch as the screen flickered again. Her fingers drifted to the tissue stuffed in her nose, pressing it deeper in what she knew was a fruitless attempt at staunching the steady dribble of blood. Her thumb came back red and sticky. Reflexively, she stuck it in her mouth. The void of her stomach ached, hungry but not. Wanting but not.

Her monitoring shift at Shaughnessy Security ended just as the infomercials started to creep into the realm of actual television. With the achingly familiar theme song of some re-run sitcom episode came the agony of another day's rest. Star wouldn't refer to it as sleeping; any little sound sent her eyes rocketing open. There was never a cinematic wake-up; she never stretched her arms above her head and smiled to the world outside her window while birds sang to her in greeting. She couldn't remember the last time she'd smiled.

Unfolding herself with a series of soft, bony clicks, she drew the curtains in the front room with one final, rueful glare down at the street below. Milky pools still bathed the cracked, weedy sidewalks. She remembered, not for the first time, the rush of warm creek water over her skin. How sunlight felt like whispered kisses, all life affirming radiance. For a breath, she could smell it: wet rocks and buzzing summer air.

Star didn't linger in the rising light. The apartment resigned itself to darkness just as she did with a quick yank of the curtains. Even her desk sighed with acceptance as it melted into the gloom. She melted too and drifted from the living room deeper into the apartment.

With the rest of her world turned off, she found herself overwhelmed by the steady drip of the bath faucet and the shh of the toilet that never stopped running for long enough to be a relief. She'd need to look up how to fix both again before it drove her over the edge.

After snapping the door shut, she went headfirst into her room. The floor mattress was a leftover from the last tenant. It had questionable stains, though the stains on the floor near the west window were more so. It was a bed. That was all it needed to be.

Her phone chimed at her from where she'd left it on the floor. It was just a reminder for another mental health appointment she didn't want to go to. The group therapies were laughable. Star didn't want to sit around with one or two other people who were just as sick and miserable as she was and pretend that things would get better. She hated that the most. Pretending. Or the fallacy of hope by way of pretending. Things were the way they were, and unless she lost her mind and decided to sign an NDA, everything would stay exactly the same.

She swiped the therapy notification away and then froze as another popped up in its place. While working, she'd missed something worse: reporting to HemoTech location 475. The lingering knot in her stomach tightened in sharp confirmation. Her breath shuddered as the previous chill between her ribs turned to ice.

The minimum mandated weekly feed. Missing one was like asking to get executed. If her body could, she would have started sweating. But it refused her. No sweating. No vomiting. Trembling and heart palpitations were all she had left.

It was too late for her to try to make it. The sun had already started rising. Being trapped in a HemoTech sounded like a real nightmare, so she hung her head and took a breath for courage.

She tapped the number attached to the text reminder and waited. It rang once.

Twice.

Three times.

"HemoTech, this is Stacey. How can I help you?" Star pictured a young woman with tidy blonde hair, smooth made-up cheeks, and all her belongings balanced in her arms so she could leave as soon as the call was over.

She swallowed hard, steeled herself, and tried to be brave. "This is Star Thomas. I missed my appointment tonight."

Her fingers shook as she pushed her tissue deeper into her nose.

A poorly concealed sigh made her wince. "What's your date of birth?" The unmistakable thunk-clang of a metal water bottle being put down crackled over the phone.

Her voice scraped in her throat as she recited the date. The edges of her too-sharp teeth stuck to the insides of her lips. She did her best to talk around them.

The click-clack of a keyboard came through the mic in the clinic phone. After typing for an inordinate amount of time,

Stacey hummed. "It looks like this is the second time you've missed an appointment, Miss Thomas, is that right?"

"Yeah, uh, the first time I was in the hospital, and they said that miss would be taken off my record."

More clacking. More humming. "Oh, yeah, I guess I do see that note here, but it doesn't excuse your absence since you were in the hospital for a blood transfusion. I'm not sure who told you that it would be removed, but we can't close those unless there's been specific criteria met or you have a notarized letter from the attending doctor you saw at the ER."

Star chewed the inside of her cheek to manage her temper, which came on hot and fast like July rain. So much red tape. So little space for her to exist in. "Can I come in tonight instead?"

"I'll have to speak to the charge nurse to get a new appointment approved so soon after a second miss. Can you hold for just a minute?"

"Yeah, thanks." The words snipped out past her teeth. Rushed. A little rude. She tried to stay cool, but the young woman on the other end stood between her and the government coming after her.

Ear-shatteringly bad music peaked her phone's speaker. She had to hold it a few inches away from her head for the wait, which turned into much longer than just a minute. Finally, blessedly, the music cut.

"Hello, is this Star?" somebody distinctly not Stacey asked.

"Yeah, who is this?"

"Oh, right, sorry. I'm James. I'm the charge nurse here at HemoTech. Stacey was just telling me that you missed your second appointment with us." He sounded... her heart leaped at the thought of him being like her in a more normal way, of him being queer.

Star's lips pressed together as she held herself back from sounding too hopeful. "It was an honest mistake. I think this should count as my first miss considering the last time I was literally in the hospital."

Please be gay or something, she begged silently. Please do me this community solid.

"I did see that. You know, these federal laws really keep our hands tied in most situations. I think I can take this miss off if you're able to come in first thing tonight and you agree to come in more often. That way, we can show that you're making a concentrated effort."

Everything melted away as she sagged, relieved. "That would be really great, thank you."

"I get it. We all have lives, right? Let's go ahead and get you scheduled out for the next month or two with, say, three appointments a week. Will you have transportation to get here?"

Heat rushed down her face, and she had to lurch to press the bottom of her shirt up against her nose before anything got onto the mattress. "Ub, yeah, sure." Her voice swelled around the consonants from how hard she pinched her nostrils together, but she hoped James wouldn't notice.

"Excellent. We'll see you after sundown, then, Miss Thomas. Take care."

As soon as the call ended, tears rushed down onto her t-shirt. She stumbled up, shoulders shaking and teeth tearing into her lip to keep her sobs from spilling out, too, to get fresh tissues.

Once her emotions were taken care of, she slid back down into bed to rest back against the wall and let her mind wander backward. She'd stay at one strike. Nobody would come for her. She would still be safe.

The relief faded in a sigh. She'd still have a strike on her record. And she'd have to leave her apartment more often.

Star didn't know how to feel. The actual act of going in would be expensive; each feed cost upwards of $400. Insurance wouldn't cover them and offer her the mercy of a co-pay.

The act of paying didn't deter her, though. There was no excuse for her not to go in more often, considering how much she saved by not being able to eat actual food anymore. Instead, she found herself lamenting the simple loss of a night spent with only herself and all the cameras on the East side.

The day came and went in a haze of petulant melancholy. When her eyes fluttered, pulled open by the television humming to life, she dragged herself up to the bathroom. She didn't bother to check her appearance in the small mirror above the toilet. Like most mornings, she knew at the very least her face would be a gory mess. Packing her nose staunched some of the bleeding, but never all. The mess always needed to be cleaned.

A trip to the HemoTech required specific clothes, ones that made her look put together. Well adjusted. They couldn't know she had a job, so something that said family money. Or a good savings account from before. Her mind whirled as she stared at her closet.

Even though she had to pause several times to re-pack her nose, she managed to get herself in order. After she slipped her only good boots on, she paused, one hand on the cool doorknob. Leaving always made her feel so small, like the world would open its mouth and swallow her right down. Her phone buzzed, reminding her that spending time afraid would come at a cost. The door opened under her fingers, though she was sure she hadn't twisted the knob enough to let it swing free of the jam.

The dark, empty hall greeted her. A stray cat darted past her down the rickety stairs and then glared back up at her before flouncing off with a flick of its bottlebrush tail. Star hadn't meant to startle it. The cat would never come if she tried to call it to her and scratch its ears in apology. None of the doctors at Restorative Genetics had an explanation for why animals avoided her other than some vague comments about scent and body movement. It was normal, they promised her. All of this was normal.

The cold, soupy night air clung to her as soon as she stepped out of the converted brownstone. Her heart raced, deconditioned from all the sitting and lying down and stress. Determined, she made it to the top of the block without stopping to catch her breath. The pools of light above her turned everything gray and sharp, though their reach remained limited as the fog thickened.

Cars thundered to life on the road next to her, released from their idle by the brilliant flash of green, and exhaust fumes hung in the mid-October air long after they passed. She tucked her scarf up over her nose and ears and continued until she stepped through the sliding front doors of HemoTech 475. A bell chimed somewhere inside. New security cameras had been installed since she'd been there last. Her sunglasses were on her face before she could even really think to take them out of her coat pocket.

"Hi there!" The high, singsong voice made her jump. Stacey was exactly how Star had pictured her: perky, blonde, and far too young to be in a building full of ReGen's medical disasters. Not everyone had the self-control Star did. She wondered if Stacey had security training or if she just had a taser under her desk for emergencies. Or the new cameras and their unblinking, shiny eyes served a live feed directly to the cops. Just in case. She sniffed.

Star grabbed a healthy handful of tissues off of the counter and shoved them up against where her nose started to drip again. "Star Thomas. We spoke on the phone."

"Oh yeah, right." Stacey sagged instantly and click-clacked away on her computer. "I have you with James tonight. He's just finishing up with somebody else, so feel free to take a seat. If you need to clean up, the bathroom's just—"

"Around the corner. I know. Thanks." Star left her sunglasses in place as she hunched into the nearest plasticky seat. For a place that's sole purpose involved taking care of people, they kept the waiting rooms too damn bright. A facade for the healthy masses. To make sure they could see her. Them. Healthy people liked things without shadows or dark corners. She used to like bright rooms, too.

A door she couldn't see opened and then closed. Somebody like her—not exactly like her—strode silently across the tiles as they left. For barely a breath, she met their eyes. Time slowed. Their nostrils flared as they straightened their posture. Star bared her teeth first. And then the tension dissipated along with the person, who sauntered out into the swirling night as if nothing had passed between them.

Star knew them the way she knew every person who'd sold out.

Their nice clothes and perfect posture always gave them away completely. They probably lived on the East side or close to it. They'd taken ReGen's money and sworn their secrecy in return. They promised the company no interviews with the media, and no posts online documenting how troubling the side effects were. Just good, cold coin. Their feeds were on ReGen's dime. She bet they came in every fucking day for more blood. Probably got it nice and warmed up, too. Her nose twitched.

"Miss Thomas?"

She recentered herself with a roll of her shoulders, let her anger and betrayal die down to a simmer as she pushed herself to stand. Star could not be so easily bought.

The charge nurse waited for her with a clipboard and a friendly smile.

"Nose bleed?" he asked. When she didn't answer right away, he started moving.

She didn't hide her appraisal of him as she followed around the curve of the front desk to the entrance to the feed rooms. He stood much shorter than she thought he'd be based on his voice. The lines on his forehead made him look constantly troubled, but she decided it was cute. It would have been, anyway, if she wasn't herself. If that sort of thing wasn't illegal. No marriage. No kids. No short, slim, curly-haired nurse husband. Star sniffed.

He did seem queer, though. The nose ring and the scar from at least two previous eyebrow piercings. A box-dye job that didn't quite cover all the previous blue. Her shoulders eased.

"It happens a lot. No big deal," she murmured, giving him an inch. If he was queer, she could work with that.

Once the main door closed behind them, she slipped her sunglasses off. The hall to the feed rooms had a warmer glow, one that didn't burn her eyes. This space existed for them, not for the public.

"Hm. I don't think I like that very much," James said. His pen scratched as he wrote something on her paperwork.

Even if he was queer, it didn't stop her from finding herself slinking up closer now that his back faced her. She held herself back half a step before she could catch his scent. Whatever it was about him that her mind had hooked itself into, she wanted to keep herself from going any deeper.

"Good thing it's not happening to you, then," she said.

He chuckled, but it sounded a little forced. Never had she seen a charge nurse before for an infusion. An intern or volunteer usually took her back, hooked her up per her request, and left her to it. Having to make small talk about her health both irritated and unnerved her. She was already under ReGen's thumb. Adding somebody else to that mix made her shudder.

"We're just at the end here," he said.

Star paused before going in. "Full house tonight?" she asked, though she already knew the answer. Full houses weren't allowed. They couldn't gather in groups of more than three, even if that group was separated and in the act of getting sanctioned care.

James smiled cheekily as he reached past her and pushed the door open for her. "No. I thought you'd like a sneaky getaway through the back exit once we're done. You seem like the type."

She raised an eyebrow but went inside. Possibly queer and good at reading people. He was growing on her every second he kept that cheeky grin plastered across his face. She wanted to reach out and dig the tip of her finger into his dimple just to feel how deep it went.

The recliner inside bounced as she collapsed down onto it. James slid around in front of her on a squeaky-wheeled stool and dropped the usual suspects onto a tray. Tubing, needles, alcohol wipes, rubber tourniquet. Her nose twitched at the sterility of it all.

She flicked her handful of damp tissues, now stained violent rose, into the trash.

"You usually take O-negative, is that right?"

"Yep." The only type that didn't give her hives and make her feel like she was on the drugs of old.

The snap of his gloves made her jump, even though she'd watched him do it. "Great. I'll go grab you a couple of bags, and then I promise I'll leave you to yourself."

"Great," she echoed.

James left after scratching his pen across her paperwork again, but he came back empty-handed only a minute later. She'd counted the seconds.

"Bad news," he said. "I'm out of O-negative. I'm actually out of everything negative."

"What? How does that—"

"Good news," he cut her off gently. "I'm O-negative and also happen to be a certified live donor."

Star gulped. Her teeth pressed more insistently against the inside of her lips. Whatever bile her body still managed stung the back of her throat.

"I can't."

"You can't... ?" he echoed, not unkindly. The way his eyes flashed to her mouth again made her stomach tighten, but she shook the feeling away with another steady roll of her shoulders.

"I can't bite."

James blinked at her once. Then twice.

He opened and closed his mouth as his expression tightened. "What?"

"I haven't ever," she mumbled.

"I'm sorry, what?"

Star folded her arms tightly over her chest and refused to look at him as she said, "I don't use my teeth. Ever."

Probably her most important rule, or at least the one that she convinced herself saved the last shreds of humanity in her soul. She wasn't some feral animal, and she refused to let herself become one.

"Did nobody ever show you how?" he asked. His tone remained confused, but he didn't seem like he thought she had chewing gum for a brain.

"Because," he continued, gentle still, "I'm fully certified, I can teach you—"

"No. If you don't have any bags, then I'll come back when you do."

When she started to stand, James reached out like he wanted to touch her. His movement stuttered, and as if he'd thought better of it at the last minute, his fingers curled in towards his palm just short of her. "Listen, if you walk out right now, I'll have to note it in your chart that you refused. That's even worse than missing an appointment."

His voice, low and urgent, sent ice through her.

"Are you threatening me?"

James's expression twisted. "What? No, I'm not threatening you. I'm trying to work with you."

When she only stared, he slowly raised both of his hands. "How about we just talk for a minute. This is our first time meeting each other and I know that can be a lot."

His hand slid forward. An offering.

"I'm James Davis. I've been a nurse for four years and I've lived in Clinton for about twice as long."

The cold in her chest softened. Barely. "Nice to meet you."

"This is where you maybe tell me something about yourself. It doesn't have to be anything huge."

The air stung as her teeth dragged across her lip. James followed the movement as his eyebrows pushed together.

"I started HRT the same year I was accepted into nursing school," he volunteered. "Two years ago, I had my chest done."

Oh, Star thought. Her shoulders sunk down an inch.

"This is freaking me out."

She waited for him to flinch. To tighten up with fear. Waited. Waited.

"Okay, I can work with freaked out. You said you don't bite, so I'm guessing it's not the needles or medical junk freaking you out?"

All she could do was nod. One little tuck of her chin while her eyes stayed glued to him just in case he did start to panic. She'd seen it before regardless of level of credentials or licensing. When she was too emotional, people always did.

"They don't help."

Another prickle of nausea rushed her as he leaned forward only enough to rest his place his palms on his knees. "I can put it all away so you don't have to see it."

"Okay."

The cabinets whispered open and closed as he shoved the whole tray out of sight. When he sat back up, his eyes were brighter. "Better?"

"Uh... yeah, a little bit." She wasn't lying. The steadily dripping melt behind her ribs fell into rhythm with the tiny twitch in the side of his neck. Her mouth watered, but not just because she was feeling the thirst.

"Great," he said. A grin warmed his face further. "What else can I do to make this feel easier for you?"

Her first inclination was to tell him to let her leave. To repeat that she could come back later when the only thing that would help became available.

"I can't do a skin-to-skin donation."

"We don't have to figure that out just yet. Why don't you ask me anything you want to know? If there's something that will help this process in general be easier for you, I want to know."

Nothing about him personally set her off. He was just as polite in person as he'd been over the phone. More so, she decided. He wanted to help her, and that meant something.

"Anything?"

He nodded. "Whatever you want."

Though being surreptitious was not her strong suit, Star tried to be more casual as she asked, "What do you get out of this?"

"My work? Helping people."

She shook her head. "No. This—" She gestured between the two of them.

Amusement pushed one of his eyebrows, the scarred one, up towards his hair. "Making time to help you feel more in control and comfortable during your appointment?"

"Right."

"Same thing; helping you. I always appreciate time with patients, but I specifically appreciate time with patients who are maybe a little more like me than I originally thought."

Her silence pushed him again. "Unless I'm misreading that."

"You're not."

Even though they were her own words of confirmation, the feeling of being fully seen struck like a blow. She knew he meant no harm, but her body reacted anyway.

The uncomfortable and wholly terrifying feeling in the front of her mouth took her breath away. Shooting pain and the acute, aching stretch in her gums sent fear ringing through her entire body, which did absolutely nothing to stop her teeth from extending lower and lower. An animal backed into a corner. That was how she felt.

She couldn't do this. Not here. Losing control at home by herself and being contained would be one thing, but with James standing between her and her safety, only chaos and punishment would ensue. Her entire body shrank at the thought of being sent off to Blood Boulevard and having to live in the open-air prison inside the city she'd grown up in.

Or she could be executed, depending on how much damage she did to the building in the process. Barbed greenbrier vines looped and locked in her stomach. Dug in. Pierced and hooked.

"Star?" James's eyes were locked on her mouth. Embarrassment turned up the power behind her pain enough to make her grunt.

Getting around him proved easy enough. He didn't have much reach. Knees shaking, she swiped blindly for the doorknob. She missed twice before she found it, but not before James caught up with what was happening and got to his feet.

"I can help you." His voice stayed low as he looked purposefully into her eyes. "I want to help you."

"Let me leave." Before I hurt you. She didn't want to do it, but she knew she would if he cornered her for too long. Some instincts could never be unwoven. She'd made it so long without hurting anyone, and now this stupid charge nurse with the pretty smile would be her undoing.

If he wasn't careful, she would break his bones with a whisper of her hands across his skin. Leave trails of bruises and brokenness in her wake. She could be his undoing, too.

Why he thought it was safe to get between her and the exit was beyond her. Even sick as she was, her adrenalized brute strength would always win out. Her mind twirled through conjured images of pages and pages of warnings telling him to do the exact opposite of everything he was doing.

"I don't want to get you into trouble. Just take a seat, we can figure this out if we think a little bit creatively."

Star bristled. Her upper body curled away from him as she let her lips pull back from her aching teeth. James didn't look startled. He looked more curious as his eyes moved from her eyes down to her teeth and then back up again.

"I know you're scared," he said. "You don't have to bite, okay? We can do something else."

A crackle of static made them both jolt. Star flattened herself against the door and cowered, her human instincts winning out for the moment. From somewhere above her head, Stacey asked, "James? Are you still in there?"

She watched as he shook himself before stretching to press under the lip of the counter. "Yes. We were discussing her availability. Everything's fine."

"Oh, my apologies."

"Not at all, Stacey."

The speaker crackled again before going silent. James focused back on her with a pleading grimace. "Please, Star. Let me help you tonight. It's our best option to strike the missed appointment without getting you flagged."

He didn't move a single muscle as she considered the offer. The room started to tip over itself the longer she stood with her knees locked. Fevers were common and normal between feeds. When she went too long. Star tried to breathe, but the rush of James's scent sent her spinning faster. Lemon grass. Olive oil. Sage. Her nose twitched.

"We can get through this and get you taken care of. I promise."

Star tried to keep track of his words. The way her mind stayed a step behind how her body reacted made it almost impossible.

"Star, I want to help. Remember why I want to help."

Air cut down her throat as she tried to breathe. Tried to calm the animal of her body. Everything hurt too strongly for her to think around and her brain fired before she could stop herself.

"I'm too hot."

"You're starting to fever." His tone dripped with ochre concern. "We really need to get you taken care of before you get too warm."

His voice swam through her ears and then inside her head. The words pulsed in the tiny spaces between her brain and skull before sinking in. Her fingers found the doorknob again. A single curl of his dark hair swung down to kiss the scars on his eyebrow as his head dipped. The cabinet opened and closed. The tray came back out.

Star looked down in time to watch him crack open the alcohol sponge. The scent immediately stung from the inside of her nose to the back of her throat as he cleaned off an inch-wide patch of his forearm. She could barely keep her eyes open with how fast the room spun. Her back twisted when the sponge clattered against the metal tray. The snap of the rubber tourniquet sent a rush of dread burning through her too. His veins bulged. Her mouth watered, and her teeth ached, and it was as if the world would tear itself apart around her if they didn't stop this.

"James, I can't—"

Desperation made it all worse. Every ache, every jolting rush of heady thirst, amplified in time with the roar of his heartbeat and hers.

"Shh," he shushed. "Let me do this for you."

He tore the finger of his glove open with his teeth and pressed along his arm until he found a place he liked. "Just another minute."

She didn't know why he had to feel around; she could see his veins so clearly even though her vision kept turning over itself. Nauseous heat washed across her shoulders and the back of her neck. She wondered whether she'd be sick before or after she passed out.

James uncapped the needle, and her jaw slackened. Her teeth screamed when the air hit them, cold and brutal and not discouraging in any way that mattered. They had a mind of their own as the urge to sink them into his warm body raced through her in a white flash.

"I can't do—Please don't—"

James made quick work of guiding the needle into his arm before sliding it back out and tossing it away too. The plastic catheter stayed put, buried in his arm the way her teeth wanted to be, as he smoothed a piece of tape down over where the connecting bit protruded.

Her mind stuttered. He hadn't cut himself open or given her a draw point to suction her lips around. For a moment, everything stilled. The roaring softened.

"Not perfect, but it'll do."

She couldn't look at his face. His words only partially registered as he twisted a thicker tube into the end of the connector. He held it out for her with an encouraging sort of nod.

When she didn't move, he winced. "Did you need me to cut this, or can you bite through?"

He hadn't offered for her to bite him. Her understanding, though present at the front of her mind, didn't click into place until she reached out and, unsteady as all hell, took his offering. The PVC tore like tissue paper. She sucked. James hissed through his teeth, and she eased her pressure. Even this far gone, she knew that she didn't want to hurt him. Hurting him meant punishment. Meant no more private apartment. It meant fear too. For him. She didn't want him to be afraid of her.

A terrified thrill shot through her as her knees buckled, but James was there. His strong hand, too cool against her burning skin, guided her as the chair came up to cushion her fall. The stool squeaked as it rolled, but she couldn't focus enough to do anything more than sag.

"Sorry," she grumbled around the tube as it tugged against her lips. Another snap of rubber startled her, but then his blood gushed, hot and heady. It shot back into her throat and almost made her spit it all out and drop the tube as she choked. She managed to stay steady as she forced the tube against her cheek and bit down to arrest the rush.

As she swallowed, there was only the cool wave of her fever evaporating. The anxious flutter in her chest eased. Around her, the room stilled.

Swallow by swallow, her body relaxed. At some point, the flow stopped, and the tube collapsed between her cheek and tongue.

"Better than a bag?" James's voice, soft and smooth, brought her back to herself.

When she managed to pry her eyes open, he had his arm resting on the recliner beside her and his legs bracketing hers. The stool squeaked again as he shifted somehow closer. His fingers found her wrist and he squeezed, numbers slipping past his lips as he counted her heartbeats.

Star let her head roll to look at him better, the relief so intense it reminded her of being high.

"You clipped the tube." Her words came out in a delicate rush. Her voice sent a shiver up her spine; she always sounded so unlike herself after feeding.

Healthy. She sounded healthy.

"I didn't want to interrupt your meditation to ask you to stop." James's eyes lingered on her, both calculating and kind. Every facet of his face sang to her.

She snorted as she tossed the soaked tissues at the trashcan under the counter. "I wasn't meditating."

"No? Could have fooled me."

His eyes dipped to her mouth, and everything inside her spun. She didn't know why her body started to move or how her hand landed in the front pocket of his scrubs. He didn't resist as she pulled him in. No pepper of fresh anxiety filled the air between them as he leaned to her too, calm and willing.

The air in the room turned thick and heavy the moment their lips met. For the first time in years, Star kissed. And it didn't feel wrong. James's hand slid from the side of her neck up into her hair and curled there. Holding, not trapping. He surrounded her, guiding their rhythm on a dime-stop whim. Fast and starving, then slow and savoring. Though maddening, Star found herself lost in him. In his smell. In the way they spoke without speaking.

All the nerves in her body sparked to life, urged on by the gentle, insistent press of James's lips against hers. She could have been a regular person again until—

"Careful." He pulled back enough to let the words pass between them as he teased his tongue against her bottom lip.

She let go of him, but he didn't leave her.

"That wasn't careful as in stop." His smirk returned in the way his words curled up around the edges. The sight of him would have made her knees give out if she wasn't sitting.

"Hard to tell," she admitted in a whisper. His fingers scorched her as he drew them to her jaw and held her still. He kissed her once, twice, then pulled back the rest of the way. Despite the space, she felt him all around her.

"It's normal, by the way," he said, his breath coming in delightfully soft puffs. "I should have warned you first. It's the fresh blood. It has... a certain effect on people."

Star nodded, dazed. His voice rushed her in waves of crushed velvet.

"Clinically speaking, you did a great job controlling yourself just now."

Star couldn't fully process his adorable babbling. Her mind, still spinning, melted as she nuzzled her cheek affectionately into his palm. He was afternoon sun on a creek bed. She didn't realize she'd mumbled this aloud to him until he let out a breath of a chuckle.

"Good. That means your fever broke. By the way, you, uh, nicked my lip, so you're a bit of a mess."

His hand disappeared from her. A soft tearing sound made her eyes shoot open, but he only held out a paper towel. No threat. No danger. Her breathing slowed. There was more squeaking as he wheeled back to the counter. The paper towel scraped against her lips as she blotted herself clean.

"I feel a bit irresponsible letting you clean up after all that by yourself."

"Don't worry about it." Her voice was too breathy. Her annoyance at the sound broke through the swirling pink clouds of happiness and brought her back down to the little beige recliner. The room sunk into a suicide Tuesday. To keep herself from reaching for him again, Star rolled her eyes and pushed herself to her feet. The room stayed exactly where it was supposed to, and so did James. These were small mercies. If he were to move in again, she knew she wouldn't be able to stop herself from— Her nose twitched.

"Call me when you get more bags in." She tried to deepen her voice past the relentless breathiness. This would not be happening again. Her mind already whirred with unhelpful, negative thoughts, berating her for letting it happen in the first place.

"See you Wednesday then. I'll make sure you get that reminder text earlier next time."

She didn't know what to do, if she should apologize or just leave. It had been her fingers that slipped into his pocket. Her lips on his first. Her teeth sinking into his—She shook her head sharply away from the fresh memory.

Without another word, Star slipped out the door and then, like he'd said, left the building through the back. The world blurred into streaks of furious color. Every single scent in the air stained the inside of her nose. She thought of the person from the waiting room and their dark sunglasses and expensive coat. This was that person's world, all the colors and the smells and the heavy feeling of being alive. It wasn't a world she belonged in, and she knew this so deeply it made her chest feel like it might cave in.

As she waited on the corner for the light to turn, she heard the familiar jingle slip out from between the gaps in the front door of the clinic. The television, though she hadn't noticed it earlier, sang out to her:

"HemoTech International, here when you need us most!"

The corner of her mouth twitched up, almost like a real smile.

Star Thomas sneezed as she scrolled through her phone. The train car bustled around her, and a guy with blue hair brushed her with his elbow as they rolled to a jerky stop at Fifth Street Station. She waited for him to move away first before darting out around him to the platform.

Fifth Street Station opened wide, the dim underground plaza shocking itself to life with the promising smell of cheap coffee and warm summer pastries. She thought about stopping, but after checking the time, she decided against it. The medical trial started in fifteen minutes, and she knew she'd have to wait for the elevator once inside Fifth Street Medical Center. Cutting edge, best in the country, FSMC. She rolled her eyes at the plaques plastered all over the entrance of the station as she pushed her way in. The sharp scent of disinfectant burned the back of her throat as she located the front desk and its winding line. It reminded her more of a movie theatre than a medical office.

"Next!"

Star shoved her phone into her pocket and stepped up. She'd been reading an article about some Hollywood A-Lister she'd only vaguely heard of getting caught manipulating stocks for a company, Hemo-something. She hadn't gotten far enough to read what happened before the person at the desk called her up.

"Hi, I'm Star Thomas. I'm here for the paid study."

The person at the desk furrowed their brow for a moment before they started typing, "Oh-kay." They hummed at her, typed more, and then slowly nodded. "Oh, I see. You're here for the NeoVita Perpetua trial. Is that right?"

"Yep, that's the one. It's paid, right?" Her palms started to sweat. The loss of her recent ex-girlfriend's income itched in the back of her mind. Chelsea. Runaway. Star sucked in a sharp breath to steady herself.

The person laughed, "Yes, I believe it is. You're all checked in, so you can go over to the elevators and head up to the seventh floor."

Another two minutes passed waiting for the elevator, and she shot up and up until the doors slid open.

The waiting room she stepped into glowed. The walls, the floor, the furniture, all of it pristine white. It almost hurt to look at as she headed towards the desk just to the right of the eleva-tor doors. An equally white woman with huge blue eyes smiled up at her.

"Hello. Are you here for NeoVita?" A tiny wisp of transparent hair curled down against the middle of her forehead.

"Yeah, I got all checked in downstairs, actually."

Star hitched her bag up higher over her shoulder and tried to pretend she could relax in such a spotless room. She knew, though, that her frizzed-out curls from a pair of braids left in for a few too many days and russet skin kept her apart from this world. A test subject. That's all she was here.

"Excellent." The woman curled the word around in her mouth. "Take a seat. They'll call you back in a few minutes."

As she sat, a door beside the desk opened, and a Black man around her age walked out. He met her eyes, flashed an excited smile, and disappeared in the elevator. The neon pink bandage wrapped around the inside of his elbow left a streak of color imprinted on her vision every time she blinked.

"Star?"

A shiver prickled at the back of her neck as she stood. The nurse looked a bit more human than the person at the desk, but Star shook that thought away. It was impolite to judge, espe-cially when she'd be walking out with her first installment of the promised $1,200 participation payment.

Being chronically ill had never had its perks until NeoVita had reached out to her through her usual specialist team. Their infusion, Perpetua, promised to give her life back, and the bo-nus of payment seemed impossible to pass up. Not when she'd been out of work for seven weeks post Chelsea disappearing, and the bills had started to pile up.

"We'll be in room three today to go over your paperwork."

Star hung back, and the hallway darkened around her as her mind faltered. "I was told I'd get my first infusion today."

The nurse gave her a flat smile and shook her head. "Oh no, today is to get your banking information and release form signed. We'll get you scheduled to come back to start your infusions sometime next week."

Her stomach twisted. "But they said on the phone I'd get to start today."

"I'm sorry for any confusion. These forms are what permit us to start treating you."

They stared at each other for all three breaths Star forced herself to take. Then, she nodded and followed the nurse to the exam room.

One week later, she found herself back in the glowing white office. Even though the back of her neck shone with sweat, she would see this through. The money was too good to pass up, and the side effects didn't seem too bad. With each heavy pump of her heart, they rang out in her head.

Excessive bleeding.

Sensitivity to light.

Increased skin sensitivity.

Low red blood cell count.

Change in tooth enamel texture—

"Star?"

The same nurse from before grinned widely as Star stood and followed her back to room three. The infusion itself was painless. Star had never been afraid of needles, which she guessed made the four pokes much easier than the nurse was used to; she even said as much.

"—took that like a champ!" she chirped.

"Thanks," Star said. "I thought it would be a lot worse than that."

It took about an hour for the cold, cloudy liquid to drain from the bag above her head. The nurse brought her a warmed blanket once the shivering started. The cold stuck with her despite the heat that couldn't seep deep enough to calm her shaking.

"It's very normal," the nurse assured her. "All very normal."

That remained the running line throughout the first three treatments. Everything was normal. Her slowing heart rate? Normal. How her teeth didn't quite fit inside her mouth the right way anymore? Normal.

Even though it all felt wrong, Star couldn't stop herself from hoping it would get better. This was supposed to be her answer. A chance to get better.

The morning of her fourth treatment, Star woke with a migraine. Splitting. She had to turn the volume on her phone down as far as it would go, and even then, the ringing on the other line as she tried to call the doctor's office sliced right through her.

"You've reached—"

"What is happening to me?" she gasped, half cradling her head in one hand. A shivering finger slipped past her lips and caught on the new, sharp edge of one of her teeth. Rotten iron dribbled onto her tongue.

"Who is this?"

"Star Thomas."

A beat. A breath. She could almost hear the woman on the other end thinking. Even that was too loud. Tears burned her eyes and turned her vision pink.

"What is happening to me?" she repeated.

"We'll send somebody to come get you. Can you confirm your address for me?"

She hung up. Everything slowed down. Her heart barely thudded inside her ears. She should be afraid that this might mean she would die. That brought nothing to her, though. No fear. Barely the bristle of her thoughts. She instead took comfort in her padded bank account. Whatever was wrong with her, she could pay for. The money, at least, felt like a mercy.

Everything ached, from the buzzer signifying their arrival to the sun scorching right through her during the short walk to the sleek Escalade at the curb. Sunglasses were pressed into her hands by a man in gray scrubs. An oxygen mask was set over her nose. Still, her calmness persisted. She would get through this. It was probably just a common reaction that they could fix for her.

They drove her across town to Fifth Street Medical Center. A strange stretcher awaited her; it looked more like a tent on wheels. The gray scrub man lifted her gently up onto the bed and then zipped her in.

"To protect you from the sun." His voice, distorted by whatever material now encased her, floated gently between her ears. The words bobbed along the surface of her mind, so captivating that she didn't notice she'd been taken inside.

"How do you feel?"

Star opened her eyes. The light ceiling of room three stared down at her. Familiar. Her eyes watered, sore and flat as she blinked away the drowsiness.

"Star?"

"Thirsty," she whispered. The words caught in her throat.

A beat of silence. Then, "What are you thirsty for?"

The answer came, to her confusion, very easily. Just as casually as if she had requested a glass of water.

"Blood."

She waited for somebody to scream. To tell her she'd lost her mind. Instead, they gave her what she wanted.

The usual transfusion of the NeoVita Perpetua drug was accompanied by two pints of O-negative. Her nurse brought in two doctors: a hematologist and a plastic surgeon. All three of them watched her the entire time.

"You'll need to start having regular blood transfusions," the hematologist murmured to her gently. "To help manage the new symptoms."

Star agreed, half high on the rush of fresh blood and still reeling from whatever had happened to her in her apartment; they wouldn't tell her exactly what.

"You only have two treatments left. Then, we'll have check-in appointments periodically to see how you're feeling."

"Right," she breathed, eyes pinned to the ceiling above her. She'd never noticed the different facets pressed into its texture. It calmed her to map the endless valleys and hills, memorizing the way they turned and bent around each other.

The voices in the room drifted. She caught bits of their conversation here and there. They planned on adding a new diagnosis to her chart. Logged new symptoms. Took photos of her face, her neck, and her body. Weighed her twice. Star waded through the experience half-awake, nodding and agreeing until she crashed back into her body hours later after being deposited back into her apartment by Gray Scrubs.

Life changed quickly after that. Star's symptoms got worse and were only temporarily staved off by regular blood transfusions. Word got out fast that she wasn't the only one.

The American government partially shut down ReGen and only allowed it to operate as the parent company to HemoTech International, ReGen's answer when the governments of the world demanded to know how they were going to handle the fifteen thousand people they'd maimed.

Then came the NDAs with their repulsive cash reward. All the money in the world for sworn secrecy. Star stayed holed up in her apartment for so long, hiding from the ReGen attorney, that she ended up in the hospital. Trying to cope with the new normal, the threat of being moved to the rumored Blood Boulevard, and the omnipresent surveillance of ReGen left her little choice. She fell in line where she could tolerate it.

Nobody could force her to sign the NDA, but without the NDA money, she had to get a job. Nobody would hire her, thanks to the public service announcements that played down her condition enough not to cause mass panic but talked it up enough to make people see her as even less than they did before. Without work, she couldn't afford the expensive transfusions that she could only get through HemoTech clinics. Regular hospitals wouldn't treat her unless she was on the brink of death. ReGen controlled everything.

Then came the laws only months later.

Both sides of the aisle worked tirelessly to make her entire existence fit into an impossibly small box. Of course, the laws didn't apply to the NDA signers. They threw parties right there on the East side of Clinton, where regular people lined up to willingly donate sips from their wrists and necks and inner thighs. Star vomited the first time she heard whispers about it.

The first HemoTech she got assigned to ran on passed-along secrets. At least, before the laws that forbade the clinics from stacking appointments like Jenga blocks were put in place.

The thought of people like her using their hush money as a free pass to feed off of healthy people was too much for her. The exploitation and the indulgence of it turned everything red. She wouldn't be bought so easily.

Wednesday came quicker than Star wanted. Dread crept up inside her chest and purred there, rattling her bones hard enough to make her shoulders shake. Still, the sun set. She showered. Got dressed. Walked the two blocks to HemoTech 475. The room was empty. No fancy coats or shiny sunglasses. Just her and Stacey and James, when he appeared at the corner of the round desk looking paler than last time.

"Come on back, Star. Glad you could make it." He had circles under his eyes, dark bags that made his copper irises dull and too still. The way he moved seemed off too. Stiff. Slow. Careful. Despite that, he lit up as she stepped closer to him.

He led her down the hall. More than once, the back of his hand brushed hers. Star barely noticed through the cloud of worry that blurred the edges of her consciousness.

She could only wait as long as it took them to get into the very last room before she asked, "Why are you walking like that? You're limping."

A glimmer of rue lit his face. "Worried about me?" He marked something on her chart, and she snapped her mouth shut. If he documented that she showed signs of getting attached to him, she could only nightmare about what the consequences would be.

"No, I didn't mean anything like that—"

"You're fine." He gave her a soft, serious look. "I like that you noticed. Even if it's against the rules for me to like that you noticed. But after last night, I don't care about ethics rules or emotional safety laws."

A breath passed between them, one of disbelief for Star. He liked that she worried about him. He wanted to break rules for her, laws.

"What happened last night?"

"There was a raid at another clinic I subbed at across town."

Sour air stung her lungs and eyes. "What?"

"Big guys with big guns broke into the clinic screaming about purging the devil plague. They came down the treatment hall and when I tried to stop them, they pushed me down the back stairs. I promise I'm okay. We'd already seen our last patient."

Star gagged, overwhelmed by the image of him being brutalized. James slid the small trash from under the sink to under her mouth. There was nothing to throw up other than a bit of bile. Thick and yellow and burning. His hand lingered on her back as he rubbed gentle circles. The flat of his palm warm and comforting.

"I don't want you to panic, but I do think it might turn into a trend with how the election is going. Dewey is pushing that anti-NeoVita agenda pretty hard now that it's making noise online."

James disappeared from in front of her as the lights cut. Her shocked cry was quickly muffled as he put his hand over her mouth. "Shh. Wait."

Over the intercom, Stacey whispered, "Code daylight, James."

There was a bang and then footsteps out in the lobby. Star's entire body went rigid. Everything in her turned black. The walls pressed in. Her vision tunneled. Just before she lost touch with her body, she felt her cardigan slide off one shoulder.

"Breathe." James's voice reached down through the darkness. Something warm curled around her, safe and comforting. "Baby, breathe."

Star breathed. Lemon. Sage. Something spicy. Cardamom. Her gums ached the second the scents washed hot over her tongue. Another breath, then a bolt of fear as her lips parted without her permission.

"James…"

"It's okay, I'm right here. Deep breaths for me."

She tried to ask what was happening, but James's hand tightened. Slowly, a dim blue light burned itself alive over the door.

A metallic slide echoed in the silence and James whispered that all the exam rooms were locked down now.

"If they don't have a battering ram, they won't be able to get in."

"We're going to die."

James shook his head. "I won't let anyone hurt you."

He'd left enough space between his neck and shoulder for her; she could dip her chin and be there. The tiny gap brought a detached clarity along with the thirst.

These right-wing, homegrown terrorists would hurt her if they were given the opportunity. Maybe even kill her.

She took another searing breath. The clarity, in some kind of melancholic desire, rippled and dimmed. James smelled too good. It was dangerous, she knew, being his close to him, and yet she found herself completely unwilling to let him go.

"There you go, try to relax. Just focus on breathing, I've got you." His hands dipped lower on her back, and she melted. The heat from his body scorched her. Brought parts of her she thought were long dead back to life.

If her isolation would end in a gunshot, what was the point of her rules? What pieces of humanity were worth killing herself over? That tiny spark that had lit her originally burst into a flume of destructive desire.

The look in James's eyes, burning with determination, turned her stomach over. Star tried to breathe but she couldn't shake the feeling creeping up the back of her throat. How many times had she already cheated death?

"Do you think you can be quiet? I want you—If something is going to happen, let me take care of you."

Heavy footfalls started at the top of the hallway. Both of them jumped when the slamming crunch of metal against wood started. They didn't have long.

Star stared at him, the ghostly light warping his eyes to something icy. "I don't understand."

"Feed from me, Star. Please. Let me do this for you."

"You—You want me to?"

He kissed her, softer than she'd kissed him the week before, like he wasn't trying to take anything from her. Like he was giving her a soft place to land.

"Please."

In the end, it was easy to let go now that she knew death would have her tonight. As if the infusions hadn't tried hard enough. As if the government hadn't tried hard enough. As if fucking Restorative Genetics hadn't tried hard enough. Now, there were fascists with guns, and by the sounds blasting through the hallway, death would have her this time.

The diamond grip she commanded over herself released. Effortless. Like letting sleep overtake her. Star let herself relax as she turned her chin. There was no reason to fight it anymore.

His neck in her mouth, warm and soft, gave way like sunsoaked, over-ripened fruit. The heady gush sent chills through her first, then came the fire. Inch by inch, her body simmered awake. The heat built. Her skin stretched too tight. The first spicy swallow lit her up like a floodlight. It didn't feel like drinking; she took all the good parts of him for herself.

Bang.

"It's okay, we're safe." he said in an urgent whisper. The arms around her—his, she realized—tightened around her as she swayed. The room tilted. Something soft cushioned her knees as her thighs collapsed down onto something much harder. Heavy hands found her hips. Her mind worked at half-speed as she recounted the path they had just taken from the middle of the room to the recliner, as far from the door as they could be. Her eyes slit open but all she could see was the beige pleather and a single curl of James's hair.

"Breathe deeper," he whispered.

The breath brought in clean air. Plasticky, faux leather and rubbing alcohol, enough to snap her back into her body. She pulled back, her face burning and eyes locked on him.

Bang.

"You can take more if you need to. Whatever you want." He smiled at her, seemingly quite comfortable underneath her despite the jump in his thighs.

It's just any other night, she told herself.

They could have this moment.

She could process his warm expression and the shining glaze over his eyes. His offer, equally as warm, curled against her tongue and purred to the beast within her. The thirst. The need.

"I need more." The confession left her on a single, choked breath.

James bared his neck for her again.

Bang.

Days could have passed, cut apart only by the interruption they both knew was coming. Star bit James up and down the expanse of his neck, made perfect by the purple and blue stained imprints of her teeth.

Cool air cut across her stomach. James wrestled the button and zipper of her jeans until he had enough of an opening to fit his hand against her. There wasn't ample room for him to work, but she lifted her hips to give him what she could.

Bang.

Her tongue laved against his skin, soothing and searching. The next crash, closer than before, sent her spiraling. Heat rushed through her fingertips as she dug her hands up under his shirt to feel more of him. To tether herself to him. She sank her teeth into him again as her hips tilted forward. Hunting. Desperate to finish before the inevitable. James met her movement and urged her to repeat it, groaning through his teeth.

They both knew he'd been too loud because the noise outside stopped. Boots pivoted, squeaking on the polished floor. Crept ever closer.

"Fuck—I'm sorry, I'm so sorry," he whispered. Her thumb brushed the scars on his chest, rigid with mostly healed tissue. Air whistled between his teeth as he arched into her.

"'S fine." She meant it. This couldn't last forever; she knew it wouldn't.

Their foreheads crushed together as the door to exam room six rattled and groaned under the first blow. James's hand, the one not buried down the front of her jeans, trembled on her hip. His panting, ocean waves in her ear, pushed and pushed her to his chest as the fingers he had inside her stilled. The gravity of the earth shifted from holding them down to holding them together. A thousand universes across a thousand galaxies pulsed with their synchronizing hearts.

"I would have fallen in love with you," she whispered. This was what people did, wasn't it? Confess everything right before they lose it all? "Probably too fast."

James nodded, his voice fracturing when he managed to gasp out, "Me too. I would have taken you on dates, movies at home and blanket forts. Do you like video games?"

"I don't know." Her chin shook so hard it kept her from smiling. It was the one thing she wanted to give him, just one real smile.

Every word left them on rushes of breath that dodged between the splintering of wood as the beating continued. It wouldn't be long. They only had a minute. Maybe less.

"I'd teach you. We'd find ones you like." He grabbed her face with both hands, held her there and kissed her hard enough to make her spin out.

A sob tried to break out of her as the door finally gave, but it caught between her throat and her mouth and stayed there. She gave him one last, miserable look as she pulled back.

"Don't!" His words came too late. What remained of the door swung open. Banged into the wall with a crunch as the knob bit into the plaster. James tried to keep her in his arms, but she pushed him back down. If this was inevitable, she wanted to look into the eyes of the man who would kill her.

Star shifted from away him as the man entered the room, gun muzzle preceding him. A single beam of light cut through the blue gloom and lit her up in brilliant white.

She knew how they must look to the outsider; her teeth and lips stained hemoglobin sin, and James's hands shaking on his lap, fingers and palm of the right one still shiny and wet. Together, they were the two things people like this intruder hated the most: a trans guy and a disabled, dying mixed girl who refused to actually die. They were supposed to be the freaks. The dangerous ones.

The gun, sharply metallic in her nose, was merely a purifier to end their transgression.

"Please don't hurt her." James's voice was only just audible over the ragged sound of her breathing.

Blood dripped from her nose. A single, penny wide splatter on the linoleum.

The man in front of her wore all black. The only piece of him she could actually make out were his eyes: blazing twin lagoon pools but flat like dead fish. There was no recognition of her being another person, only the cold determination of a man who already had his mind made up.

Just as she started to take another breath, the room erupted in a blast of heat and orange light, the muzzle too close to miss its mark.

Sweetest Midnight

by Lyndall Clipstone

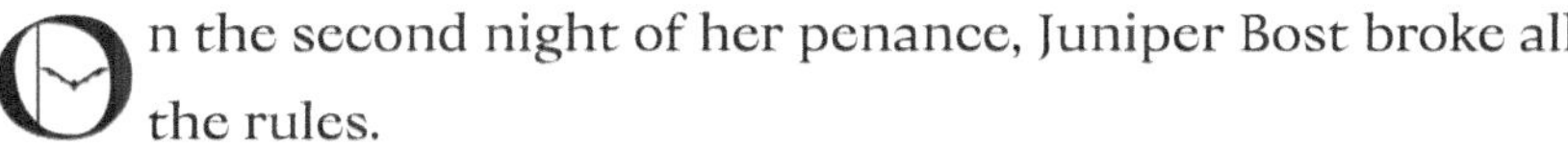n the second night of her penance, Juniper Bost broke all the rules.

The cottage where she'd been sent was at the crest of a hill, at the end of a dirt trailhead. Maine in the summertime. Low moonlight and endless stars, the hush of the woods and the *lap lap lap* of the lake. Just a few short weeks ago, she had been in rehearsals for Die Vara's *Rebirth,* and everyone knew she'd be chosen as the principal dancer. God, what an idiot she was, for it to all come out like this—from the favorite to a disgrace. From bright future to the threat of losing it all.

This summer in exile would save her. That was the offer she'd been given when Die Vara found out what Juniper had done. She could leave the company or she could or face this penance, and prove she could be trusted again. So Juniper chose exile.

She was to stay at this cottage as a companion to a girl she'd never see. The daughter of one of the company's bene-factors who suffered from terrible nightmares. The directives were clear: never go upstairs into the girl's private rooms, never leave the grounds, and take five pink pills from the unlabeled bottle each night before bed.

The first night, Juniper followed the rules to the letter. As the sun slunk low and daylight dwindled, the woods around the cottage were eerily still. In town, when she arrived, it was crowded and busy. Idyllic as a storybook upstate summer: sailboats and flags, everyone here to escape the hot press of the city. The lakeside cottage was only six miles out, but it felt like another world.

Juniper prepared herself as instructed. She put on the nightgown they'd left for her, bridal and billowing. She lined the pills on the counter. A trail of shiny pink orbs that tasted of nothing as she swallowed them down. Outside, the trees sloped toward the water where the dock lay cruciform against a lake as flat as glass. Sunset turned the surface to the color of blood.

Juniper swallowed the pills and thought of her charge for the summer. She wondered if the girl was also preparing herself for bed. The house was so quiet: no creak of floorboards, or echo of footsteps from overhead. No sign of life from the girl who was so stricken by nightmares that she needed a warm body asleep in the bed beside her.

A warm body. That was what Juniper had become now.

But her body was her instrument, honed for years into a form that could express the strange and beautiful choreography of the dance company. Die Vara was known for her forthright and occasionally brutal methods. Hours spent on a single movement—leap, gasp, leap, gasp—until it was perfect. And maybe this was another lesson designed to carve Juniper into a new, more desirable form. Emotional rather than physical manipulation. Maybe Juniper was spending the summer alone by the lake, drugging herself to sleep in an empty house, an empty bed.

She didn't care. Juniper was here to earn back her place in the company. She was here to follow the rules.

The only problem was, on the second day, Juniper realized she couldn't dance.

She awoke in an empty bed. If the girl had even been there, she left while Juniper still slept. As she prepared herself to rehearse, pulling a woolen wrap-sweater over her leotard, the house was as silent as a many-chambered shell. Hollowed and echoing, and Juniper was certain that she was alone.

She went down to the docks to practice. The wooden boards that jutted out onto the glass-flat lake were smooth as the stage floor in the company's rehearsal space. As she stretched beside the stillness of the water, Juniper closed her eyes and pretended she was back there. In the grand ballroom with its post-war architecture, surrounded by the other girls as they stretched and smoked and shed layers as their bodies warmed. The anticipation like a held breath as they waited for Die Vara to arrive.

Juniper began to dance. But everything felt wrong. Her body was leaden. Her muscles wound impossibly tight: hamstrings inflexible, her hips aching. A strange bruise throbbed on her wrist, aching and purple as a flag iris. She tried to ignore the pain the way Die Vara would demand. She'd been trained to push through discomfort, to perform even when injured.

She moved through the routine she had rehearsed every day before her exile. Bend, leap. Gasp. Fouetté. Her ankle twisted and she landed wrong, falling heavily to her hands and knees. Juniper was used to falling. She was used to forcing herself past her limits for Die Vara's artistic vision. But this moment— grazed palms and throbbing knees, the bruise on her wrist aching and aching—was an executioner's blow.

Her plan was clear. Nights of drugged, dreamless sleep beside her unseen companion. Days of rehearsal, practicing the steps of *Rebirth* so when she returned, Juniper could retake her place as principle in the performance.

The whole point of this summer was to earn back her place. Juniper *needed* to dance. If she couldn't rehearse while she was here, her exile would be for nothing. An entire summer without practice would set her back a year at best.

At worst, it would be the end of her career.

Juniper didn't want to break the rules. But if it was a choice between broken rules and a whole lost summer, there was no choice at all.

So, on the second night, Juniper Bost left the pink pills unswallowed.

She went into her downstairs bedroom, a converted parlor with a wall of windows that overlooked the lake. Anyone else would use this space for summer parties. Bonfires on the shore, watching Fourth of July fireworks in the clear night sky.

Juniper put on her bridal nightgown and climbed into the large, wrought-iron framed bed. She closed her eyes and slid into shallow sleep.

She was so tired; it was easy at first. Sleep lapped at her like the shallow waves of the lake. When the sound of footsteps came, padding softly over the floor, Juniper kept her eyes closed. She ignored the shift of the mattress, the weight of a second body on the bed. The girl, it seemed, was real after all.

Fingers slid over Juniper's wrist. The touch was cold and dragged a shiver from her that she couldn't hide. She bit the inside of her cheek. She forced herself to remain still. To pretend. With her eyes closed, with her body still, she told herself that she hadn't *really* broken the rules.

Then, the cool whisper of breath on her skin. The tender inside of her wrist, just above the large, iris-purple bruise. It throbbed at the soft rush of air. A brush, a press, an ache. Juniper forced herself to keep her eyes closed. Lips rasped her bruise in a shallow kiss. A strange shot of desire arrowed through her. She bit the inside of her cheek again and tasted blood. She swallowed down a gasp. Until this moment, Juniper hadn't even believed this girl was real and now here she was, fingers circled around Juniper's wrist and her mouth—*her mouth*—pressed to Juniper's skin with a cold, shivery kiss.

No. Not a kiss.

A *bite*.

A swift sting, the drag of teeth across the bruise, and Juniper's eyes snapped open. She wrenched her hand free, scrabbling back against the wrought-iron bed frame. The room was dim, with only the barest palings of moonlight coming in through the window. Limned in silver, the girl was like something Juniper had imagined, a dream. She was beautiful as a doll: flawless skin, spun-gold hair and thick-lashed eyes. Her skin was so pale, like carved marble.

The girl regarded Juniper levelly, her gaze intent, unblinking. "You're supposed to be asleep."

"I know," Juniper said. She shifted forward, drawn as if by a compulsion. The crumpled sheets rustled beneath her knees as she leaned closer to the girl. Her heart began to pound.

This girl was not a stranger. "*Lenore?*"

The name on Juniper's tongue felt like a spell. Lenore Delune had been the principal dancer when Juniper joined the company. Talented and perfect, Lenore had been Die Vara's favorite, praised in a way she had never done for any of the other dancers. Until Lenore left the company without explanation five years ago.

Five years. That much time had passed since Juniper had seen her, but Lenore had not changed at all. She looked to be the same age as Juniper, even though that was impossible. Only her hair was different: grown fantastically long, as though it hadn't been cut at all since she left. It fell to her waist in glinting waves that shimmered when she moved. This couldn't be real—it couldn't be Lenore, but at the sound of her name, she offered an uneasy smile.

"Juniper," she said. "You've grown up since last I saw you."

"And you haven't changed at all."

At this, Lenore laughed. It wasn't a cheerful sound. Her smile curved, turned sharp like a blade. Her irises darkened to twin pools of ink. "Oh, I have changed. Just not in the way you'd expect."

She crept closer on all fours, crawling across the distance between their bodies. The way she moved was feral, and her dark eyes and widening grin sent a cold shudder all through Juniper's body. Lenore's mouth was open. Her teeth were fanged, *sharp*.

Juniper swallowed a gasp. She clutched her wrist, her heartbeat desperate. The mysterious bruise, the kiss that had woken her... it now made a terrible kind of sense. "You bit me."

It hissed out, choked as a sob. The words belonged to someone else. Juniper was far above the scene, staring down at her own trembling body. Her dark hair, her bridal nightgown. She thought of vampires from films. Pallid, brooding creatures who wore silken capes. She thought of the battered paperback she carried everywhere the year she turned fifteen about a lost boy called Nothing. The strains of the Bauhaus song *Bela Lugosi's Dead* ran through her mind.

As she watched Juniper's expression change, Lenore gave a rueful smile. "This would have been much easier if you'd stayed asleep. If you hadn't broken the rules."

Juniper scrabbled back, trying to put space between them. "Wait. Please. I can explain."

"*Can* you?" Lenore crept closer, and her eyes gleamed in the dark. She was still the same girl Juniper remembered, blonde and fair and delicate. Beneath the familiar traces though, was carved a strange new form. She was feral. She was *hungry*.

"I need to be able to dance," Juniper said quickly, fighting to keep still when she wanted to flee. "The pills made me so groggy that I couldn't rehearse. And if I can't practice then the whole summer will be a waste."

This gave Lenore pause. She narrowed her eyes at Juniper. Incredulously, she said, "You still want to go back."

"I—yes. Of course I do." Juniper thought of rehearsals in the grand ballroom. The tick of a metronome. The thrill she felt after a perfect series of steps. Even with all the heartache, all her shame, she had to return to the company. Die Vara, *Rebirth*, all of it—that was her life. "You won't tell her, will you? That I broke the rules."

Lenore made a low, thoughtful noise. "Maybe we can come to an arrangement."

She reached out to Juniper and tucked back a tendril of dark hair behind her ear. Her fingertips brushed Juniper's cheek. Her skin was glacially cold. Juniper sucked in a breath. That touch, that cold, it was the final proof this was all, impossibly, true.

Anyone with an ounce of self-preservation would have refused. Left the cottage, the town, the state. Run away and never looked back. But no one who danced for Die Vara knew self-preservation. Juniper Bost had shaped her body into a tool of muscle and sinew and bone that craved belonging and approval. This was no different from any other grueling aspect of her time in the company.

She lay down. Carefully, she drew the sheets over her body but left her arm free. Hand extended, wrist bare. She turned her cheek against the pillow, and she closed her eyes. "Nothing needs to change. I'm asleep. You—you'll do whatever you need. And I'll never know, I'll never remember."

The mattress shifted as Lenore stretched out beside her. Cold fingers traced down Juniper's arm, and she closed her lips against a shiver. Fear and desire spilled through her in equal measure. Once, she would have given anything for Lenore to touch her like this. She felt the brush of lips against her skin. Soft, soft, and wretchedly cold.

"Keep your eyes closed," Lenore murmured.

Juniper did as she was told. As Lenore's teeth pricked through her skin, she squeezed her eyes shut and thought, *At the end of the summer, this will all be over.*

Juniper slept through the entire day, swallowed up by exhaustion. Everything that happened—Lenore, sharp-toothed, a *monster*—felt like a dream when she finally woke up, alone. Only the throbbing mark on her wrist proved that Juniper hadn't imagined the events of the night. Tangled in the sheets, she thumbed the bruise, watched the sun sink low over the lake and turn the water to liquid crimson.

She dressed in her leotard, went down to the docks. This time, when she began to practice, her steps came easily. None of the wrongness, the numbed feeling in her body that had come from the pink pills. Her wrist ached from Lenore's bite. She was slightly woozy from her lost blood. But when Juniper moved through her warm-up, the sequence was like a natal path imprinted onto her body. The first steps from *Rebirth* were a long-held exhale.

In the hush of the Maine summer twilight, there was only her feet on the boards, the hum of insects, and the blue hour dusk. As Juniper danced, she imagined herself back in the company. On the stage at opening night. The ritual all the dancers did before the curtain rose, encircled together in the glow of the lowlights as they toasted with cups of rich, red wine. The taste of it—herbs and berries and darkness—always lingered on her tongue throughout the entire performance.

In this imagined scene, when the curtain rose there was only one person seated in the audience. And as all the other dancers melted away, Juniper was left alone, standing in front of Lenore.

She opened her eyes. Looked back toward the house. There was a faint glow from the kitchen where Juniper had left on a lamp. Outside, beneath the window, a figure. Lenore stood close to the wall, outlined by the spill of lamplight through the glass. Her hair turned to gold and her eyes glowed like fireflies. Juniper faltered, suddenly shy at being watched. Lenore, unblinking, moved closer, her footsteps noiseless and feline through the grass.

"Don't stop," she said, and there was an ache in her voice. A yearning that made Juniper hold out her hand, beckoning.

"Dance with me."

Lenore hesitated but shook her head. "No. I won't dance Die Vara's steps ever again." A brief flare of anger hardened her features, then she sighed, lashes veiling her gaze as she softened. "Please continue. I want to watch you."

A cool shudder of *want* spilled over Juniper, like she had plunged into the lake and swallowed a gasping breath of the water. She thought of Lenore's fingers on her cheek, twined in her hair. The bruise on her wrist gave a throb that echoed lower, between her thighs. She kept her hand outstretched. "Will you join me if it isn't Die Vara's dance, but our own?"

Somehow this felt even more dangerous than what they had done last night. Lenore's gaze shuttered. She pressed her lips together, then, cautiously moved forward to take Juniper's hand. Her fingers were cold, her palms smooth as lakeshore stones. Up close, there were bluish shadows beneath her eyes like splotches of watercolor.

Juniper moved through a series of simple steps, a routine she had learned in her childhood dance classes before she joined the company. Lenore caught up the rhythm. It was discordant at first, each of them in their own separate worlds. But soon Lenore began to match Juniper's motions, and they danced not just alongside each other, but together. The tempo picked up. They parted and spun and leapt. Divided to opposite ends of the dock then spiraled back together with a magnetic force.

Juniper *never* felt like this dancing with the company. Each time they joined, the cold press of Lenore's hands turned her mouth dry. The weight of Lenore's gaze on her skin was like silken ropes, binding her, grounding her. By the time they finished the sequence, Juniper was breathless. Her heart raced. Her hair, fallen free of its pins, spilled down around her shoulders like a caplet of ink. She gazed at Lenore, panting, enraptured. Desire held her, a clenched fist.

They stood together on the docks, the lake quietly murmuring beneath them. Juniper looked at Lenore, and tried to see, really see, the truth of her. The fangs. The bloodlust. The feral way her eyes had darkened. But in the last velvet edges of twilight, Lenore was all lush-hued, pastel shades, gold and peach and lilac. Juniper stretched out her hand, unable to keep from reaching. Lenore turned away at the last moment, and walked over to the trees that encircled their cottage clearing.

Juniper followed her, helpless as a thrall. Lenore looked back over her shoulder as they reached the edge of the woods. "What did you do," she asked, her voice quiet, "to be sent to me?"

Heat burned over Juniper's skin, and she felt a hot blush cover her cheeks. She took a deep breath, tasted petrichor and earth. In spite of everything, it was so painful to confess.

"It's like you said: I broke the rules." Juniper said, feigning a casualness she didn't feel. Lenore didn't respond. She arched a brow, clearly wanting more. With a sigh, Juniper went on. "I broke... the moral code."

There. Now it was said and done. The confession fell heavily between them. They both knew what it meant. Any relationship between the company dancers was forbidden—emotional, physical, or otherwise. Lenore leaned closer to Juniper as though she could sense the warmth of her skin. Her eyes ran hungrily over Juniper's flushed cheeks. "Who did you break it with?"

Juniper shook her head. "It wasn't *with* anyone. Die Vara found letters I had written. Letters I never sent."

Lenore was silent as she parsed this out. Brows knit, jaw hard. Finally, she said, "Die Vara cast you out because of *letters*, and you still want to go back to her?"

Juniper gazed down at the docks. She could still feel the worn-smooth boards beneath her feet. Die Vara made the rules clear to all her dancers. Romance was forbidden. *Feeling* was forbidden. It was for their own good, she said. All that energy, the aching and wanting, should fuel nothing but their dance. That was how they made art.

And it did feel like art to Juniper. The way her body fell into the rhythm of the steps, the delight at the flow of movement. Leap, gasp, leap, gasp. She wanted to dance. She wanted to belong. Determination beat within her, a second heart. It had driven her to this exile and to this arrangement with Lenore.

It was worth it, wasn't it? It was what she wanted.

Somehow, she couldn't make herself answer.

Instead, she slowly reached to her tangled hair. Drew it away from her neck. Her skin was flushed, sheened by a layer of perspiration. She could feel the throb of her pulse. Lenore watched the movement and swallowed thickly.

Wordlessly, they moved together like it had been choreographed. Lenore took Juniper by the shoulders. Spun her, so her back was pressed against the tree. Rough bark scratching her skin, and the solid press of the trunk caged her. Her hand came up, clasped at Lenore's waist. Even through the fabric of her shirt, her skin was cold. It should have felt wrong, this proof that Lenore wasn't human. Instead, desire rose through Juniper, sharp and piercing.

She'd wanted to do this for so long. To hold Lenore close, to be held by her, to feel the weight of her body. Now it was real, and the truth of it was electrifying. A fever dream made real. A desperate, mewling sound spilled from her mouth. Lenore licked her lips. Her eyes turned dark as she lowered her head to Juniper's neck. Her breath shuddered out, fierce and desperate. Her lips brushed against Juniper's throat. But after a brief, gentle kiss, she drew back and reached instead for Juniper's hand.

Juniper wanted to protest. But the sight of Lenore, bowed to her wrist like a penitent, stole all the words from her mouth. Lenore closed her eyes and bared her teeth. When she bit down, Juniper buried her face in Lenore's golden hair and let everything else fade.

The following night, when Juniper felt the mattress dip as Lenore crept into the bed, she sat up and switched on the lamp. Bathed in the light, it was like it was the first time she'd seen Lenore so clearly. She was *beautiful*. Otherworldly and frightening, with her spun-gold hair and her carved marble skin, watercolor shadows beneath her thickly lashed eyes.

"When I knew you, before, you were... human," Juniper said. The word felt strange in her mouth. Lenore nodded slowly. "So how did you become like this?"

"I am what Die Vara made me."

Juniper reached to Lenore, cupped her cheek. Felt the cold silk of her skin. Slowly, her thumb slid over Lenore's plush lips. This felt like danger, like tracing the edge of a sharpened blade. Especially when Lenore's eyes narrowed, and her attention dragged to the soft hollow of Juniper's throat. Her tongue licked slowly at Juniper's thumb. Then, obediently, she opened her mouth.

Lenore's teeth were sharp. Not like the fangs of a carnivore, but serrated, filed *points*, as though they'd been shaped with a dentist's tool. Juniper looked at them and felt a twinge at her wrist. She thought of Lenore in her arms as they stood beneath the trees—her fragile body, her cold, cold skin. "What do you mean?"

"Perhaps it's unfair to say that she made me. My hunger has always been. At first, I wanted only to dance—and then I only wanted her recognition. I wanted her to love me. Being her principal dancer sated every appetite I had... then I was injured my last year with the company. It was going to be the end of it all, until Die Vara offered me a new role. A way to serve the company, to be special and *needed*, eternally."

Juniper's stomach twisted. She thought of Lenore, how she had been when they were dancers together. Juniper had ached for her, even though they'd never spoken. She had watched Lenore, brilliant and loved and golden, and she had burned for her. Now, Juniper wanted to gather up Lenore, hold her close, keep her safe.

"You deserve better than this. At least my exile is only for the summer. But you—you'll belong to Die Vara forever."

"I can't say there haven't been regrets," Lenore said, and her voice was so quiet that Juniper had to lean closer to hear. "But this is my life now. Whenever a girl breaks the rules, she's sent here."

Juniper circled her hand over her bruise. Cold breath. Teeth at her wrist. "You drink our blood."

Lenore dipped her head, pained and solemn. "I drink your blood. And in turn, *my* blood is offered up to Die Vara, and to the very best of her dancers. To enhance and preserve their skills."

Juniper wrapped her arms around herself. A wave of nausea crested as she remembered their opening night ritual. All of the dancers in a circle on the stage. Die Vara, pouring red wine into small silver cups. Their hands, raised in toast. The sour-sweet taste of the wine—no, *not* wine—

"You drink our blood," Juniper said again, but it didn't sound any more real the second time. "And then we go back to the company and the cycle continues. Until another girl breaks the rules."

Lenore nodded. Tears filled her eyes. It was the first time, in all of this, that she had looked ashamed. Her tears were crimson, bloodied, and it should have been horrifying. Juniper felt only tenderness. She wiped Lenore's tears away, leaving smears of crimson on her fingers.

She and Lenore, they were so similar. When Juniper first became a dancer, it was for the love of it—for the pure delight and joy at making art with the movement of her body. Now, it was all corrupted. Her joy had been lost, replaced by her drive to win the approval of Die Vara, a choreographer who exiled girls to feed a monster. A monster who, in turn, would then be fed back to those same girls.

"My letters, the ones Die Vara found... They were for you." Juniper had sworn to keep it secret forever, but now the confession rushed out, impossible to hold back. "I wrote them to you."

Lenore's eyes snapped open. Her mouth parted, incredulous, baring her serrated teeth. "To me?"

Juniper nodded vehemently. "I was so ashamed of myself. That I couldn't be more controlled with my emotions. That I was foolish enough to write down how I felt about you, even if I wasn't brave enough to send them. I knew the rules and what it would mean for my place in the company. But now..." She paused, then reached out to stroke the traces of bloodied tears from Lenore's cheek. How could she feel such tenderness for a creature like this? And yet, it overwhelmed her. "Now I'm only ashamed that I never told you how I cared when I had the chance."

Lenore crept toward Juniper. Sorrow dripped from her body like lake water. Her fingers slid over Juniper's knee, her touch like ice through Juniper's nightgown. Up close, she was even more inhuman. Her skin like marble, her eyes as crystalline as a glacial sea. But Juniper wasn't afraid. She drew Lenore into her arms once more. They were so close that the ice of Lenore's breath feathered over Juniper's mouth. She shivered, licked her lips, and then closed the distance between them.

At first, she didn't move, and Juniper was worried she'd made a mistake. Then Lenore made a yielding, desperate sound, and she kissed Juniper back. She tasted of rose petals, red wine, rare meat. Her teeth were sharp, but she was so, so careful. Her tongue was cold, slick, like a piece of clear ice. Juniper imagined it melting against her own hot fervor, little rivulets of meltwater dripping down her throat. She wove her fingers through Lenore's golden hair and pulled her closer.

When they finally parted, everything felt hot and aching. They curled together at the heart of the bed, their legs intertwined, their hair sifting together—brunette and gold.

"Lenore," Juniper said quietly. "What if there is another choice?"

"What do you mean?"

"We gave our lives to the company. We let Die Vara shape our bodies into instruments of her artistic vision, because she was a visionary, and it was like magic to dance for her. But is this price we pay for art, for perfection, worth it? You and I are both bound in a pact we can't undo. Trading our time and our blood to someone larger and more powerful. What if we simply... walked away?"

Lenore was quiet, her brow creased into a sorrowful frown. "I can't leave Die Vara. I need her."

"You need blood. But Die Vara isn't the only one who can give that to you."

Juniper trembled as she said it aloud, this ruinous offer. But when Lenore's fingers slid over her throat, marking the rhythmic beat of her pulse, Juniper knew this was what she truly wanted.

"To run away," Lenore whispered, "would not be enough. There will always be another dancer. Someone who will be desperate enough to accept Die Vara's cruelty."

Juniper laid her hand over Lenore's, deepening the press of Lenore's cold fingertips into the hollow of her throat. Lenore groaned softly. Her lashes fluttered. Her lips parted, and she ran her tongue across her sharp, sharp teeth.

And Juniper felt fierce and hungry, just as monstrous as Lenore, when she said, "I think... she needs to be stopped."

Lenore nodded, her golden hair rustling against the pillow. "And we could stop her."

"We could."

Juniper kissed Lenore again, then turned on her side as Lenore settled against her. The cold, slender weight of her fit so perfectly to the contours of Juniper's body. It was as though they had always been made for this, to be together. Lenore nuzzled into the crook of Juniper's throat. First a kiss—her cold, chapped lips. Then the press of her fangs. She waited, teeth a cool half-moon against Juniper's skin. Her tongue rasped over Juniper's aching pulse.

They curled together, their motions like a new kind of dance. And Juniper saw a new future unfold ahead where there had only been a singular path before. Herself and Lenore and their own feral choreography. Bodies and movement and bloodlust and love.

Juniper wrapped her arms around Lenore's waist and urged her closer. "Go ahead," she whispered, with her head tiled back. "I'm yours."

A Note from the Editors

This book was a frantic project that Margaret and I conceptualized in early 2025, and it has blossomed into something larger than we ever intended. This anthology is a direct response to the violent hate and disenfranchisement that the LGBTQ+ community is facing. We are so proud of what this book has become.

Margaret and I met many years ago over our shared love of one particular vampire story: *Twilight*. It feels fitting that the first professional project we embarked on together was a vampire project. When I first approached Margaret about this, it wasn't quite yet a vision fully formed. Rather, it was the inkling of something that could be more. Margaret is the one who suggested this anthology be a charity project, and that we center queer love, not just as a welcome contribution, but the primary focus of the project. She has shaped not only this anthology, but the future of this company as we continue to brainstorm new fundraising projects for the future. While most of this note is from us both, Margaret, to you I must say: thank you, thank you, thank you. I am lucky to call you a colleague and a friend.

This book is for the queer community. If you are queer and still at home with your unaccepting family, if you are the only queer person in your town, if you don't have queer friends, or have been ridiculed or threatened for being who you are, we are sorry. We see you. We are in solidarity with you. We hope vehemently that you find the peace and joy that Aileen has with Veronica, that Gwyn has with Rodrigo, that Lenore has with Juniper. While our identities can mean suffering, they also mean an intense, indescribable joy.

Of course, this book would not have been possible without the authors. Not only the authors who are a part of this anthology now, but also the ones who submitted their incredible stories. To the authors who are featured here, we hope we have fully expressed our profound gratitude for each of you. If we haven't, allow us to tell you now that your stories are captivating, electric, and the heart of this project. A book is only as good as its author, and we had the privilege of working with not just one but eight amazing talents. If you are an author who submitted a story, thank you. We still regularly think about the submissions we regretfully turned away.

Thank you to the Contrarian Publishing staff, both public-facing and private. In particular, thank you to Leah Block and Darrian Kirksey. You two are rock stars!

Thank you to each and every bookstore with which we partnered to launch this book to even greater heights. Indie bookstores are the backbone of publishing. Dear reader, we implore you to support your local bookstore.

Now for some more personal thanks from each of us.

From Margaret:

This project has been a sea of pleasure. From pitch meeting to final print, it has been a joy to dive deep into the wine-dark sea of vampire lore and symbolism with Jamie, and I am eternally grateful for her wholesale support of my passionate pedantry.

My love, affection, and immortal dedication belong to my Fang Gang sisterhood (Ali Regan, Holly Thomas, Meredith Ammons, Rachel Lloyd, and Katherine D'Souza), who walk the shadowed path alongside me with indulgence.

Lastly, I offer my utmost gratitude to Stephenie Meyer and Anne Rice, whose vampire stories have changed my life, time and again. The beauty of the Savage Garden awaits all in need of inspiration. 5x5. Grá a bhfuil grá agat dó.

From Jamie:

I can't thank everyone, but first to Kin, thank you for cleaning the house and cooking dinner after you get home from a long day at work so I can work around the clock to make Contrarian what it is. I love you. Thanks also to Lisa Tsang, Jiwoo Sung, Callias Zeng, Samantha Rose Baldwin, M.B. Thurman, Ash Harvey, Vee Elle, and Writer's Block. What would I do without you guys?

Thank you, Stephenie Meyer, for writing the story that made me fall in love with books and set me on the path to becoming an editor.

If anyone at The Trevor Project happens to read this, thank you for the work you do. I had the luxury and privilege of a therapist and a supportive friend group as a teenager, granting me a comparatively easier time with my own queerness. Not everyone is afforded the same. Thank you for saving our lives.

And finally, from us both, thank you to all the contributors who made this book possible by donating to our crowdfunding campaign, and even just by sharing. Thank you for your support not just of Contrarian Publishing, but of queer voices and queer stories.

Bibliography

Auerbach, Nina. *Our Vampires, Ourselves.* University of Chicago Press, 1995.

Craft, Christopher. "'Kiss Me with Those Red Lips': Gender and Inversion in Bram Stoker's *Dracula.*" Representations, vol. 8, 1984, pp. 107–133. University of California Press, https://doi.org/10.2307/2928560.

Le Fanu, Sheridan. *Carmilla.* London, 1872; Project Gutenberg, 2003.https://www.gutenberg.org/ebooks/10007.

Polidori, John. "The Vampyre." London, 1819; Project Gutenberg, 2004. https://www.gutenberg.org/ebooks/6087.

Stoker, Bram. *Dracula.* Archibald Constable and Company, 1897.

Sontag, Susan. *Illness as Metaphor.* Farrar, Straus and Giroux, 1978.

About the Authors

U.M. AGOAWIKE is a Nigerian-Canadian author of speculative fiction in various mediums. They write short stories with vibes for plot and SFF books featuring everything but the kitchen sink. Their debut novel, *Black as Diamond*, is forthcoming in 2026 from Bindery Books and Ezeekat Press.

ANDI ASTRA is a queer, multidisciplinary illustrator and creative based out of Hilo, Hawaii. While studying English Literature at Eastern Michigan University in 2015, Astra began creating science fiction and alien centric art under the name Spooky Girl, using these themes to explore their own identity and relationship with femininity. Since then, Astra has built a successful career as an illustrator, and has begun to expand their universe by writing stories that explore the strange, queer and ethereal.

L.A. BARRON finds sanctuary in the soft underbelly of horror and speculative fiction. Whether it's online or in their collection of hard cover journals, their work orbits themes of devotion, the physicality of emotions, and the rot that lives inside us all.

The *Blood, Sweat, & Queers* anthology is their formal debut to the world of writing. Their addition to the anthology pays homage to all those who bled before us; whose stars burnt out too soon to see how far we've come, and how far we still have to go.

They live in the Pacific Northwest with their partner and small menagerie of pets.

LYNDALL CLIPSTONE writes dark tales of flower-threaded horror. She is the critically acclaimed author of The World at the Lake's Edge duology, *Unholy Terrors*, and *Tenderly, I am Devoured*. She currently lives in Adelaide, Australia, in a hundred-year-old cottage with her partner, two children, and a shy black cat.

AUSTEN LEE has been spellbound by storytelling since childhood, fascinated by how a single tale can transport, transform, and haunt. They write stories that explore the strange and the unsettling. When not writing, Austen is immersed in tabletop games, teaching in the U.S. and abroad, and rarely seen without a briefcase full of notes, a dog, and a cat.

A lifelong bookworm and performer, ANNA MCG always knew she wanted to pursue a career in the arts. She has performed at the Forever Twilight in Forks Festival and immersive events for M.B. Thurman's Summoned Series. Her debut story, *When the Day Met the Night*, is an ode to her eternal love for vampirism and literature.

She lives in Colorado with her high school sweetheart and their four cats.

MAE MURRAY is a writer and editor hailing from Arkansas, now living in eerie New England. She occasionally contributes essays and film criticism to Fangoria.com and Dread Central. She is the recipient of the 2022 Brave New Weird Award for Superior Achievement in Short Fiction. *The Book of Queer Saints*

Volume I was her editing debut and a 2023 British Fantasy Award nominee in the Best Anthology category. Her debut novel, *I'm Sorry If I Scared You*, released in 2024.

EZRA WREN (they/them) is a queer fiction author who identifies as non-binary, bi/pan and demi. Wren is a lover of all things literature, music and art. Their favourite thing to do when they're not writing is read, watch anime and suspenseful series, and sit by the water. Wren lives with their husband, German Shepherd Groot, and cats Benny and Nebula in Norway, but is originally from Malta. They are partial to cake, sunshine and highland cows, in exactly that order.

Wren also writes dark fantasy under the pen name J. M. Rose, and is independently publishing their Lorcanverse body of work. Their first book, *Usurper*, published in March 2025.

About the Editors

MARGARET HALL (she/her/hers) is a scholar of vampire literature, an author, a teacher, a director, and a theatre historian. Margaret is a staff writer for Playbill Magazine, the pre-eminent theatre publication in the United States, as well as a teacher at various accredited programs, including Juilliard and New York University. She is the youngest known nominator in the history of the Drama Desk Awards.

Her debut biography, *GEMIGNANI: Life and Lessons from Broadway and Beyond*, explored the life of esteemed Broadway music director Paul Gemignani. An unflinching advocate for the societally marginalized, Margaret is an autistic woman, and the founder of the non-profit Autistic Theatremakers Alliance. She has received both a Bachelor of Fine Arts in Drama, and a Masters in Musical Theatre History from New York University. Grá a bhfuil grá agat dó.

JAMIE RYU worked for Big 5 powerhouse publishing companies like Macmillan and HarperCollins before forging her own path as the founder of Contrarian Publishing. With ample editing experience and a degree in Comparative Literature from New York University, she is well-equipped to help writers unlock the full potential of the stories they're meant to tell and aid them in pursuing their goals, whether that be traditional publishing or indie publishing. She is a proud, queer Korean American woman, and is sadly married to a man (a wonderful man, but a man nonetheless).

This book was made possible by

M.B. Thurman

Trent Thurman

Holly Thomas

Sandra Kralik

Anna McG

Sarah Gallagher

Ash Harvey

Lyn Solomon-Linville

Pam VanOverbeke

Arianne Hartsell-Gundy

Evelyn Rude

Jennifer Donovan

Taylor Szuba

Samantha Rose Baldwin

Jennifer Peshansky

Shawn Barma

Jessica Blanton

Shrike

Baz Pugmire

Tara Hester

Briana Cox

Thank you